...ood time! Rule 2: Be coy, not shy... ...body splash

...orts, music! Then immerse yourself in it! Rule... ...with your

...k eye contact! Rule 6: Make him feel special, like he is the only guy in the

...le 8: Let your inner beauty shine! Show him the wonderful treasure that

...le 10: Have a sense of humor! Guys like to laugh! Rule 11: Act distant

...long with! Rule 13: Do not be bossy! Do not tell your crush what to do!

...e 15: Have an outside interest that you can talk to him about! Rule 16: Be

...pany of your crush! Rule 18: Respect yourself! Demand that your crush

...mething you do not want to do! Do only things that you and only you are

...Guys like danger.) Rule 21: Be mysterious! Show him that there is some

...moments before you answer! Rule 23: Leave some things to his imagination!

...ule 25: Compliment your crush two times a week! Rule 26: Do not feel you

...ng on a guy if it turns into an obsession! His loss if he can't see the jewel that

...r crush likes you! Rule 29: Do not write your crush an anonymous Email

...ne that you have a crush on someone unless you know you can trust them not

...im! Rule 32: Do not act shy, speechless, or tongue-tied around your crush!

...nd listen to sad love songs if your crush does not notice you! Rule 35: Get to

...5: Do not pretend to be a different person when your crush is around! Rule

...like you are the stuff! Any guy is lucky to have you! Rule 39: Do not be

...clingy, or possessive! Rule 41: Do not crush on a boy who has a girlfriend!

The Crushes

Also by Pamela Wells

The Heartbreakers

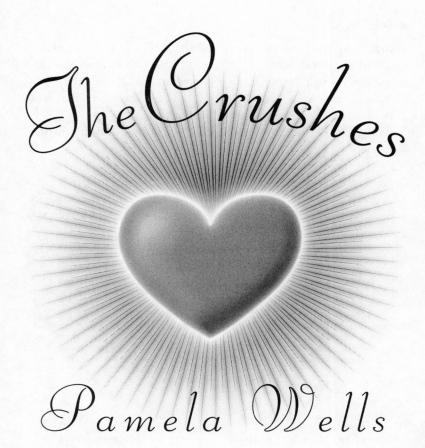

The Crushes

Pamela Wells

Point

Acknowledgments

I would like to thank my genius editor, Abby. It is wonderful to know my manuscripts are in such experienced editorial hands. I can't thank you enough for polishing my work until it shines. Abby, your continued faith in my work means a lot to me. I appreciate it more than I could ever express in words.

This book is dedicated to my friend, my father, and my mentor, Tommie.

This all started many years ago as our dream. I am now living this dream and I am so sad that you are not here to see it come to fruition with me. None of this would be possible without your support, advice, and always telling me never give up! I miss talking about life with you. I miss you dearly! May you rest in peace!

Copyright © 2008 by Pamela Wells

Library of Congress Cataloging-in-Publication Data

Wells, Pamela.
    The Crushes / Pamela Wells.—1st ed.
        p. cm.
    Summary: Four high school friends have an unexpected summer of crushes—and heartbreak.
    ISBN-13: 978-0-439-02693-2 (alk. paper)
    ISBN-10: 0-439-02693-8 (alk. paper)
    [1. Dating (Social customs)—Fiction.   2. Interpersonal relations—Fiction.
3. Friendship—Fiction.]   I. Title.
    PZ7.W4667Cr 2008
    [Fic]—dc22

                                                            2008011746

12 11 10 9 8 7 6 5 4 3 2 1   8 9 10 11 12/0

Printed in the U.S.A.
First edition, December 2008

The display type was set in Liberty and NotMaryKate.
The text type was set in Horley Old Style.
Book design by Steve Scott

The Crushes

June

ONE ⟿

Usually hospitals had a distinct sterile smell, but Children's Hospital of Birch Falls smelled like cinnamon buns. Sydney Howard passed a room and saw a small blond boy ripping apart a cinnamon bun with his fingers.

That explained it.

It was mandatory for all students at Birch Falls High to take at least four weeks of a volunteer course before they graduated. Sydney had wanted to volunteer somewhere with her friends, but Raven and Alexia had completed their volunteer hours their freshman year at the senior citizens center. Kelly was volunteering at the animal shelter, but all their volunteer spots were full.

Sydney's guidance counselor had talked her into volunteering at the hospital. Apparently, they were shorthanded for the summer and were taking all the volunteers that applied.

While Sydney wasn't exactly a kid person (there was that time she made her little cousin cry when she told him there was no Santa Claus) she was always up for a challenge.

"This is the east wing of the Children's Hospital," Melanie, the human resources manager, said, keeping her voice low as she swept through the halls. She was a nice woman in her late twenties, with a pixie haircut and black horn-rimmed glasses, who was responsible for coordinating the volunteers.

The tour group of about six people rounded a corner into a new wing.

"And this is the west," Melanie said. "Each of you will be assigned a department. I'll let you know where you're at when you come in next Monday."

The group moved around a TV cart in the middle of the hallway. There was a video game console on the shelf below the TV, and the shelf below that was full of video games.

"Oh, sorry, Mel," someone said from behind the group. Everyone turned around to see a guy about their age grabbing hold of the cart. A few of the girls standing next to Sydney instantly perked up.

"I was just coming to move this," the guy said.

Melanie rolled her eyes. "Sure you were. Everyone, this is Quincy, another volunteer and also my younger brother."

"Quin, please," he said, grinning. "Why do you torture me, Mel?"

Sydney couldn't help but appraise Quin. She was close enough to see he had caramel brown eyes partially hidden behind rectangular black-framed glasses. He was tall, at least six feet, and seemed to have compact shoulders or maybe just a really nicely tailored white Oxford shirt. His jeans fit just as nicely but were baggy in all the right spots.

He'd used a rubber band to tie back black hair. When down, Sydney guessed, it probably hit just below his shoulders. Where did Quin come from? He certainly didn't go to Birch Falls High. And he was close to her age, if not a bit older.

He flicked his eyes to her and Sydney quickly looked away, the blush in her cheeks clearly spelling out the guilt she felt for staring.

"Nice to meet you, guys," Quin said before wheeling the TV cart away.

"Okay," Melanie said, "let's move on."

The group followed Melanie down the hall, but before they rounded another corner, Sydney looked back over a shoulder to catch sight of Quin one last time.

There was something different about him, something intriguing. Sydney just didn't know what *it* was. She looked away and hurried after the volunteer group.

Returning home, Sydney pushed her bedroom door open and saw Drew sitting on her bed. He'd been there since that morning reading *The Messenger* by Mark Goodman. When Drew started reading, it was hard to get him to do anything else.

His dark hair was overgrown and starting to hang in his face. He didn't seem to notice, but it was starting to drive Sydney crazy. She thought he looked so much better with short hair. He just didn't do long hair well. Not like Quin did.

Quin.

Why was she even thinking about him?

She plopped down on the bed next to Drew and grabbed one of the black throw pillows, putting it in her lap. She tugged on the corner where a loose string hung. She wound the string around her index finger waiting for Drew to say something.

"I just put a pizza in the oven," she said, snuggling in closer to him. "Are you hungry? It doesn't look like you've moved all day."

He held up a finger to give him another minute. Sydney pursed her lips and continued to pick at the pillow.

Finally, he slipped one of Sydney's sticky notes inside the book and closed it up. He set it on her nightstand and turned to her. "Pizza sounds good." He put his arm around her shoulders and ran his fingers through her hair. She closed her eyes, enjoying the attention.

"So, how was your first day volunteering at the hospital?"

Sydney kept her eyes shut as she said, "It was good. The girls in my volunteer group are nice. The guys, they want to be doctors so at least that means they'll take this job seriously and . . ." She trailed off, Quin's name on the tip of her lips. She wanted to tell someone about Quin. It was that weird excitement of discovering something new. You wanted to tell the whole world about it, but she couldn't tell Drew without him taking it the wrong way. It wasn't that she wanted to date Quin; she just wanted to get to know him better, wanted to figure him out.

"I think I'll like it there."

"That's good."

Sydney nodded. That was a safe answer, right? It wasn't like she was deceiving Drew, because there was nothing to lie about. She loved Drew. *Loved him*-loved him. At the beginning of this year when he'd broken up with her, she'd felt like a part of her had died. Sydney and Drew had been together for over two years now. She didn't count the few months they'd been broken up. That was just a hiccup in their relationship, and she'd never let anything come between them again.

She'd learned a lot being single. She'd learned that she'd taken Drew for granted and that to have a good relationship, you had to meet halfway. The breakup changed her for the better. She knew now more than ever that every second with Drew counted.

But the most important thing about the breakup? Sydney had gotten to know herself a little more. She'd let loose a bit, learned that life was not about schedules and homework and pressed khakis.

Drew had been right about one thing — it was time to have fun, get out, live a little. Sydney was trying to do just that, trying to put the spark back in their relationship. Unfortunately, it was harder than she first thought.

"Syd?"

Sydney opened her eyes. "Huh?"

"Your timer is going off."

"Oh, right." The timer beeped in the kitchen. She got up just as Drew's cell rang playing Lune's new song, "Did I Hurt You." He flipped the silver RAZR open and said, "Hey."

Out in the kitchen, Sydney shut the timer off and the usual silence of the house settled around her. Her dad was still at work, and her mom was in Hartford finishing up for the week.

A few months ago, her mother was practically living in Hartford and came home every other week. She'd since promised Sydney she'd take more time off to spend with her family. She seemed to be doing well so far.

Sydney enjoyed having her mother around. She felt like she hadn't really had a mother since Mrs. Howard became an executive at SunBery Vitamins in Hartford. And, while Mr. Howard tried hard to fill the void left by his wife's absence, he wasn't very good at it. He tended to forget things like paying the bills and buying groceries. At least his cooking was getting better.

After shutting off the oven, Sydney set the baked pizza on the stove top. She pulled out the utensil drawer, looking for the pizza cutter. Her father never put things back where he found them. Neither did Drew. Those two had a lot in common.

Finally, after searching forever and finding the pizza cutter in with the pans, Sydney threw slices on Drew's plate and on hers. She was headed down the hallway when Drew came out of her bedroom.

"Where are you going?" she said.

He grabbed a piece of pizza off his plate. "Going to Todd's."

Todd, her friend Kelly's brother, was Drew's best friend, unfortunately. Todd was obnoxious and annoying and immature. How did Kelly deal with living with him? Sydney was glad Todd wasn't *her* older brother. She'd be tempted to move out.

"Now?" Sydney asked. "He can't wait a few minutes for you to eat with me?"

Drew took a bite off the end of the pizza and shrugged. "He needs help with something. I'll come back later." He passed her, chomping on the pizza some more as he disappeared into the kitchen.

Sydney hurried after him. "So you're just going to hurry off, then?"

He pulled open the back door and stopped. "Come on, Syd." He was using that tone of voice. The one that said Sydney was being unfair. Was she, though? She'd just gotten home, she'd made them pizza, and now he was taking off to hang with his apish friend.

Sydney wanted to point all this out, but she was trying so very hard not to nag. She needed to communicate calmly.

"Sorry." She set the paper plates on the counter. "I just . . . you know . . . wanted to hang out."

He leaned over to kiss her forehead. "I'll be back. Promise."

"All right. Love you."

He grinned. "Love you, too."

Sydney watched him cross her yard and climb inside his truck. Despite the fact that they were back together now and seemed to be going strong, she still worried every day that she'd lose him again. She couldn't let that happen.

TWO ～⚬～

Alexia Bass watched the seniors at Birch Falls High stream into the gymnasium for their graduation ceremony. She'd already seen half the graduating class. Ben had to be coming out soon.

The gym was as hot as a thousand suns and stuffed like a turkey. It took Alexia nearly fifteen minutes to find a seat: a very tiny six or so inches on the fifth bleacher up.

She was sandwiched between a can-barely-sit-still little girl and a paunchy man who smelled like cigars. This was not the way she'd envisioned Ben's graduation. It was too bad Kelly's brother, Todd, went to a different school and had graduated last week. Alexia could have sat with Kelly's family. Or, if she weren't so chicken, she might have asked Ben's parents if she could sit with them down on the first row. Ben's parents weren't exactly warm and inviting, though. Not like Ben was.

A few more seniors entered the gym, and still no Ben. Where was he? He better not have skipped out and left her hanging. Not that he'd ever do that. At least, he would never leave her hanging; the skipping part he *would* do. To Ben, there would be nothing funnier than skipping your own graduation ceremony. Ben would use that as a story for his kids and then his grandkids, too.

Streamers and balloons adorned the stage at the far end of the gym. There was a table stacked with leather-bound diplomas. Several metal folding chairs held school faculty.

Alexia looked out over the sea of spectators and saw a few familiar faces.

In the back of her mind, she'd known this was coming, but she'd always hoped that, for some crazy reason, Ben would wait for her to graduate before leaving Birch Falls. Not that she would ever let him do that. He had to get out and go to college.

It just hurt that they were already putting distance between them. That couldn't be good for a relationship. Would the strain be too much? Alexia didn't want to consider it right now, not with their summer vacation starting. Worrying about something she couldn't control would ruin the time they had together right now.

A shrill whistle sounded, the heat waves carrying it up the bleachers to Alexia. She looked up and saw Ben. His eyes were on hers and he grinned, his forest green tassel hanging in front of his face.

Alexia smiled back and waggled her fingers at him.

It was amazing how, even after dating a few months, Alexia still got butterflies whenever she saw him.

He headed over to his seat near the stage while the last of the graduates entered the gym.

After the ceremony introduction, the principal and the

valedictorian each made a speech. Before they handed out diplomas, a slide show played on a projector screen. Ben was smiling in all of his pictures.

When he was away at college, Alexia would miss his humor the most.

Oh, stop thinking about it! she chided herself.

When the ceremony was over, Alexia joined the exodus to the front lobby to get fresh air outside with the rest of the crowd. She waited beneath the sycamore tree where she and Ben had taken to meeting during their lunch hour.

Would this be the last time they'd meet here?

Ben came out of the open double doors, his twin brother, Will, at his side. Despite the fact that they were identical twins, it wasn't hard for Alexia to tell them apart.

Will carried his graduation cap beneath an arm. Ben didn't have his, probably because he'd tossed it in the air at the close of the ceremony. His forest-green gown was already unzipped. Beneath it, he'd worn a white T-shirt and his usual khaki cargo pants. Will probably had a suit on beneath his gown.

"I'll meet you at the car," Ben said to his brother.

"I won't wait long," Will answered and ambled off to the parking lot.

Ben came up alongside Alexia, putting his arms around her shoulders. "Hi," he said.

"Hi."

He leaned over and kissed her softly. An excited chill ran up her spine despite the sweat still lingering there from the overheated gym.

"Congratulations," she said when Ben pulled away. "You're officially done with high school."

He nodded and leaned his forehead against hers. "Officially done. I cannot wait to spend the summer with you. There will be virgin strawberry daiquiris, afternoons spent lying out in the sun, and many make-out sessions."

Alexia whapped him on the arm.

"Hey, now, I have a wet Speedo contest later. You can't damage the goods."

Alexia threw her head back and laughed. "A wet Speedo contest?" She rolled her eyes. "That would be fun to see."

"And sexy."

Alexia smiled, but lately that word made her tense up.

There came a point in every relationship where sex went from thoughts and whispers to full-on conversations. She and Ben had reached the latter, and it was starting to make her nervous.

On the one hand, she really loved Ben and wanted to share that important event in her life with him. On the other hand, part of her wanted to wait longer. Not because she was afraid of regretting it or that she doubted Ben was the "right" one.

It was the simple fact that her parents had brought her up to believe the *first time* was a special event and that she should think about it before making a decision. She didn't want to jump into anything.

Ben kissed Alexia's forehead, bringing her out of her thoughts. He took a step back. "I have that stupid photo thing with my family, so I can't hang long. And then Will and I are celebrating with some friends later. Though Will seems to have a different definition of 'celebrating' than me. We'll probably end up making goal lists and future-income graphs in Microsoft Excel or something."

Alexia laughed. "There's nothing wrong with goals, you know."

"I know. I have goals. I just don't want to put them in a spreadsheet."

Cocking an eyebrow, Alexia said, "What kind of goals, exactly?"

"Well," — he puffed out his chest and set his hands on his hips — "there's this girl who I love more than sunlight and someday I'll marry her and then we'll have three and a half kids and a goat and a picket fence. How are those for goals?"

Alexia wanted nothing more than to share the rest of her life with Ben, and the fact that he was thinking the same thing made the butterflies in her stomach dance.

"Sounds good to me, except for the goat."

He came a little closer. Close enough that Alexia could take in his familiar smell. It was a woodsy scent with an undertone of Tide laundry detergent.

"So," he said, his voice low and eager, "have you thought about *it?*"

She didn't need clarification of "it."

It was sex.

And yes, she'd thought about it. She thought about it every waking moment.

"Yeah," she said.

"I take that as a 'Yes, I've thought about it, Benjamin, but can't you see this is an important decision, and I don't want you pressuring me!'"

She grinned. "That's pretty close."

"Take as much time as you need to think about it. I want you to be sure."

Relief loosened the muscles in her shoulders. If it had been any other guy, he probably would have lost patience with her by now. She could always count on Ben understanding.

He leaned over and kissed her quickly on the lips. "I have to go before Will leaves without me. I'll call you later."

"Okay. Have fun."

He waved good-bye as he rounded the corner of the school for the back parking lot. Alexia sat on the cool grass beneath the sycamore tree, leaning her head against the bark.

Why did sex have to be such a big deal? Why did the thought of making a final decision put her stomach in knots? She wished she could just do it and get it over with, but that wasn't the right answer either. Sighing, she got up off the ground and went home.

♥   ♥   ♥

Alexia slammed the front door, shutting out the June heat. Thankfully, her house was air-conditioned to a comfortable sixty-five degrees. She felt like she was baking all the way home, the sun beating through the driver's-side window of her car. It didn't help that sex was on her brain.

She found her older brother, Kyle, in the kitchen, making what appeared to be instant mashed potatoes but which had the consistency of melting snowballs. He either hadn't dressed for the day or wasn't planning to leave the house, since he was in a pair of Yale sweatpants and a white T-shirt. And Kyle wasn't the type of person to go out in public wearing sweatpants.

"Hey," Alexia said as she took a seat at the kitchen island. "Mom and Dad here?"

Kyle shook his head. "They're scouting locations for a new office."

Despite the five-year difference between them, Alexia and Kyle got along well. He'd always been a good sounding board. He never pulled the parental role and talked down to Alexia. He was a good median between her best friends and her parents. They didn't talk a lot when he was away at school, but she enjoyed having him around the house on his summers off from Yale. He'd just graduated last month with an undergraduate degree in anthropology. From the sound of it, he didn't know what he was doing next.

"Kyle?" Alexia said.

"Yeah?"

Kyle had always told Alexia that if she ever needed anything, she should come to him if she wasn't comfortable talking to their mom and dad. Sex was one of those areas, but did she really want to talk to her *brother* about it?

She knew she could take anything to her best friends and that they'd never make fun of her, but she felt like such an inexperienced prude talking about losing her virginity when her friends had already gone through it. Well, Raven and Sydney had anyway. Kelly was still a virgin, but she said she didn't think sex was a big deal and that she was confident she'd know when to do it.

"Um." Alexia picked at a fingernail as she tried to think of a way to broach the subject.

Kyle shut off the stove burner and started to scoop his instant mashed potatoes into a bowl. He didn't seem to notice her stalling.

"How old were you when you had sex for the first time?" she blurted out.

Kyle froze mid-scoop. He looked across the kitchen island at her, unblinking. Finally, he set the pan down and pressed his hands into the counter as if to balance himself.

"I was fourteen."

"Fourteen!"

He ran his hand through his red hair and avoided looking Alexia in the eye.

"Do Mom and Dad know?"

"No! And don't tell them. Mom would flip out. I mean, not that it's a big deal now. It'd just break her heart." He inhaled deeply. "Why are we talking about my sex life anyway?"

Now it was Alexia's turn to avoid eye contact. She didn't say anything because she wasn't sure what to say.

At any rate, her silence clued her brother in.

"Oh," he said, drawing that one word out into five syllables. "You and your boyfriend are thinking about it?"

More like *she* was thinking about it. Ben had already made up his mind. Of course, it didn't help that he had already lost his virginity. For him, this was nothing.

"Do you love him?" Kyle asked.

"Yes. Or at least I think I do."

"Is he pressuring you into having sex?"

Was he? Not really. It wasn't as if he asked her every single day. He never pushed her when they started making out and things got heavy. He never made her feel bad for avoiding it.

"No," she decided.

"Do you want to have sex?"

"Yes and no."

"Do you trust him?"

That was an easy question to answer. "Yes."

"Then you'll know when the time is right. It's like riding a bike without training wheels. Eventually you'll get to the point where you just do it because it feels right and then afterward you're like, 'Wow, that wasn't so hard.'"

Alexia furrowed her brow. "Did you just compare sex to riding a bike?"

"Yes I did."

"And you went to Yale?"

He puffed out his chest. "And graduated with honors."

Alexia scooted off the chair and pushed it back beneath the edge of the counter. "Thanks, Kyle, for . . . you know."

"I think if anyone would make the right decision about sex, it's you. You've always had a good head on your shoulders." He paused and curled his upper lip. "God, I just sounded like Dad, didn't I?"

Alexia laughed. "Yes you did." She stuck a finger in his potatoes and licked her finger. She cringed. "And apparently you cook as bad as he does, too."

Kyle sighed. "Want to order pizza with me?"

"I would love to," she answered, "but I'm supposed to meet my friends at Bershetti's for a late lunch."

Kyle tossed the potatoes in the garbage. "Well, it looks like I'm ordering pizza alone, then."

Alexia laughed. "Good idea."

THREE ~⁄⁓

Kelly Waters got out of her car, looked to the Family Center Gym straight ahead and then to the McDonald's off to her right. Stupid Big Macs. Why did they have to be so good? She locked her car and headed inside the gym, trying to ignore the scent of French fries enticing her to join the dark side.

If the extra padding at her hips and beneath her biceps and on her thighs and — everywhere else on her body — was any indication, Kelly really, *really* didn't need to ingest more junk food.

It was time for a diet. Maybe if she hadn't spent the last several months as a single woman eating too much ice cream and watching way too much TV, she wouldn't have gained ten pounds.

Thankfully, once she got inside the gym, the enclosed space and air-conditioning blocked out the divine scent of fast food. A woman in her late twenties with a pink ribbon in her hair greeted Kelly from behind the counter. "How can I help you today?"

Kelly threw her car keys in her backpack. "I'm here for a kickboxing lesson. My brother won it in a radio station contest, and he told me I could use a couple of his lessons. I mean, if that's okay with you guys."

"Sure." The woman flipped through several files in a wire rack on her desk. She pulled out one marked CONTESTS and had Kelly sign a chart beneath several other names. "What was your brother's name?" the woman asked. "I need to mark down that one of his lessons was used."

"Todd Waters."

The woman wrote down Todd's name and the date. "You're all set, then. You can go ahead into workout room one, and I'll let Adam know you're here."

"Thanks." Kelly followed the plastic signs that said WORKOUT ROOMS down a hall and to the left. There she found several doors labeled one through six. The door on room one was open and she went inside.

Her tennis shoes squeaked on freshly polished pine floors. The sun shone through tinted glass on the wall of windows across from her. In the far corner were two blue mats, probably for tumbling.

Kelly set her bag in the corner and went to the windows.

Someone cleared his throat behind Kelly. She whirled around.

"You aren't Todd," the guy said.

Kelly couldn't even shake her head. When Todd offered the free kickboxing lessons, Kelly had assumed she'd get a thirty-something woman as an instructor with an intense attitude and muscles to match.

She'd assumed wrong. This guy was very, *very* close to oh-my-god hot. Kelly couldn't pull her eyes away from his *extremely* toned biceps or his *extremely* defined abs. It didn't help that he was wearing one of those stretchy shirts that stuck to every crease of muscle on his upper torso.

"So, where is Todd?" he said.

"Um . . . well . . ." Her heart was beating rapidly in her head. She could hardly hear herself think. "I'm his brother." She closed her eyes and rubbed her forehead. "I mean, he's my brother. He asked me to come today in his place."

The guy shook his head. "So he doesn't lose his free sessions. I get it." He approached Kelly, giving her a better view of his face. He had one of those perfect, straight-arrow noses and marble green eyes. Even relaxed, his dark brow etched into a scowl. Dark brown hair fanned into a deliberate mess. The sunlight shining through the windows turned his chin stubble golden.

Kelly couldn't tell how old he was — maybe eighteen or nineteen. Either way he seemed light years out of her league. He might even have been out of Raven's league, and she was like an exotic model lost in East Coast suburbia.

"I'm Adam," he said.

Kelly nodded in acknowledgment. Now she was beginning to fear her clumsiness. What if she fell on her butt in front of this guy? She'd feel like a total freak. There was still time to escape, wasn't there?

"Let's get started, then." Adam opened a closet and dragged out sparring gear. "These are boxing gloves," he said, holding one out for Kelly to slip into. "Despite the fact that it's called kickboxing, you'll be using both your hands and your feet."

Once Kelly's hands were in the gloves, Adam slipped round black pads onto his hands.

"Ready?" He clapped the pads together and then squared his feet.

"Yeah," Kelly said when really, she was nowhere near ready.

♥   ♥   ♥

An hour later, Kelly was sweating more than she ever had in her life. Her legs were sore. Her arms were dead, but she felt great. Not only was Adam an awesome instructor, but he never once made her feel weak or dumb. Even when she stumbled on a kick and nearly fell over.

"So," Adam began as he put away the gear, "tell your brother to show up next time or I'm kicking his butt."

Kelly scooped up her bag and smiled. "I'd like to watch that, actually."

Adam laughed. "If you keep up with lessons, *you* might be able to kick his butt."

Kelly smiled. "That's true." She waved good-bye.

By the time she hit the heat outdoors, she'd already come up with five excuses to get her brother out of kickboxing next week. He was so done at Family Center, and Kelly was a new, loyal member.

FOUR

Raven Valenti sat back in the driver's seat of her car and closed her eyes, rubbing her hands over her face. She didn't want to be here now, in the airport drop-off zone sending Horace to Detroit.

"Do you really have to go?" she said, looking over at him now in the passenger seat.

They'd been together just a few short months. Not to mention it was summer break! She wanted to hang out with him and make beautiful, sweet music.

Okay, maybe that was a little cheesy, but it was the truth. Their band, October, was doing so well. Ever since they played open-mike night at Scrappe, they were busy most weekends playing gigs. Why stop now when they were so popular? Couldn't Horace go to his dad's later? Like next year?

"It's only a month," Horace said, grabbing Raven's hand. The worn leather cord wrapped around his wrist tickled her arm. "My dad would be bummed if I didn't show up," he finished.

With her free hand, Raven tugged on the charm necklace hanging from her neck. Horace had given it to her just a few days ago. The charm was a sterling silver musical note. It was simple, but it meant a lot to her.

Caleb, her ex-boyfriend, had never bought her something meaningful. It just proved that Horace was the sweetest guy Raven had ever had, which was exactly why she was so afraid of screwing something up.

With him gone, she was doubly likely to screw something up. Horace kept her sane and grounded. If he was all the way in Detroit, how could he keep her from doing something stupid?

She sighed and squeezed Horace's hand.

Please don't let me screw this up, she thought.

Horace leaned over and kissed her softly. Raven still got butterflies every time they locked lips. They hadn't said "I love you" yet, but right now, she had the urge to pull away and whisper it. Probably Horace wouldn't even flinch, probably he'd say it back, but Raven was afraid of exchanging sentiments.

She wasn't out of the danger zone just yet and saying "I love you" would only make it worse when she messed up.

No, no, *if* I mess up. Because I'm going to do everything in my power *not* to mess up.

"I have to go," Horace said.

Raven nodded and tugged again on her necklace. "I'll miss you."

"I'll miss you, too. I'll text every day, okay?"

"Okay."

He got out of the car and grabbed his bag from the trunk. Raven followed him to the doors of the airport. People rushed in and out. A taxi honked its horn behind Raven.

She wrapped her arms around Horace's neck, tears biting at her eyes. She'd promised herself she wouldn't cry, but sending Horace off like this was more painful than she'd imagined.

Horace leaned his forehead against hers, his reddish-blond hair tangling with her own dark hair to form a curtain between them and the busy airport traffic. "I love you, Ray," he breathed.

Raven's stomach knotted into a million double knots. She felt ill and exhilarated all at the same time. She should have known this was coming. It was the perfect moment and Horace was good at spotting them.

She did love Horace, she loved him more than she'd ever loved any of her boyfriends. Saying "I love you" wasn't a big deal. It was the responsibility of the trust that went with it. That's what scared her.

She kissed him quickly on the lips and whispered, "I love you, too."

Horace was only going to be gone for a month. How much could really happen in that short a time?

Raven went into her mother's workroom. Mrs. Valenti sat at her desk flipping through pages and pages of stickers. Raven's little sister, Jordan, sat on the couch chatting on her cell phone.

"Hi," Raven said, plopping down next to Jordan. Jordan whispered, "Hey," before turning back to her phone conversation.

"What are you up to today?" Mrs. Valenti asked.

"I'm meeting my friends at Bershetti's for a late lunch. After that, I'm not sure."

Jordan got off the phone. "Speaking of Bershetti's, I applied there today."

"I still don't know why you won't work at Scrappe," Mrs. Valenti said.

Scrappe was her coffee shop/scrapbooking store. Raven worked there about twenty hours a week with Horace. She liked it, despite the fact that her mother was her boss. Jordan said she'd rather clean public bathrooms with her toothbrush than work at Scrappe.

Her reasoning? "I get enough of Mom bossing me around at home. I would totally go bonkers if she bossed me around at work, too."

"If you won't work at Scrappe, though, Bershetti's would be nice," Mrs. Valenti said. "They have a good Italian atmosphere there. You'd fit in nicely."

Raven and Jordan were half Italian, and their mother never let them forget it. Jordan looked just like their mother. Raven looked more like their father, who was African American, though she did have the Italian Valenti hair.

"There's a totally cute boy that works at Bershetti's, too," Jordan said. "Have you seen him?"

Raven shook her head. "I haven't been in there in a while. What's his name?"

"Nicholas. Nicholas Bershetti." Jordan nearly went starry-eyed. "He goes to the private school on the upper north side."

"Chisholm Academy?"

"Yeah." She grinned. "Private school makes him so much hotter."

Raven rolled her eyes. "Most private school boys are snots."

"Well, Nick isn't." Color touched Jordan's cheeks. There was a permanent smile on her face. She was practically glowing.

Part of Raven was envious. She missed that feeling that came with having a crush. Excitement, trepidation, optimism. As if anything could happen.

But Raven had someone now. Someone extremely good to her.

Probably that was better than the crushin' feeling. Yeah, definitely better.

♥   ♥   ♥

Raven threw the bag of trash in the big trash can and closed the lid to wheel it out to the street. She hated this chore. She'd tried getting out of it by hurrying out of the house to meet her friends, but her mother caught her at the back door.

"Before you leave," Mrs. Valenti said, "make sure you take out the trash."

Raven grabbed hold of the handle, tipped the can back on the two wheels, and lugged the thing out from behind the garage. She rounded the back corner of the house and heard a scraping noise coming from the street. It was like metal scraping against wood.

Someone rode a skateboard down the street toward a homemade railing about knee height. He jumped and slid the skateboard down the railing.

Raven watched as he made a perfect landing and then kicked the board up with a foot.

It wasn't until he looked over at her that she realized she'd stopped in the middle of the driveway to gawk.

"Hey," he said, tipping his head.

"Hi." Raven tried to kick-start her brain into thinking again and dragged the trash can the rest of the way down the drive. She set it along the curb and was about to hurry inside, when the boy skated over to her.

"You live here?" he asked.

She pursed her lips and nodded.

The boy was new to her. She'd never seen him around town before, let alone on her street.

Blue eyes peered at her from beneath the straight brim of a DC baseball hat. He had on baggy jeans, a black T-shirt, and white DC shoes. The skateboard slung beneath an arm said BLAKE across the length of it with a silhouette of an alien at the bottom.

From what Raven could see beneath the baseball hat, his dark hair was cropped close to his scalp.

"My grandpa lives across the street." He pointed over his shoulder at the two-story Tudor. That was Mr. Kailing's house. Raven didn't know he had grandchildren. He mostly kept to himself and never had people over. He was nice, though. Last summer when Raven had a flat tire, Mr.

Kailing had come out and changed it for her. He might have been close to seventy, but he still got around well.

"Your grandfather, huh? That's nice," she said, nodding quickly. "Well, I have to go."

"Hey, Blake!" someone called.

The boy, presumably Blake, glanced at Mr. Kailing's house and Raven couldn't help but look, too. The man who'd yelled from the front porch had one of those deep, husky voices that you couldn't help but follow.

A large black man waved from the porch.

"That's my . . . uh . . . uncle," Blake said.

Raven raised her brow. "Really?"

Blake *looked* one hundred percent white, but maybe he had some African American in him? Like Raven. Mr. Kailing was white, but that didn't mean one of Blake's parents wasn't black.

Blake dropped the skateboard and put a foot on it. "It was nice meeting you. . . ."

"Raven."

He smiled. "Raven." He propelled the board forward with his left foot. "I'll see ya 'round, Raven," he called over a shoulder before disappearing inside Mr. Kailing's garage.

The man standing on the porch waved Raven a peace sign before heading back inside. The screen door closed behind him.

Raven went inside her own house and passed Jordan in the living room.

"Why are you grinning like a goon?" Jordan said.

"What? I'm not."

But she was.

FIVE ～

Now that she had a boyfriend, Alexia was finding it difficult to have "friend" time. She had had good intentions to split her time between her friends and Ben, but it seemed that when she had a free afternoon, her friends were either working or out with their boyfriends.

Not to mention, spending time with Ben always seemed sweeter. She felt like such a terrible friend for thinking that, but it was true.

It felt like it'd been forever since they all got together, so they'd made plans to get together today. Alexia pulled into the Bershetti's parking lot and parked next to Sydney's SUV.

Inside, Alexia pulled her sunglasses off and stuffed them in her bag.

Bershetti's was a nice-size Italian restaurant in the middle of Birch Falls. It was owned by the Bershetti family, who had opened it some fifty years ago. It'd been updated since then and was one of the nicer restaurants in town.

A deep Concord purple Venetian plaster covered the upper half of the walls while white wainscoting spanned the bottom half. A thick chair railing met the two around the entire restaurant. Candle sconces hung on the walls every three feet or so. There were real plants everywhere. Some sat in the window partitions between the lower-level dining room and the upper dining room. They hung in planters from the ceilings.

Alexia's mom told her that most of the plants were herbs and that Mrs. Bershetti used a lot of them in her food.

The host, a forty-something woman with silver and black hair, greeted Alexia with a wide smile. "How many?"

"I'm meeting my friends here," Alexia said, scanning the restaurant over the host's shoulder. "Oh, there they are."

Kelly, Sydney, and Raven sat in the lower level of the restaurant in the very middle. Kelly waved.

Alexia made her way through the upper level of the restaurant and down the five stairs to the lower level. She sat down next to Kelly, across from Raven and Sydney.

"I'm so happy we're all together!" Kelly said, clapping her hands. "I've been bored out of my mind. Being single isn't so fun anymore."

Unfortunate but true, Kelly had taken over Alexia's previous role as the single girl of the group, though something told Alexia that Kelly was dealing with it better than Alexia had. There was nothing like feeling unwanted and uncool. Being boyfriendless until your junior year of high school was bordering on lame.

"I'm glad we're getting together, too," Raven said. "I sent Horace off to Detroit today. I feel like if I stayed home, I'd go stir-crazy."

Despite the foul mood Raven seemed to be in, she looked stunning per usual. She had on a white flowing skirt that grazed her knees. She'd gone with a plain purple tank top that seemed to match the Venetian plaster on the walls. She'd pulled her dark, wavy hair back in a ponytail and slipped on a white headband.

Sitting next to her, Sydney was Raven's complete opposite. Sydney's straight black hair hung loosely around her shoulders. She had on a white polo and had worn jeans despite the summer temps.

The girls all settled in around the table and started talking, but Alexia couldn't help but watch her friends inconspicuously over the top of her menu. At the beginning of this year, they'd barely hung out. That is, until Kelly, Raven, and Sydney all lost their boyfriends on the same night.

It was because of Alexia's Breakup Code that all three girls had gotten over their heartache. And in the long run, all four of them had gotten closer.

When they were together like this, Alexia couldn't help appreciating her friends, appreciating the little time they seemed to have to hang out together.

Sometimes she wished they still had the Breakup Code or something similar to it to keep them together. The Code had bridged any gaps between them.

"Oh my god," Kelly said, bringing Alexia out of her reverie.

"What?"

They all followed her wide-eyed expression to the front of the restaurant, where a group of guys had entered.

"That's the guy I had my kickboxing lesson with today," Kelly breathed.

Her cheeks had gone pink.

"You took kickboxing today?" Raven said.

"What guy?" Sydney asked. "Which one is he?"

"The one in the front," Kelly answered, still staring. "The one with the biceps."

"Holy crap," Raven said as the group of guys made their way toward the lower-level dining area. "He's hot!"

"I know." Kelly raked her teeth over her bottom lip. "You should see him in one of those Under Armour shirts."

Sydney rolled her eyes and picked her menu back up. "He's probably a muscle moron."

Kelly shook her head. "He wasn't a moron. He knew every muscle in the human body. Muscles I had never heard of."

Alexia appraised the guy Kelly couldn't stop drooling over. The sleeves of his navy blue T-shirt hugged the dip between his deltoid and bicep. The rest of the T-shirt wasn't formfitting enough to show definition so it was left to Alexia's imagination.

Alexia wasn't a huge fan of guys with muscles, but coupled with a smoldering scowl, strong cheekbone structure, and striking green eyes, Kelly's mystery man had Alexia's attention.

Seems he had the attention of every other girl in Bershetti's, too. Well . . . except for Sydney's.

When he and his friends passed the table, Kelly's kickboxing instructor stopped and shot a white smile at Kelly.

"Hey! How are you feeling?"

Kelly's mouth hung slightly agape. She stared at the guy for several long seconds before Raven kicked her beneath the table.

"Sore," Kelly said. "A little bit sore."

"That happens on the first day. It'll take a day or so and you'll feel fine."

"Yeah." Kelly nodded and kept nodding as if she was stuck in that gesture.

"Hi," Raven said, offering her hand. "I'm Raven. A friend of Kelly's."

"I'm Adam." He reached across the table to shake. "Kelly did kickboxing with me today." He looked over at her, smiling quietly as if kickboxing was their little secret, as if Kelly had done him a huge favor by working out with him.

Kelly blushed and looked away.

Alexia didn't blame her friend. She'd only witnessed that smile as a bystander and *she* wanted to melt.

"Well, I better go before my friends start harassing me. It was nice to meet you all. Nice to see you, Kelly. You should come back next week with your brother."

"Yeah, okay." She nodded as he walked away.

"Wow, he was hot," Raven said. "How have I not seen him before?"

"He's new," Kelly said. "He's a sophomore at the University of Pennsylvania but came here for the summer to work at Family Center. His uncle owns the place."

"UPenn?" Sydney arched an eyebrow, clearly impressed with his school yet unwilling to admit it.

"So that makes him . . . what, like nineteen?" Raven said.

Kelly nodded.

"You should ask him out," Raven went on. She tugged on the necklace, hanging near her collarbone, that Horace had given her.

"What! No!" Kelly shook her head. "Did you see him, Ray? He's like so out of my league!"

Raven sipped from a glass of water. "No one is out of your league, Kel. No one."

Kelly's mouth hitched up into a subtle smile. "Thanks." The expression fell and she shook her head again, her strawberry blond hair sliding in front of her face, hiding her expression. "Even if he would go out with me, I don't know how to ask him out. I'd be so lost. Will was the one who did the asking when we got together. No way could I be the pursuer."

Alexia sat forward, butterflies fluttering in her stomach. "A crush code," she said just as suddenly as the idea had struck her.

Sydney set her menu down. "A what?"

"To help Kelly get that guy or whatever guy she wants. We could create a crush code for her to follow just like the Breakup Code."

"No way," Kelly said. "Come on, you guys. I don't need another code to follow, and I would never in a million years get Adam!"

"We could all use it," Alexia said, "as a way to keep our own relationships strong."

"I'm in," Raven said. "I could use it while Horace is gone to *not* fall for a crush."

"Yeah," Sydney said. "And I could use it to put the spark back in my relationship with Drew."

"Let's start now. Here." Raven handed Alexia her napkin.

"No." Kelly shook her head for emphasis. "No-no-no-no."

Sydney pulled a pen out of her bag. "The Breakup Code worked for all of us. A crush code might work, too."

Kelly sat back against her chair, grumbling to herself. This would be good for her, Alexia thought. She just had to give it a shot.

Alexia grabbed the pen and began to write.

The Girls' Thirty-eight Crush Rules — How to Turn a Crush into a Boyfriend!

We hereby instate the following code to ensure that we will get any crush we want to notice us — for today we become Women of the Crush Code.

Rule 1: *Be playful, fun, and flirty! Boys like girls who know how to have a good time!*
Rule 2: *Be coy, not shy!*
Rule 3: *Wear raspberry body splash — it drives boys wild!*
Rule 4: *Find out what your crush likes — hobbies, sports, music! Then immerse yourself in it!*
Rule 5: *Seduce him with your eyes! Make eye contact throughout your conversations with him. Never break eye contact!*
Rule 6: *Make him feel special, like he is the only guy in the world!*
Rule 7: *Be adventurous and daring! See life as an adventure!*
Rule 8: *Let your inner beauty shine! Show him the wonderful treasure that lies within you!*
Rule 9: *Be yourself! He will like you for the real you!*

Rule 10: *Have a sense of humor! Guys like to laugh!*

Rule 11: *Act distant but interested! Guys love a challenge!*

Rule 12: *Be agreeable and easy to get along with!*

Rule 13: *Do not be bossy! Do not tell your crush what to do!*

Rule 14: *Make him notice you! Get his attention! Draw him into you!*

Rule 15: *Have an outside interest that you can talk to him about!*

Rule 16: *Be interested in things that interest him!*

Rule 17: *Always look your best in the company of your crush!*

Rule 18: *Respect yourself! Demand that your crush respects you as well!*

Rule 19: *Do not allow your crush to pressure you to do something you do not want to do! Do only things that you and only you want to do and are comfortable with!*

Rule 20: *Take chances and appear to live life on the edge! (Guys like danger.)*

Rule 21: *Be mysterious! Show him there is some mystery about you!*

Rule 22: *Don't answer questions right away! Take a few moments before you answer!*

Rule 23: *Leave some things to his imagination!*

Rule 24: *Become his friend! Talk to him but do not become one of his boys!*

Rule 25: *Compliment your crush two times a week!*

Rule 26: *Do not feel you have to tell your friends who you are crushing on!*

Rule 27: *Do not keep crushing on a guy if it turns into an obsession! His loss if he can't see the jewel that you are!*

Rule 28: *Do not spend more than two months trying to find out if your crush likes you!*

Rule 29: *Do not write your crush an anonymous Email or letter, because he might think someone else sent it!*

Rule 30: *Do not tell anyone that you have a crush on someone unless you know you can trust them not to tell your crush!*

Rule 31: *Do not send your friend to tell your crush you like him!*

Rule 32: *Do not act shy, speechless, or tongue-tied around your crush!*

Rule 33: *Do not stalk or stare at your crush!*

Rule 34: *Do not get depressed and listen to sad love songs if your crush does not notice you!*

Rule 35: *Get to know your crush slowly! (You may discover that you don't like him!)*

Rule 36: *Do not pretend to be a different person when your crush is around!*

Rule 37: *Learn to listen! Do not just talk about yourself!*

Rule 38: *Carry yourself like you are the stuff! Any guy is lucky to have you!*

As the waiter served the girls their dinner, Alexia capped her pen and handed it back to Sydney. "There you go," she said to Kelly. "I'll take this home tonight and type it up. I'll get you a copy tomorrow. You should probably start right away."

"Or not!" Kelly said. "This is insane, you guys. No way am I pursuing Adam. He'd probably laugh at me."

Raven took a big bite of her salad, crunching into the lettuce. After she swallowed, she said, "He doesn't seem like that type of guy. Besides, did you see the way he smiled at you?"

Alexia nodded. "He thinks you're cute at the very least."

"It's worth a try," Sydney said, twirling spaghetti around her fork.

Kelly rolled her eyes.

"I'll get you all copies tomorrow," Alexia said. She smiled to herself as she ripped apart a garlic breadstick. She'd wanted to bring the Breakup Code back, but this was ten times better.

How could this fail?

SIX

Rule 2: *Be coy, not shy!*

The elevator doors dinged and slid open on the second floor of Children's Hospital. Sydney stepped out, holding fast to the strap of her American Eagle messenger bag. She'd be lying if she said she wasn't nervous to start her volunteer shift.

She emerged beneath a lit sign hanging from the ceiling that said WEST WING. Directly in front of her, taped on the wall, were posters advertising the twenty-sixth annual Birch Falls Carnival in July and another canned food drive through the end of the month. Next to those flyers was a poster announcing a photography contest on June 19.

That sounds like fun, she thought absently. Too bad she wasn't good enough to enter.

She went to the right down the hallway and came upon a nurse's station. All around it were hospital rooms with large sliding glass doors so that you could see clearly into each room.

There were balloons floating around the beds. Flowers topping the bedside tables. Crayon drawings hung on the wall behind the nurses' station. Noisy cartoons filtered out from various rooms. Machines dinged and beeped.

Sydney went up to the nurses' station and spoke to the petite woman there. "Hi," she said. "I'm Sydney, a new volunteer."

"Oh! We've been expecting you. I'm Pat, the head nurse on this wing." Pat was a forty-something woman who wore bright pink scrubs and white Crocs. She extended a delicate hand across the counter and said. "It's nice to have you, Sydney."

"Thanks."

"I think I'll get you started with Quin. He's been around here awhile so he knows all the important details. If you go down this hall right here and turn into the third room on the left, you'll find Quin there. If you have any questions, just let us know."

"All right. Thanks."

Sydney followed Pat's directions and went into the third room on the left. Quin sat in one of the green rocking chairs next to the bed. He was in another white Oxford shirt, this one unbuttoned and untucked to reveal a black T-shirt. He had on jeans and scuffed brown leather boots.

In his hands, he held a paperback book with a ghost and werewolf on the front cover. The title was printed in a shiny silver script that said *Dead Wolf.*

Quin read out loud while a little boy lay in bed, his tiny frame drowned in white sheets and blankets. Canary blond hair fanned over the pillow while the boy's pale skin nearly matched the starched white pillowcase.

Quin finished reading and dog-eared the page. "Hey," he said, nodding at Sydney. "I heard you were coming in today. Sydney, right?"

"Yeah." She walked around the bed and offered her hand in a friendly shake. "And you're Quin?"

"Yes, and this" — he pointed at the boy lying in bed — "is Micah."

"Hi." Sydney waved. Micah nodded, uninterested.

Quin put his hand on the little boy's shoulder. "Read more later, dude?"

"Sure." Micah reached over for his TV remote and hit the power button. Cartoons brightened the TV screen as Quin ushered Sydney into the hall.

"So I guess I'm supposed to show you the ropes." A piece of hair fell loose from his ponytail and hung along his temple. He swiped it back absently, tucking it behind his ear.

"I guess."

"It's not as scary or boring as it sounds. You'll have fun here. I promise." The smile he flashed could have brightened any room, let alone a hospital room.

"Well, I'm looking forward to it."

"Let's start with the basics, then. This whole section is the West Wing, but there's West One and West Two. We're in West Two right now." He led her out into the main hallway and pointed to the nurses' station. "That's Station Two. They're in charge of rooms 409 through 418."

They headed back the way Sydney had come and passed the elevators. They came upon another nurses' station and more rooms with sliding glass doors. If Sydney didn't know any better, she'd have thought this was the same nurses' station they'd just left. The counter and rooms were set up exactly like West Two. The only difference was the nurse behind the counter had long red hair and wore black scrubs.

"This is West One," Quin said, "and Station One. They're in charge of rooms 400 through 408. And if you come around this way" — they walked around the nurses' station, where a few nurses nodded a hello — "you'll find the media room."

The media room was large, with two TV centers. There were bookcases spanning an entire wall. There were books, DVDs, and VHS movies.

"The kids can check out the movies and books while they stay here," Quin explained. "We're in charge of that. Getting the movies and books between here and the rooms."

Sydney nodded.

"The kids can come here to hang out, too," Quin went on, "if they're well enough. There are video games hooked up to the TVs."

"Okay," she said.

He smiled. "Are you always this quiet?"

"Umm . . ."

"Just shy?"

Shy? Hardly. Drew said she was born without the shy gene. Being shy was one of the rules in the Crush Code, wasn't it? She hadn't had the opportunity to memorize the rules yet.

Maybe she should try holding back around Drew. Keep a little mystery in their relationship? It was certainly worth a try.

"I wouldn't say I'm shy," she answered. "I'm just trying to take it all in." It was important to her to have all the details right. There was no point doing a job if you couldn't do it well.

"I know it's a lot, but you'll do fine. And the kids are so happy to have company that they're going to love you no matter what."

"I hope so."

"Tell you what . . . I think I have an idea. Something to help loosen you up. Come on."

Sydney didn't like the ominous sound to that.

♥   ♥   ♥

"Are you serious?" Sydney said.

Quin nodded. "The kids love it."

It was a big dragon costume the color of pea soup.

"Umm . . ." Sydney did *not* want to put that stupid thing on. She would rather scrub toilets than put that thing on. Why couldn't *she* be the one reading books to the kids?

"I've done it," Quin added, as if that made it any better. "And trust me, when you're done, you'll feel great." He paused, then, "Well, great and a bit sweaty."

Sydney grimaced.

♥   ♥   ♥

The dragon tail swished behind Sydney as she made her way from the changing room to the kids' hospital rooms.

"Let's go to West Two," Quin said leading the way.

Sydney could barely see out of the dragon's head. Her eyeholes were actually in the dragon's open mouth and it was covered with a black netting to hide her eyes. She'd only been inside the costume for ten minutes and already sweat rolled down her spine.

"Here," Quin said, opening the first sliding door he came to. "They're going to love you."

Yeah, right. She felt like the biggest moron. She probably *looked* like the biggest moron. She could barely walk in this thing. It felt like she had on one of those blow-up sumo wrestler costumes. And flippers on her feet.

When she managed to get inside the first room, the little boy in bed sat up and smiled wide. "Tony!"

"No," Quin said, "this is Trina. Tony's little sister."

The boy's eyes got wide. "Ohhhh," he said.

Quin nudged Sydney in the back. She was surprised she even felt it.

"Um, hi," she said. "What's your name?"

"Lars."

Sydney shuffled over to the hospital bed, hoping she wouldn't catch her big dragon feet on any cords. The little boy's IV stand was on the other side of the bed and all the monitor cords were behind him. Her path looked clear enough.

She shook the boy's hand. "It's nice to meet you, Lars."

"You, too. Can you tell your brother I said hi?"

"Sure." Sydney glanced at Quin. What else was she supposed to say? Hope you get out of here soon? Is the hospital food good?

"Hey, Lars, ask Trina what she has in her pocket."

"What do you have in your pocket?" Lars asked, sitting up straighter.

Sydney glanced down at the kangaroo pocket in her dragon belly and pulled out a bag.

"Let him pick something," Quin whispered.

Sydney held the bag out before her. "Pick something from my treasure," she said, remembering that dragons supposedly collected treasure in the myths she'd read.

Lars dug his hand inside and pulled out a golden egg. He popped the egg open and a bracelet fell out. "Cool! Thanks, Trina!"

"You're welcome."

They said good-bye and headed on to the next room.

It took nearly two hours to visit all the children who were well enough to have visitors. They skipped a few rooms where Sydney saw children tucked in their beds, their eyes shut tight, their monitors beeping behind them. Sydney wondered if they were going to wake up eventually and wished there was something she could do to make them better.

When she took the costume off later that day, she realized Quin was right. Putting a smile on those kids' faces was worth stuffing herself inside that costume. And it felt good to loosen up. Drew would have been proud of her.

SEVEN ~

Rule 23: *Leave some things to his imagination!*

"I miss you," Raven said through her cell phone.

"I miss you, too," Horace answered, his breath sounding soft through the phone. Raven flopped back on her bed and closed her eyes, imagining his arms wrapped around her. Why did he have to go away for the first half of the summer? At least he wasn't going to be gone for the *whole* summer.

"So what have you been doing?" Horace asked.

The first thing that popped into Raven's head was Blake. She hadn't been able to get him out of her head since she met him. There was something about a skater boy that . . . well, she couldn't describe what it was, he just had it. Maybe she could describe it as the cool factor. Skateboarding was one of those sports that was well known enough to make you famous, but not so well known that you lost who you were because of the money and attention.

Skaters were *real*.

"Ray?"

"Huh?" she said.

"Did you hear me?"

No she hadn't. Because she'd been thinking about skaters. And a particular skater boy.

Quit it, she screamed in her head. Focus on your boyfriend. The guy you *love*.

"Sorry," she said. "Jordan was making faces at me from the hallway."

"I said, I have to go, but I'll call you later, okay?"

She sat up in bed and sighed. "Yeah, okay." They'd already been talking on the phone for thirty minutes and had pretty much used up all their conversation starters.

"I love you."

"Love you, too," she replied and said good-bye.

♥   ♥   ♥

"Hey, Ray!" Jordan yelled through the house.

Raven came out of her bedroom. She found her little sister in the living room in a hooded zip-up sweatshirt and cutoff Abercrombie sweats. "What?"

"Want to go for a walk with me?"

Raven had been cooped up in the house all day. A walk would do her good.

Outside, the sun was beginning to set, turning the sky bright orange and pink. The day's heat had retreated and Jordan zipped up her sweatshirt. Raven was in a long-sleeve shirt, the material thin enough to let a bit of night's breeze through.

The neighborhood Raven and Jordan lived in was a small subdivision with light traffic and a lot of outdoor activity. As they headed down Alpine Drive, they passed a father and son in their front yard playing catch with a baseball. A woman speed-walked past them, her rottweiler surging ahead of her on a retractable leash.

Raven looked across the street at Mr. Kailing's house but saw no lights on in the windows.

"So," Jordan began, "I got the job at Bershetti's."

Raven raised a brow. "Really? Are you excited?"

Jordan nodded her head emphatically. "Totally. I mean, have you seen Nicholas Bershetti? He's like Milo Ventimiglia's twin brother. He's so hot and I'm going to be working with him!"

Raven smiled while envy knotted in her gut. She missed that crush/pre-relationship excitement.

"So when do you start?"

"Tomorrow, at eleven in the morning. It means I have to get up early, but that's cool because Nicholas works the same shift. I checked the schedule when I was there yesterday.

"What do you think I should wear?" Jordan mused.

"Maybe —"

Raven was cut off by the sound of skateboard wheels rolling across the asphalt. Blake flew past. He headed straight for the curb and Raven tensed, thinking he was going to crash. Instead, he jumped the curb, flipping his board as he did. He landed perfectly on the sidewalk and whirled around, tipping the board up with a foot.

"That was awesome!" Jordan said, clapping.

Raven agreed, but she wasn't about to say so out loud.

"Wait up, son!" someone called behind them.

Raven glanced over her shoulder to see Blake's uncle

saunter up. He was so big that his arms stuck out like tree branches at his sides. He wasn't fat, just extremely bulky.

Blake grabbed his board and slung it beneath his arm. He was wearing baggy black pants and a white T-shirt with a black tree printed from the shoulder down to the hem. He had on a black DC hat today, but the same white DC shoes. Raven noticed a diamond in one ear.

"I'm Blake," he said, extending his hand to Jordan.

She shook. "I'm Jordan."

"Nice to meet you. You must be Raven's sister?"

Jordan nodded.

"You two look alike. You're both beautiful as hell."

A blush touched Jordan's cheeks. She looked at the pavement.

"Come on, Jordan." Raven linked her arm through her sister's. "We have to go."

"Already?" Blake set his board down and kicked forward, following them as they turned back toward their house.

"We just started our walk," Jordan said.

Raven gave her sister the shut-up look, but Jordan just shrugged.

"Hey, Raven," Blake began, coasting beside them on his board, "why are you giving me the freeze-out?"

"She's just like that," Jordan said.

Raven frowned.

"Does she warm up once you get to know her?"

Jordan nodded.

"Hey, Mil-D!" Blake called to his uncle. "Keep up, man."

"Mil-D?" Jordan furrowed her brow. "Is that his name?"

"Yup."

Mil-D trotted up, his chest heaving. "It's my nickname. Short for Milton Downs."

"It's cute," Jordan said.

Mil-D grinned wide. "Well, thanks."

"You're going to make him blush," Blake said, punching Mil-D in the gut.

"Come on now, son!" Mil-D rubbed his plump stomach.

Blake gave himself a few more pushes on the board so he could catch up with Raven. "So, Raven, what do you do for fun around here?"

"I work."

"That's it?"

"She does music."

Blake raised a brow. "Does music?"

"Writes it, sings it." Jordan nudged Raven. "Tell him."

She'd rather keep her personal life to herself. The more she shared with Blake, the more he'd know about her and the more he knew . . . the closer he'd be.

Wasn't that one of those new rules from the Crush Code? Something about leaving things to the imagination. Maybe she should tell him about herself . . . that way she'd be going against the Crush Code.

No, she should keep quiet, that's what she should do. How would she feel if she found out Horace was in Detroit hanging out with some random chick? And having conversations about their music? Raven would be jealous, and she'd feel betrayed. Not that she didn't trust Horace — she trusted him completely — she just didn't trust other girls. Horace was a cutie, and he was extremely good to Raven. Any girl would kill to have him.

And Raven didn't want to lose him.

When they reached the house, Raven started up the front lawn.

"Ray!" Jordan called. "Where are you going?"

"I have things to do."

Raven heard her sister say, "No she doesn't. She's just trying to get away from you, probably because she thinks you're hot and she has a boyfriend and feels bad."

Raven tensed. How did her sister know all that? Was Raven that transparent? Or did Jordan just know her that well?

"Anyway, I should go," Jordan said. "See you guys around!"

"Later," Blake said. His skateboard hit the ground and he zoomed off down the road, Mil-D trailing behind.

Raven watched him round the corner to the next street, from the *hopefully* inconspicuous spot on her front porch.

Why were the Forces That Be screwing with her like this? Why did a hot guy have to move in across the street from her at the very moment in her life when her boyfriend — whom she loved — was out of town for a month?

Did she have to lock herself in her bedroom? She could already feel that early crush feeling sneaking up on her. Things were not looking good.

EIGHT

Alexia's phone went off in her bag playing Kay-J's new pop hit, "Settled Over You." She winced and dug in her bag, quieting it. It was a new text message from Kelly.

What ru doing?

Alexia looked around the tiny office in the back of Cherry Creek Specialty Store. There were papers stacked a mile high on the metal desk. Sample cookies filled a basket atop the filing cabinet. Some weird New Age music played softly from a CD player in the corner.

Alexia had applied at the store just a week ago, and she was now, officially, an employee.

I'm @ the store, she texted back to Kelly, *waiting for my boss so i can fill out papers.*

It took Kelly a total of seven seconds to respond. *Bummer. i was going 2 ask u 2 come 2 the gym w/ me.*

I wish I could, but u know i'm a working gurl now.

I know! good luck w/ that!

"Yeah," Alexia mumbled and slipped the phone back in her bag.

According to Alexia's parents, a "real" summer job built character, which was why she was at Cherry Creek Specialty Store at ten A.M. on a Saturday morning. Thankfully, Alexia had a good feeling about the store. The owners, an older couple well into their sixties, were extremely warm and inviting and the store itself had a good vibe.

It wouldn't be so bad, right?

Alexia wasn't one to complain about hard work, but she'd wanted to work at the bookstore. She'd heard employees got forty percent off their purchases! And who wouldn't love working around books all day long?

Her parents, both psychologists, had quietly suggested she look elsewhere, somewhere where she'd get dirty. Character was not built on bookshelves. Alexia argued that characters were, quite literally, on bookshelves, but her parents didn't find that amusing.

Lately they'd been pushing her on everything. From school, to a summer job, to her relationship with Ben. When her parents were out touring, promoting the books they wrote, she got along just fine with them.

Now they were taking a break from tours *and* they were in the middle of switching offices. Their lease on their old office had run out while their new one was still being built, which meant the brunt of their work was done from home.

Suddenly they were everywhere and very much into Alexia's business, including what kind of summer job she worked.

Bella, one of Alexia's bosses, walked into the office. "Okay, thanks for waiting. How about we get that paperwork out of the way and then go on a tour of the store?"

"Sounds good."

Twenty minutes later, with the necessary paperwork completed, Bella led Alexia from the small office by the back door into the kitchen. "Here's where we make our sandwiches." There was a long white countertop with several compartments filled with meats and veggies and other sandwich necessities.

In the middle of the kitchen was an island, pots and pans hanging above it. There were several shelves below it with more pans and utensils and other small kitchen appliances.

Bella led Alexia to a small room off the kitchen.

"And this is the break room. You can leave your bag in here. There are aprons in the cupboard above the sink. You're welcome to put whatever you want in the fridge."

Alexia hung her messenger bag on one of the hooks behind the door, then grabbed an apron. They were forest green with the Cherry Creek logo — a river with a cherry tree — printed across the front.

Just as she tied the apron on, the back door opened and closed. Several voices rose and fell as the new arrivals made their way to the kitchen.

"Oh, and here's the rest of the morning crew," Bella said as they filed into the break room.

"This is Nancy," she said, nodding at the fortyish woman. "Rachel." She was the one with long blond hair. "And Jonah."

Jonah was about Alexia's age, if she had to guess. He had sandy blond hair and a warm smile.

"Hi," Alexia said, nodding at everyone.

"Nice to meet you," Jonah said, ducking behind her to grab an apron.

Alexia didn't recognize him from school and wondered if he went to Chisholm Academy.

"Well," — Bella clapped her hands together — "you guys ready for another busy day?"

♥　♥　♥

By the end of her shift at four o'clock, Alexia's feet felt like they were going to fall off. Her forehead was slick with sweat, her apron covered in purple onion juice and avocado mush.

If this wasn't a "real" job, she didn't know what was. The lunch rush had been chaotic and the cleanup afterward lasted even longer. Who would have thought so much went on behind the scenes?

Alexia tossed her dirty apron in the hamper and grabbed her bag.

Jonah met her in the break room. "How was your first day?"

Alexia thought about her response. She didn't want to come across as whiny. "It was tough," she said. "It was a lot more work than I thought it'd be."

He nodded, blond hair falling over his forehead. He swept it back with quick fingers. "It'll get easier," he said, giving her an encouraging smile. "When do you work next?"

"Um . . . Monday."

"Me, too. I'll see you then." He said good-bye.

Alexia grabbed her things and hurried home to put her feet up.

♥   ♥   ♥

Every muscle in Alexia's body was screaming. She felt like she'd run a mile, biked two, and balanced a basket on her head for another four.

She lay back on her bed, relishing the soft comfort of her pillow-top mattress. If she didn't move for the next twenty-four hours, it still wouldn't be long enough.

Eyes closed, she listened to her breathing, feeling sleep slinking in just as her bedroom door burst open.

"Lexy?" Ben said.

She opened her eyes and smiled at him as he looked down at her.

"Tough day?" he asked.

She managed to nod.

"Well, I brought something to make you feel like royalty, which would make me the slave and you can totally order me around so long as it includes making out with you."

She laughed as he sat down beside her.

"Here." He handed her a plastic bag and she dug inside.

"Aww, Ben!"

There was a Subway sandwich and a chocolate chip cookie the size of a hamburger.

"And ice water, too," he said, nodding at the plastic mug on her dresser.

"You're too good to me."

"Yes I am."

She ribbed him and he yelped. "I wasn't serious."

He leaned down to kiss her softly on the lips. "And neither was I."

"Mmm, I liked that."

He quirked an eyebrow. "Yeah?"

She nodded and he bent over to kiss her again, this time lingering longer on her lips. She pulled him closer, weaving her fingers through his messy hair. He put an arm over her, his hand reaching beneath her T-shirt.

Tingles erupted at the contact of his skin against her tummy. And then all her nerves seemed to light with fire.

Ben slipped his tongue along her lips, and she did the same, pulling him more on top of her. He pulled back, breathing hot and heavy.

"You have to stop teasing me like this," he whispered, pushing against her. "You're going to drive me insane."

That was an early crush rule, Alexia thought. It said to tempt and tease the crush, but she hadn't meant this when she wrote it, which is why she deleted the rule. Somehow the deleted rule still lingered in her mind.

"You're right," she said, shrugging out from beneath him. "I'm sorry."

He lay back against the pillows, closed his eyes and rubbed at his brow.

"I really am sorry, Ben."

"I know." He didn't look at her yet. "I just . . ." He sat up. "I love you and I want to share everything with you and you're so damn hot."

She grinned, face hot with flattery and something else.

He scooted off the bed. "I should go anyway. More family stuff tonight. I just wanted to bring you over a treat, but then you tried seducing me." He came around the bed and kissed her atop the forehead. "I'll come by later tonight and massage your feet for you. I bet they hurt."

"They do, but you —"

"Shh." He put a finger against her lips. "It's my job to take care of you, and I take my job very seriously."

Smirking, she nodded. "All right. I'll see you later, then."

"Love you."

"Love you, too."

She followed him downstairs, and she watched him leave from the living room window. When he reached his car, he stopped at the front bumper and bowed in her direction.

She giggled and waved as he got inside his car.

Everything about their relationship was perfect.

Everything except for the whole situation with It.

NINE

Rule 1: *Be playful, fun, and flirty! Boys like girls who know how to have a good time!*

Rule 18: *Respect yourself! Demand that your crush respects you as well!*

Kelly's brother, Todd, took in a deep breath as they entered the Family Center Gym. "Ahh," he said, "smells like rubber mats and sweat."

"You're such a pig." Kelly rolled her eyes.

"Yes he is," Drew added, sharing a knowing smile with her.

"Aren't you two cute?" Todd said, sauntering ahead.

Kelly swallowed, and felt her face warm with unease. Whenever someone grouped her with Drew, she got uncomfortable. It was only a few, short months ago they'd shared a moment. Kelly didn't know what it was or where it would have gone had she explored it further. She'd ended it before it even started.

She shook aside her thoughts before they went too far.

She and Drew were friends, and more importantly, he was going out with Sydney.

"I'm just going to pretend I don't know you," Kelly said to Todd. "So stay far away."

"Good idea," Drew said as he signed Kelly and himself in at the front desk. With that taken care of, they entered the main gym area together. Kelly slowed once she'd passed the threshold and looked around. A very small part of her (well, okay, maybe a medium-size part of her) was hoping she'd run into Adam.

She still thought the Crush Code was silly and that even if it did work, Adam was so out of her orbit he might as well be Saturn to her Earth.

At any rate, she'd told Alexia she'd give it a try but had been putting it off since they developed the new code on Friday.

Now, here she was at the gym bright and early the following Saturday. She'd been in the school's gym, but until last week, she'd never been inside this one. There was a sea of white machines before her, the mirrored walls reflecting everything so that the room looked ten times bigger and that much more intimidating.

When she'd complained to her brother and Drew, they'd agreed to accompany her. It was really Drew she'd wanted along since she knew Todd would be a total dink anyway.

Drew was always helpful.

"Where do I start?" Kelly asked him.

He dropped his truck keys in his gym shorts pocket and led Kelly to the row of treadmills that spanned an entire wall. Each machine had its own flat screen TV attached above it. The Discovery Channel was playing reruns of *Deadliest Catch*.

"Warm up first," Drew said, hopping on a treadmill. "Ten minutes of walking fast or jogging, then we'll start with weight training if you want."

"Sounds good to me."

Kelly got on the treadmill next to Drew and started out at three miles per hour. At two minutes into the workout, she upped the speed to four miles per hour and jogged slowly. Drew upped his treadmill, too, but completely outpaced her. She'd forgotten how good a runner he was.

Using the mirrors, Kelly scanned the gym behind her, looking for Adam. Every few seconds she'd check the entrance and then the locker room door. So far, no sign of him.

Five minutes into the workout, sweat beading on her forehead, Kelly decided to kick it up more and went to five miles an hour. Her legs screamed in protest, her lungs tightened. It'd been a week since she'd exercised. She was so going to pay for this tomorrow morning.

She looked up when movement at the front door caught her eye.

Adam walked inside looking even better than he had the last time she'd seen him. Was that possible?

Staring at him in the mirror, she lost her balance. One foot stepped off the treadmill, causing her to stumble and lose her footing entirely. She went down on the conveyor belt, and it winged her off the treadmill onto the floor.

"Kelly!" Drew jumped off his treadmill.

Adam ran up.

Todd burst into raucous laughter.

"Are you okay?" Adam asked.

Mentally or physically? Because physically she was fine, mentally she felt like she was about to die.

The Crush Code popped into her head. She only knew rule number one by heart.

Be playful, fun, and flirty! Boys like girls who know how to have a good time.

Now was as good a time as any to try out the Code. She really needed something smart to save herself in this situation.

She turned to Adam and gave him a demure smile. "I'm fine, thanks. I just saw you walk through the door looking gorgeous as ever, and I couldn't seem to focus."

Adam's face turned a bright shade of red. He dodged her attention, averting his gaze to the floor. "Well, thanks . . . I guess."

Had she really flustered him? Or was it an act? It didn't seem like an act, but how in the world could someone as good-looking as Adam get embarrassed at a little flattery? He had to know he was hot. Probably he heard that kind of thing all the time.

Drew cleared his throat and hoisted Kelly to her feet. "You sure you're fine?" He ran his fingers over her cheeks, pushing hair away from her face as he looked her over closely.

"I'm fine. Really."

Except she felt like a moron because she'd fallen in front of Adam and Drew and . . . maybe a bit embarrassed that she'd flirted with Adam so blatantly.

When the attention on her started to wane, Adam introduced himself to Drew. The boys started chatting and Kelly escaped to the bathroom to make sure she didn't have skid marks on her face or something.

Satisfied with her appearance, she returned to the main area of the gym. She overheard Drew invite Adam to the next poker night.

"Yeah, that sounds cool," Adam said. "I'll be there."

And so would Kelly.

TEN ~

Rule 24: *Become his friend! Talk to him but do not become one of his boys!*

Sydney plopped down on a bench in the back lobby of Children's Hospital, her cell phone up against one ear, her other hand holding tightly to an 8x10 photo she'd had printed out last night at a copy shop.

On her first full day at the hospital, she'd seen a flyer announcing an amateur photo contest. At the time, she hadn't given entering a second thought, but the contest had stuck with her, and the deadline to enter was today.

The photo she'd picked was one taken earlier this year of Drew's friend Kenny running through the park, the sun shining muted rays on him. It was by far one of her favorite pictures, and she'd always wanted to share it with someone, someone who was honest and would tell her whether or not it was good.

A panel of judges on a photo contest would be honest, but did she really want to know? She liked the picture, wasn't that enough?

"Hello? Syd?" Kelly said through the cell phone.

"Oh, sorry." Sydney turned away from the photo and looked out the lobby windows at the people rushing left and right. Some wore business suits, others colorful hospital scrubs.

"You said you had something to talk to me about," Kelly said. "What's up?"

Sydney glanced again at the picture of Kenny. She'd called Kelly for encouragement because Sydney knew Kelly, out of all her friends, would push her more than anyone. Raven wouldn't care one way or the other. "Just do whatever you want," Raven would say.

Alexia would come up with something neutral, like, "Do what feels right to you."

But Kelly, she'd shriek and cheer Sydney on and tell her she was being silly by not entering. And that's what Sydney needed.

Sydney told Kelly about the contest and the picture she'd taken of Kenny.

"I just wanted your opinion," Sydney said, "should I enter?"

"Well, yeah! Of course you should! What can it hurt, right? Besides, you're perfect at everything. I highly doubt the judges would laugh you right out of the contest."

Perfect? Hardly. Sydney's love life was certainly not perfect.

Nothing about her life was perfect right now. But Kelly was right, Sydney had little to lose if she entered the contest, and she only had until seven o'clock tonight to make a submission. If she let the deadline pass and held onto her picture of Kenny, she'd always wonder, What if? Sydney hated *What ifs*.

"Thanks, Kelly, for listening."

"Hey, no problem. So does that mean you're entering?"

Sydney stood up from the bench and headed toward the front of the hospital where the photo drop box was located. "Yeah," she said, "I'm entering right now."

♥   ♥   ♥

Sydney eyed the clock that hung on the wall behind the nurses' station in West Two. One thing Sydney hadn't figured on was working just a few floors above the contest submission box. She had an hour before the deadline, before someone swooped in and emptied the box, taking Sydney's photo with them.

That would be it, no going back. She would be subjected to a panel of judges, her picture analyzed and scrutinized and . . .

"Muffin duty today, Sydney," a heavyset nurse said, rolling a muffin cart in Sydney's direction. "It's tonight's after-dinner snack. Pass one out to each child and any of the parents who are visiting. The only rooms you should skip are 403 and 408, since those children are on strict diets."

In school, Sydney was used to being in control. She knew the work and she knew it well. Here, it was a completely different situation. She was at the mercy of the staff to help her along. One little slip and these kids would suffer because of her.

She hated feeling out of control.

After writing down the restricted room numbers, Sydney wheeled the cart away from the nurses' station and headed toward the first room. The little boy was sleeping and his mother declined a muffin. In the next room, the little girl, clutching to her stuffed rabbit, nodded emphatically when asked if she liked chocolate chip muffins.

"Here you go, then," Sydney said as she handed the muffin over along with a napkin. Her mother and older brother both took one, too.

So far, so good.

Sydney went back to her cart and rolled along to room 403.

Strict diet, she thought, remembering the nurse's orders.

Sydney glanced inside the room. The little boy was on his side facing the hallway. The blanket was kicked off his legs. Tubes snaked from his hand and his mouth. The machines behind his bed beeped and whirred.

And, sitting close to the child's bed, holding his tiny hand, was Quin. His back was to her and his black hair was untied, creating a curtain between his eyes and Sydney.

But if he'd been able to see, he'd have most definitely caught her staring.

There was something awe-inspiring about a guy Sydney's age who sat in a Peds ICU room with a little boy who was a stranger to him, holding his hand while he slept.

Sydney finished passing out muffins just in time for her break. Plopping down at the round table, she brought out her cell phone and hit number two on speed dial. The phone rang several times before Drew's voice mail picked up.

Sydney hit END and then number five on speed dial. Kelly answered on the third ring.

"Hey, Syd. What's up?"

Sydney clacked open a can of Sprite. "Is Drew over there?"

"Umm . . ."

Sydney could hear music playing in the background. It was that new singer, Kay-J. She'd apparently gone double platinum, or whatever it was, and was on all the top billboard charts.

"Hold on a sec," Kelly said, turning the music down. "I'm in my room. I heard a car pull up not too long ago. Maybe it was Drew."

Sydney pulled an orange from her bag and peeled back the rind. Her day so far had been pretty uneventful except for entering the contest. She really had nothing to talk to Drew about, but that didn't stop her from *wanting* to talk to him. Just hearing his voice on the phone made her happy. And she figured, the more they communicated, the stronger their relationship would be.

Like Rule 24 said, *Become his friend!*

Sydney figured a good relationship started there, with a friendship. She and Drew, they'd skipped that part and gotten right to the making out. If their relationship was going to survive this time, she had to be his friend *and* his girlfriend, someone he could trust, someone he felt he could talk to.

And most importantly, someone he could count on to listen, to be understanding.

That was the new and improved Sydney.

"Yup, he's here," Kelly said a minute later. "Hold on."

The phone switched hands. Drew came on the line. "Hey. Did you get off work early or something?"

"I'm on break."

"Oh. Everything okay?"

"Fine. I just . . . I don't know, I missed you."

"Oh." He sounded surprised. A good surprised. Maybe Sydney needed to do this sentimental thing more often. "Well, I miss you, too."

Silence filled the line. Sydney peeled off a slice of orange and bit into it. "I guess I really don't have anything else to say. I just called to tell you I love you."

He laughed that easy Drew laugh. "I love you, too. And hey, Syd?"

"Yeah?"

"You can call more often like this. You know, just to tell me you miss me. I kinda like it."

Sydney grinned wide. "I can manage that."

ELEVEN

Rule 30: *Do not tell anyone that you have a crush on someone unless you know you can trust them not to tell your crush!*

The early afternoon sunshine spilled over the porch railing as Raven swung slowly in the hammock. She chewed on the end of her pen, trying desperately to ignore the sound of a skateboard hitting cement across the street.

On her lap sat a journal, one she'd made at Scrappe a few weeks ago specifically for her lyric scribbling. There were musical notes glued to the front of the white notebook. Across the bottom of the cover, she'd drawn the words *Musical Ramblings* with a purple calligraphy pen.

So far, she had about ten pages full of rhymes and thoughts but nothing substantial. There were so many things she wanted to say in a song, but she wasn't sure where to start. The major thing she was experiencing right now was heartache. She wanted Horace here, now, not thousands of miles away.

It'd been so long since she'd seen him (okay, only two weeks). She was finding it hard to conjure an image of him in her mind. And if she didn't think it extremely dorky, she would have asked him to send a picture message of himself so she had something to look at.

She closed her eyes, daydreaming about Horace, when the front door of the house opened and Jordan clomped out in a pair of espadrille sandals.

"What are you doing?" Jordan asked, plopping down in one of the wicker chairs across from the hammock.

Raven sighed. "Trying to write a song. Something. Anything! But I can't concentrate with all that noise he's making." She nodded her head in Blake's direction.

Jordan smiled. "Yeah, because you really don't get any enjoyment out of watching a hot skater boy get all sweaty and stuff."

"Very funny."

"Just admit it, you're crushing on him."

Raven put pen to paper but drew a blank. "I have a boyfriend, Jordan. I do not have a crush on Blake."

"Having a boyfriend has nothing to do with it."

Oh, it had everything to do with it because Raven having a crush was the same as Superman being exposed to red kryptonite. Raven would go bad in a second if she had a crush. She couldn't let it happen.

Blake kicked off his driveway and rode out into the middle of the street. He did some sort of kick flip or something (Raven wouldn't pretend to know what all those skateboarding tricks were) and landed smoothly on his board.

She sat up straighter in the hammock to watch him. It was hard to admire his body in all those baggy clothes, but she could see the intricate muscles working in his forearms as he balanced and then grabbed the board when he slid down the stair railing in front of Mr. Kailing's house.

If that small part of him looked that good, then what did the rest of him look like?

Oh stop! she chided herself. Get it together.

"Hey, Raven!"

Raven jumped and lost her balance in the hammock. It rolled over, tossing her out and onto the porch floor.

Jordan erupted in a shriek of laughter.

Raven scrambled to her feet. "Shut up!" she whispered.

"Come on over!" Mil-D called, waving frantically.

"I can't," she said.

"Yes she can!" Jordan said.

"What are you doing?" Raven gritted her teeth. "You're . . . you're . . . such a meddler!"

Jordan stood, smacking her lips together. "I might be a 'meddler' but you're crushing on him, and I like watching you squirm because of it." She giggled again and shoved Raven off the porch. "See ya, sis."

Grumbling to herself, Raven went across the street. She could feel Blake's eyes on her as she passed him.

"Thanks for the invite," she said, once she was in close enough range of Mil-D to have a normal conversation. "But I'm really busy right now."

From here, Raven could smell something barbecuing in the back of the house.

"You're never too busy for food, girl. Stay."

Blake skated up behind Raven. "Yeah. Stay for just a little while. My grandpa skipped out on us for bingo so we're grilling the goods he bought last night."

"Umm . . ." Her stomach growled when she smelled the cooking food. It did sound good. . . .

No, she was busy and Blake was . . . sweaty and looking extremely good. But she was starving and, really, what could it hurt? As long as she didn't indulge in anything inedible, she was safe.

"Fine," she said. "But just for a little while."

♥　♥　♥

Raven had expected to sit down at the table, eat, have light conversation, and then leave. What she got instead was a lot of insight into Blake's life. It turned out, Mil-D was not, in fact, Blake's uncle. He was Blake's bodyguard.

"Then why did you say he was your uncle?" Raven asked as she wiped her hands on a napkin. They were sitting in Mr. Kailing's backyard on his deck. The sun was still bright behind her, warming her bare shoulders.

"Because some people treat me differently if they find out I have a bodyguard." Blake shrugged and tore apart another piece of barbecued chicken. "Besides, Mil-D's been with me so long, he's like family."

"Aww," Mil-D said, "thank you, son." He gave Blake a hearty pat on the back.

Blake laughed, shaking his head.

"So," Raven said, looking between the two guys, "he's your bodyguard because you're actually a somewhat famous skater?"

Blake gave a half-hearted shrug.

"Yes he is," Mil-D filled in. "You should see him when we go to New York. The boy's like a mini Tony

Hawk or something. Little high school girls fawning all over him."

Blake slapped Mil-D on the arm. "Shut up, dude. They do not."

When Blake turned his back, Mil-D looked at Raven and nodded.

Raven leaned into her cushioned patio chair, biting her lip. How had she managed to *not* notice there was a semi-famous celebrity living across the street from her? And more importantly, how had Jordan missed it? She was usually on top of celebrity news.

"You know what else?" Mil-D said. "My boy here, he's sponsored by some pretty big names. Red Bull, Volcom, Etnies . . . kid's sick."

Raven raised her brow. "Really?"

Blake pulled the brim of his hat down even more as if to hide beneath its shadow. "Dude," he muttered.

"Sorry, son. I just like to brag about you. Can't I be proud?"

"Wow, that is cool," Raven added reluctantly. She didn't want Blake to get a big head, but still . . . what he did and how successful he was at it had Raven more than impressed.

Maybe being around Blake wasn't so bad after all.

Alexia scraped spinach dip from a plastic dish and slopped it in the garbage. The stuff looked like mushy sea-weed in a creamy dressing, but she had to admit, with bread, it tasted really good.

She'd been at Cherry Creek Specialty Store for over a week now and she felt like she was finally getting the hang of it. Of course, there were still many things she didn't know. Thank god for Jonah.

He was always patient with her, no matter how many questions she asked. He'd been at the store the longest, which meant he knew everything. Even some of the employees who'd been there for months occasionally had to ask him questions.

Bella came into the kitchen, her hair mussed at the top, wispy strands floating around her forehead. "You're doing great," she said to Alexia. "We sure had a rush today."

Alexia nodded and set the plastic dish in the large industrial sink. "Saturdays are always busy in here, huh?"

"They are." Bella turned the oven off, then grabbed a pan of cooling bread. She set it on the countertop to slice. "It dies down in the wintertime."

Jonah pushed through the swinging doors at the front of the kitchen. "Can I take my lunch, Bella?"

"Sure. Why don't you go, too," she said to Alexia.

"Are you sure?"

"Yeah. We can handle it."

Jonah grabbed a sandwich from the refrigerator. "Alexia, you want one?"

"Umm . . . sure. Turkey, please."

He grabbed her a turkey and brought it over to the sandwich counter.

"Want to come with me outside?"

"Sure."

They headed out the back door and to the small patch of grass on the store's lot. There was a metal table there with four bistro-style chairs. Alexia sat and Jonah picked the seat across from her.

A line of elder maple trees kept the hot afternoon sun at bay. A slight breeze cooled the sweat at the nape of Alexia's neck.

"Nice day, huh?" Jonah said.

"Yeah. I wish I wasn't working, though. So I could really enjoy it."

Jonah laughed. "Yeah. Don't we all." He ripped his sandwich in two and took a bite. "For some reason, my girl-friend works, despite not having to. She's odd like that." He smiled as if his girlfriend's eccentric qualities were her most endearing.

"How long have you guys been together?"

"Two years."

Alexia widened her eyes. "Wow. That's a long time."

He nodded before taking a drink of his soda, then, "I love her a lot and maybe it's old-fashioned of me, but I'd like to think there's only one love of your life. I think she's it."

"Really?"

Alexia wasn't sure if she agreed with having only one major love, but she liked that Jonah admitted to being old-fashioned and romantic. She admired that. Ben was romantic. Too bad he wasn't old-fashioned. If he was, he'd want to wait until they were married to have sex. That would save her a lot of stress. She could spend the next five to ten years (okay, maybe not ten) blissfully relaxed while she waited for her marriage to come along.

Then she wouldn't be constantly thinking about It and worrying about Ben breaking up with her if she didn't do It.

He didn't seem like that kind of guy, but Alexia was definitely not like the other girls he'd gone out with. What if he realized he missed having sex and found someone else?

Her friends would say that she didn't need Ben if he turned out like that anyway, but Alexia really loved him. Maybe she didn't need him, but she sure did want him.

TWELVE ～∽

Rule 4: *Find out what your crush likes — hobbies, sports, music! Then immerse yourself in it!*

Sydney was due at the photo contest awards ceremony at four in the afternoon. She'd gotten up somewhere around nine A.M. and was already showered and dressed. She sat at the dining room table, her knee bobbing nervously. She tapped her pen against her open journal.

She'd sat down intending to write a bit about how she was feeling, but she couldn't seem to concentrate.

"Syd?"

Sydney looked across the table at Drew. He was working on his essay for his college applications. Drew wasn't going to waste one moment of the summer, not when his senior year was so close.

"What?" Sydney said, setting her pen in the open spine of her journal.

"I can't seem to concentrate," Drew said, grinning. "And you aren't exactly concentrating either."

Sydney sighed and rubbed her forehead. She'd never been so nervous in her life. Entering the contest at the hospital had sounded like fun, but now that she knew people were examining the photo and judging it, she wanted to take the submission back.

"Get up," Drew said. "I have an idea."

"What kind of an idea?" Sydney asked, looking over at him warily.

He shut his notebook, then her journal, and held his hand out to her. "I'll take you to the fish store. It always helps calm you down."

Ever since her mom and dad took her to the New York Aquarium in Brooklyn, Sydney had been in love with marine wildlife. Seeing fish just relaxed her, and she hadn't been to the fish store here in Birch Falls in what seemed like months.

Drew was right — going might calm her down — something she desperately needed if she was going to make it to the awards ceremony without hurling.

"All right," she said, slipping into her tennis shoes. "Let's go."

♥   ♥   ♥

Drew turned left down Franklin Avenue, which would take them to the I-99 East.

"Umm, is it too late to ask you to take the side streets?" Sydney said as Drew flicked on his blinker and got into the on-ramp turn lane.

He glanced over at her. "I'm already getting on the freeway. Besides, it's quicker this way."

"Yeah, but . . ." She trailed off as the stoplight turned green and Drew turned. He sped up, hitting fifty miles an hour quickly and bringing the car up to seventy as he merged onto the highway.

"I just like the side streets," Sydney said. "The highway is so . . . boring. It's just traffic and concrete."

Drew took her hand in his, squeezing gently. "We'll take the side streets next time. And you can bring your camera if you want. We can make a day of it."

She nodded, liking the sound of that. "Okay."

At one in the afternoon, traffic wasn't too bad. Drew drove at a steady seventy-five miles an hour passing only two cars on the way to the fish store. Sydney stared out the passenger-side window, silent, zoning out as the green interstate signs became a blur.

When they got off the freeway, slowing down felt good. Sydney snapped out of the quiet. "I've been thinking about buying an aquarium," she said as they waited beneath a stoplight.

"Oh yeah? I've been thinking about getting a dog."

Sydney instantly tensed. "What kind of dog?"

Sydney liked dogs, she just didn't like big dogs. When she was eight, the neighbor's chow mix bit her on the hand when she got too close to his food. Ever since then, big dogs freaked her out to the point she felt like panicking whenever she was around one.

"I don't know," Drew said. "I guess whatever kind I find that I like."

"Just not anything too big?"

He shrugged, barely glancing at her. "I guess it'll just depend on what I find."

He pulled into the parking lot of the large strip mall, and they got out, the sun shining through thin, white clouds. Sydney took Drew's hand as they walked up. This felt good, the two of them together, getting out and doing something.

"You mind if I go to Pet Shop real quick? See the dogs?" Drew asked. "Then I'll come to the fish store."

Sydney nodded, letting go of his hand. "Sure."

They parted, Drew going inside Pet Shop on the left, Sydney going inside the fish store on the right. Inside the small specialty shop, the outside world faded away. Here, there were no ceiling lights, only the soft glow of aquarium lights. With dozens of aquariums lined up together on every side of the shop, it almost felt like Sydney was in the ocean itself.

"Hi there," a man said behind the counter. "Anything I can help you with?"

"Just looking, thanks."

Sydney bypassed the shelves of empty aquariums, the display of aquarium stones and sculptures, heading directly to the fish. She started at the goldfish, ducking down to watch their orange bodies darting around one another. She moved on to the guppies and fancy goldfish and then the tropical fish.

A display tank took up almost an entire wall. A sign above it said THE GREAT CORAL REEF. There was green fluorescent mushroom coral and yellow colony polyp among other things. There were a few anemones and sponges.

Two vibrant clown fish swam lazily in front. A blue tang poked its head out from behind a rock as an auriga buttefly-fish swam past.

Sydney moved on to the other same-species tanks, stopping to admire the black sea horses. They were, by far, her favorite. She could sit and watch them all day as they seemed to float in the water.

How much would it cost to put together a new tank? Would her dad help her with the expenses? Maybe Drew would — "Syd!"

She startled and straightened as Drew rushed over. "Come to the pet store," he said, grabbing her hand and dragging her next door. He held the door open at Pet Shop, smiling like a kid in a toy store. Sydney went in, and a cacophony of barking dogs sounded from the back. It smelled like wet dog and dry cat food here. Not a bad smell, just not something Sydney was used to.

"In the back," Drew said, winding through the aisles of dog and cat food and then the hamster cages and plastic exercise balls. They finally reached the back corner of the store, where an arched opening led to another room. Above the archway read PET LAND in big, blocky letters.

Sydney went in beneath the archway and looked around. On one side of the room, puppies yipped from small kennels and on the other side, larger, adult dogs barked and jumped against their cages.

"Hey," a woman crooned. "Calm down, you guys." Several of the adult dogs quieted, sitting on their hind legs eyeing the short, petite woman intently. She had long black hair braided down her spine. Oversize square glasses sat low on a crooked nose.

"Oh, you're back," she said to Drew. "This must be your girlfriend, then?" She offered her hand to Sydney and Sydney shook it.

"Hi," Sydney said.

"Your boyfriend here said he couldn't adopt anything without your blessing." The woman smiled. "But you look like a girl who can handle a Husky."

"Um . . . Husky?"

The woman went behind a partition wall and came back out with a large, fluffy dog on a leash, its tail wagging happily behind.

"His name is Bear," the woman said. "And I think he was meant for you two."

Drew crouched down and scratched Bear beneath the chin. "I think he likes me," Drew cooed. The dog was mostly white save for a patch of light brown fur at the top of his head and a spot on his back.

"Isn't he cute?" the woman said, the leash hanging loosely from her hand. "He has eyes just like you."

Sydney had to admit, if Drew had a twin in dog form, here it was. But adopting it? Sure, it was sitting there nicely now, but what happened when Drew took it home and Sydney accidentally got in the way of its food?

Her shoulders tensed, remembering that dog from so long ago, snarling and snapping at her. She shuddered, rubbing her fingers over the scar on her right hand where the neighbor's dog had bit her. The bite itself hadn't been that bad. It'd bled, of course, but she hadn't needed stitches. Sydney's mom had wanted the dog put to sleep, but the neighbors, Mr. and Mrs. Yates, had sworn over and over again that the dog would be kept behind a privacy fence.

They kept to their word but moved just a year later.

"So what do you think?" Drew asked, looking up at Sydney expectantly.

She'd never told him about the dog bite so long ago and the lingering effects of it.

She reached over tentatively and patted the dog on the back, far, far away from its mouth and teeth. It turned slowly, watching her with those striking blue eyes. Sydney stepped back, putting her hands safely in her shorts pockets. "He's pretty."

"Isn't he?" the woman said, running her hand down the dog's back. "I wish I could take him home, but I have too many already! My husband would kill me if I brought one more home."

"Cathy?" Drew said. "Can you give us a minute with him?"

"Sure." The woman, presumably Cathy, handed Drew Bear's leash and disappeared into an office in the back.

Standing now, the dog reached Drew mid-thigh, that's how big he was. Drew pulled his fingers absently through the tuft of fur on the dog's forehead. "He only has today, I guess," Drew said softly. "Nobody has adopted him yet because he's so big."

"He *is* big."

Big dog meant big teeth and an even bigger bite. Another image of the neighbor dog snarling flashed through her mind. Sydney blinked, trying to keep the chill at bay.

"I think we should adopt him," Drew said softly.

We? Sydney thought. She half grinned, liking the way he put it. He wanted to adopt a dog together, like they were starting their very own family or something. Family was the one thing Sydney was lacking lately.

"He's house-trained," Drew added as if he were trying to sell a used car with leather interior.

Maybe it would be fun, having a dog that Sydney and Drew saved together. And getting a dog would follow rule number four because Sydney was immersing herself in something Drew liked.

"All right," she finally said. "Let's adopt him."

"Did you hear that, Bear?" Drew said. "You're saved!" Bear barked several times before coming over to Sydney. He sat on his hind legs and glanced up at her as if to say, "Can I lick you or something?"

"He fell in love with you quick," Drew said. "Just like I did."

Sydney smiled. She was hesitant about the whole thing, but saving this dog seemed to make Drew happy, and he was the only thing she had left.

THIRTEEN ～ॐ～

Rule 9: *Be yourself! He will like you for the real you!*

Sydney crossed her legs, hoping to stop her fidgeting. A moment later, her foot tapped impatiently on the carpet, making her knee bob up and down. Her trip to the fish store had calmed her down, but then Drew had talked her into adopting a dog, a big dog at that, and . . .

She let out a breath. Right now, she needed to focus on the photo contest awards ceremony.

Drew sat on one side of her, Raven on the other. Alexia, Ben, Kelly, and Todd were all there, too. Sydney hadn't expected them to come, but Kelly surprised her by telling their friends. They'd all been waiting for Sydney in the front lobby of Children's Hospital at the start of the ceremony.

To be honest, Sydney was glad they were here. Sure, losing in front of them would be disappointing, but she liked having their support for something she felt so awkward with. Photography was new to her. Not to mention, some people might think it a waste of time. But her friends didn't and that made Sydney grateful.

Within the ten minutes the group had been seated, the room filled up. They were in the conference room on the first floor of Children's Hospital surrounded by at least a hundred red chairs. The panel of judges, two men and two women, sat quietly in their chairs on a dais at the front of the room.

Sydney's knee bobbed faster.

"It's all right," Drew whispered, setting his hand on her leg. "No matter what, at least you entered, right?"

She nodded.

At five minutes after four, the room quieted as a man took the podium on the dais. He was older, mid-forties, with thinning gray hair and black-framed glasses. "Good afternoon," he said. "I'm Eddison Gerald, director of public relations. I'm glad you all could be here. Welcome to the fifth annual Children's Hospital photo contest. For those of you who are new, every year we take photo entries from amateur photographers. Those photos are hung in our art hall for the children to view, to give them something beautiful to look at as they go through difficult treatments, working toward better health.

"And, to encourage submissions, we award first, second, and third prizes every year. Now let me introduce you to our panel of judges."

He stepped back, pointing to the man seated on the far left. "We have Roy Harrison, a critic at the Yale School of Art. Katie Taylor, a professor at the New York Institute of Photography. Jamie Munson, director of photography at *Shutter* magazine, and leading photographer Cook Porter whose photos have been in magazines such as *National Geographic*. Please welcome them."

The room applauded. Sydney clapped quietly, her fingers trembling. She didn't recognize the names of the judges, but if their credentials were any indication, they were prominent figures in the industry. Who was she to enter her photo? They'd probably seen her entry and laughed, picking it apart.

"Can we go?" she whispered to Drew.

"What, now?" He frowned. "It just started. I don't want to stand up in the middle of it."

"You okay?" Raven asked. "You look pale."

"This was a bad idea," Sydney said as the clapping quieted down. "Those judges are serious about this, and I'm just an amateur!"

"It's an amateur contest," Kelly pointed out.

"Now," Mr. Gerald said, stepping up to the microphone, "along with a free two-year subscription to *Shutter* magazine, our winners will receive some other valuable prizes. Third place will receive a hundred dollar prize. Second place will receive a two hundred dollar prize and first place will receive a five hundred dollar prize."

The room applauded again, the sound seeming in rhythm with Sydney's rapidly beating heart. She wasn't going to win, but she really, really wanted to place somewhere in the top three. Did she actually have talent? Should she continue to explore photography?

This moment seemed like a declaration of her future path. She pictured herself going away to art school, becoming a photographer, traveling the world, taking photos that meant something.

But if she lost today, maybe she'd continue down the path she already had planned. School at Yale, a degree in something serious like science or business.

Suddenly that didn't sound so exciting.

Mr. Gerald raised his hand and people quieted.

"Third place goes to . . ."

A woman entered the room through a side door. In her hands she held a picture frame covered with a white cloth. She stepped up on the dais, standing next to Mr. Gerald. He grabbed a corner of the cloth and pulled it off quickly, exposing a photograph of a pink flower and a bee sitting in the middle.

"Macy Bernard."

A girl near the front of the room stood and made her way up to the dais. She shook Mr. Gerald's hand and accepted a framed award certificate with her name on it.

"Second place goes to . . ."

Another woman entered the room and went up onstage carrying a picture. Mr. Gerald pulled off the cloth to show a picture of a large maple tree, bare of leaves, standing tall against a storm-darkened sky.

"Michael Shallen."

An older man went onstage, took his award certificate, and stood off to the side with Macy.

"Now," Mr. Gerald said, "for our grand prize winner."

The last picture came out, covered in a white cloth. The woman holding it smiled wide, her feet soundless as she went up the two steps to the dais. She stopped at Mr. Gerald's side and looked out as if trying to spot the winner in the crowd.

Sydney squeezed her eyes shut, tried to slow her beating heart. She felt light-headed, her fingers trembling, her breath coming too quickly.

I can't be the winner, it's not me. . . .

"Oh my god," Kelly said.

"Is that . . ." Raven trailed off.

Sydney opened her eyes. There was her picture, framed in a beautiful mahogany frame, held up for the entire room to see.

"Sydney Howard!" Mr. Gerald said.

The room clapped. Sydney's friends stood up, whistled.

"Go up there!" Kelly said. "Go on!"

Sydney stood on shaky legs. She'd won? That was her picture, but maybe there'd been a mistake.

She made her way to the dais, went up the steps to Mr. Gerald's side. He shook her hand, congratulated her. She thanked him and took her award certificate, her name written big and bold in elegant cursive writing.

She'd won and, in her heart, she was now Sydney Howard, amateur photographer. It was an official title, she thought, a title that reflected who she was on the inside. She wanted to shed the old Sydney, the prim, perfect, proper Sydney. The one who took all the AP classes and had Yale, Harvard, and Stanford on her to-apply college list.

It was time to do what she wanted to do. It was time to be herself.

FOURTEEN ～👁

Rule 5: *Seduce him with your eyes! Make eye contact throughout your conversations with him! Never break eye contact!*

Rule 8: *Let your inner beauty shine! Show him the wonderful treasure that lies within you!*

Rule 22: *Don't answer questions right away! Take a few moments before you answer!*

Kelly pulled out a chair at the restaurant table and plopped down. It smelled like refried beans and taco meat inside. It was Sydney's idea to come to the Mexican restaurant, though she'd had to fight with Drew over it.

He wanted Italian, she wanted Mexican. Since it was her night of celebration, she'd eventually won the argument and here they were. Alexia sat on Kelly's left side, Raven on her right. Drew, Sydney, and Todd were on the other side of the table, Ben at the head.

Spanish music played from a jukebox highlighted red with neon lights. Musical instruments hung on the walls along with a flamenco skirt and pictures of a Spanish band who'd inspired the opening of the restaurant in Birch Falls.

For a Thursday night, the restaurant was packed. The group had to wait more than ten minutes for one of the bigger tables to open up in back. Now that they were seated, the waitress took their orders and hurried into the back, her bright red skirt swinging around her calves.

The table was a mix of several conversations. The guys talked sports while Raven and Alexia chatted about music. Sydney was decidedly quiet for having just won a contest, despite the fact that she was glowing. She wouldn't come right out and say she was proud of herself for winning, but anyone could tell just by looking at her. A permanent smile was on her face and every few minutes, she'd get this faraway look in her eyes like she was somewhere else.

Kelly didn't blame her. The picture Sydney had taken of Kenny earlier this year was a really good picture. Kelly wouldn't pretend to know anything about photography, but the sun shining down on Kenny, it was like heaven had opened up or something. That had to be a sign of good photography skills, right?

But Drew . . . he didn't seem that impressed with the whole thing. He'd congratulated Sydney, offered to treat her to dinner, but he just didn't seem as excited as he should be.

Maybe because he expected this kind of thing from Sydney? Because she was good at everything she did?

Then again, Kelly had sensed a bit of distance between the two for some time now. It wasn't anything she could explain in words, it was more a physical sense. Not to mention, he'd been spending a lot more time over at Kelly's house hanging out with Todd.

"You should have seen him last weekend," Todd said, giving Drew a friendly pat on the back, his voice growing louder by the second. "We're down by six, right, and we're twenty yards off from the end zone and Drew catches the ball and he takes off! He's dodging guys, jumping over them. Dude, I haven't seen him play like that in forever!"

"I'm sorry I missed it," Ben said.

"Yeah," Todd added, "because you're just a boy toy now, always hanging out with your girlfriend instead of your guys."

Ben snorted. "You're just jealous!"

Todd rolled his eyes, but quieted down. "No I'm not."

Drew laughed and shook his head. He met Kelly's eyes across the table.

Never break eye contact!

Rule five, Kelly thought. There was more to the rule, but she suddenly couldn't remember it. The very first thing Kelly noticed about Drew when she met him so long ago was his eyes. He had uncanny blue eyes, eyes that Kelly had fallen in love with as a little girl.

Sydney nudged Drew, and he looked away.

Kelly blinked, straightened in her chair. She tried tuning into Raven and Alexia's conversation, but she couldn't help listening in on Sydney and Drew. Sydney wanted to go for a walk in the state park after dinner, he wanted to hang out at Kelly's house with Todd.

When Drew finally agreed to the walk, Kelly's heart sank. It was fun having Drew over at her house. Maybe instead she'd invite Adam out somewhere, if she could summon the courage to ask him out.

♥   ♥   ♥

Two days later, Kelly still hadn't asked out Adam. What if he said no? She couldn't take the rejection.

Instead of going out on Saturday, she'd taken an extra shift at the animal shelter.

"Come on, Clove," she said, trying to coax the gray adult cat forward. He cowered in the back corner of his kennel, amber eyes wide, watching her. He wasn't hissing yet, which was a good sign. But then again, cats could attack without giving any notice.

That's why Kelly had on plastic safety glasses and thick gloves. Morris, the animal control officer, always made fun of her when she put the gear on, but she wasn't willing to lose an eyeball because of some crazy cat. Better to look silly than be sorry.

She never would have worn this stuff if Will were still working here, though.

Thankfully, once he graduated from Birch Falls High, he put in his two weeks' notice with the shelter. Kelly had the whole summer to enjoy working with the animals without having to worry what Will thought of her.

Of course, if she still *had* Will, or anyone for that matter, she wouldn't have picked up this extra shift at the shelter.

Being single, she had a lot of free time on her hands. It benefited the shelter, at least. She was working here over twenty hours a week and was loving every minute of it.

After coaxing Clove from his kennel and settling him into a clean one, Kelly left the cat room. She went down the short hallway to the front lobby, stopping abruptly when she saw Adam standing on the other side of the counter.

"Adam!"

He looked up and half laughed. "You look so official in those gloves and glasses."

Rule number . . . what was it? Whichever it was, it said to let your inner beauty shine! And she totally just screwed that rule up!

She shook off the gloves and tore off the glasses.

Morris tried to mask his snort/laugh. Kelly shot him a death look, but he couldn't stop himself. He would never let her forget this moment.

Adam picked up a cardboard box. "They found these behind McDonald's," he said. "A litter of six kittens."

Morris took the box over the counter and handed it to Kelly. She set it on the floor.

"Aww!" She picked up a black and white kitten and nuzzled it with her nose. "I love kittens."

"Me, too," he said.

"Really?"

Adam shrugged. "My grandma had a farm when I was little and there were always kittens running around. She used to say they were like sunshine and velvet."

Kelly scratched the kitten behind the ear, then ran her fingers over its soft furry back. "They are kind of like velvet, aren't they?"

Morris sauntered off to get the paperwork ready for the intake. Kelly set her kitten back in the box and lifted it up.

"Here." Adam came around the long counter and took the box out of her hands. "Let me help."

"You're sure?"

He nodded. "Just lead the way."

♥   ♥   ♥

Kelly petted an orange tiger kitten once more before setting him inside the big kennel with his brothers and sisters. They had a clean litter box, fresh food, and water.

"Thanks," Kelly said, turning to Adam. "That was nice of you to bring them in and help get them settled."

"My pleasure." He pulled his car keys from his jeans pockets. "So . . . uh . . . do you have to work tomorrow night?"

She managed to shake her head no.

Trepidation roared up Kelly's throat like a tidal wave. Was Adam going to ask her out? It sure seemed like he was going to ask her out. What was she going to say if he asked her out?!

"Would you like to go to Bershetti's with me?"

Kelly just stared at him. He *was* asking her out. She smelled like a litter box and probably looked like one, too. And he was *still* asking her out? Was this some kind of joke? Did Raven or Alexia put him up to this?

No, they wouldn't, which meant . . .

He was asking her out!

Adam raised his brow. "Kelly?"

Adam and Kelly . . . that did have a nice ring to it, didn't it?

"Kelly?"

"Yes!" she blurted.

He grinned.

She took in a deep breath, hoping to calm her rapidly beating heart. "I mean, yes, I'd love to go. Sunday at Bershetti's at, say, seven?"

"Sounds good." He continued to fidget with his keys. "I'll see you then." He tipped his head by way of saying good-bye. Kelly waved, feeling like the biggest goober in the world. At least he hadn't taken back the dinner offer. That was a good sign, right?

FIFTEEN ∽ᄋ

Rule 20: *Take chances and appear to live life on the edge! (Guys like danger.)*

Raven handed the vanilla frappé to the woman on the other side of the counter. "Thanks," she said, putting a smile on her face, hoping she didn't look as crappy as she felt.

Working at Scrappe wasn't the same without Horace around. It seemed quieter. Duller. Raven was counting down the days. Only seventeen more to go.

Seventeen? She exhaled. That seemed like forever.

She ran hot water through the espresso machine and picked up the dirty dishes. "Hey, Katie?" she called to the other worker. "Since it's slow, I think I'll take my break if you don't mind."

"No, go ahead."

Raven escaped to the back of the store and went to her mother's office. She sat on the pumpkin-colored suede couch, tucking her legs up beneath her.

Checking her cell phone, she found a text message waiting for her.

Call me as soon as u can.

It was from Horace!

Raven hit number two on her speed dial, her heart rate increasing with every ring on the other end.

"Ray," Horace said when he picked up the line. "How are you?"

Raven's heart seemed to drop right out of her chest. "Better now." She smiled to herself, laying her head against the back of the couch. "God, I've missed you."

"I miss you, too."

"So, tell me, what have you been doing over there in Detroit?"

Horace told her about going to a baseball game, checking out the Motown Historical Museum, and going to a few local music hangouts.

"The music here is awesome," he said. "Me and you should come here together next summer."

Raven closed her eyes, imaging it. It'd just be her and Horace in a car driving across country without her mother nagging her in the background.

"Hey," Horace said, bringing Raven out of her thoughts, "I was at this place the other night and this guy I met, Tommy, told me about a contest coming up. It's a singing contest."

"Oh yeah? Like *American Idol* or something?"

"No. It's a search for a backup singer for that pop singer, Kay-J."

Kay-J had the number one song on the billboard charts for the last ten weeks in a row. They were probably capitalizing on her fame by doing a reality show about finding a backup singer. Sell it while it's hot, right?

"That sounds cool," Raven said.

"I think you should enter."

Raven laughed. "Yeah, right." She thought Horace was joking, but when he didn't respond, Raven said, "You're serious?"

"Of course I am, Ray. You're a wonderful singer."

She blushed, smiled. People had been telling her for the last three years that she had a great voice, that she was destined to be a star, but none of those compliments compared to Horace's.

"I don't know, Horace. I mean, it's in New York for one. My mom would never let me go, and two, backup singing for Kay-J? I don't think I'm *that* good."

"You are, Ray. You just can't see it."

She clutched the phone harder knowing that she had to get back to work but not wanting to hang up.

"I'll think about it, okay?" she said.

"Okay."

"I should go. I've been on the phone" — she looked at her cell screen — "for twenty minutes. Katie's probably wondering where I'm at."

"Text me later, then," Horace said. "Love you."

Every time he said those words, Raven's throat felt like it was going to close completely. Love, *real* love, was such a huge commitment!

"I love you, too," she replied. She said good-bye and went back to work.

♥   ♥   ♥

"Have you researched any colleges?" Mrs. Valenti asked as Raven swept the front of the store.

Raven, her back to her mother, rolled her eyes and said, "Yeah."

After a pause, Mrs. Valenti said, "Well? What did you find?"

Despite the fact that Raven's mom had accepted her daughter's love of music, she was still dead serious about Raven going to college. And an Ivy League university at that.

Mrs. Valenti had visions of Yale and Harvard and Princeton dancing through her head. Raven would be satisfied with graduating high school; anything beyond that, she didn't really care. She wasn't even considering college. If she hated high school, wouldn't it be fair to assume she'd hate college just as much?

What she wanted to do was graduate, take a road trip, play music, and see what happened from there. Her mother had spent the last ten years planning her life. Raven just wanted to go off the grid, live outside the rigid expectations of her mother. And those plans included Horace. Detroit would be their first stop and then . . . Nashville? Raven didn't do country, but Nashville did have an undeniable musical culture.

Raven propped the broom up against the wall. "I really like the looks of Yale."

Like she'd ever get in there. Seriously. She was more likely to win a clown contest.

"Yale has such a pretty campus," Mrs. Valenti said. She whirled around on her heels and headed toward the back room, her flats clipping along the ceramic tiled floor. "I have a new brochure I picked up the other day. I'd forgotten about it until you said something. Let me go grab it in my office."

"Yeah, okay," Raven said, wishing she could put her headphones on right now so she wouldn't have to listen to her mother.

Jordan sauntered up. "Mom driving you nuts?" She was still in her uniform from Bershetti's — black pants, white button-up shirt — but looked stunning.

"She won't shut up," Raven muttered. "You wait until you're a senior."

"Oh, I can wait." Jordan sat at one of the black café tables when Raven resumed sweeping. "Hey, did I tell you what Nicholas did?"

"No." Raven straightened. "What?"

"He texted me this — here, I'll just show you." She pulled her cell phone out and scrolled through her messages. "Look."

Hey new grl---ur doing good

"Isn't he sweet? I was all worried that I sucked because I was messing everything up, and he must have noticed how upset I was. Then I got this text message. Anna said he asked Dee for my number, and she gave it to him."

Raven smiled. Her sister's excitement was infectious. "That was nice of him."

"I know, right?"

The bell above the front door dinged. Raven and Jordan looked over.

Blake and Mil-D entered. Blake led the way as always, Mil-D sauntering behind, his body swaying like a sumo wrestler's.

"Hey," Blake said, tipping his head Raven's way.

A smile spread involuntarily across her face. She squashed it quickly.

"We close in about fifteen minutes," she said.

Jordan whapped her on the arm.

"What?" Raven raised her brow.

"Stop being such a jerk."

"I'm not."

Blake and Mil-D made their way to the counter and ordered two drinks from Katie.

"Why are you so mean to him?" Jordan whispered. "He's cute. And super nice."

"Because . . ." Raven couldn't come up with a good enough excuse.

"Because why?"

"Just because, okay?"

Grabbing the broom again, Raven swept a pile of dirt and straw wrappers and tossed it in the garbage with the dustpan. She tried escaping into the back room before Blake had a chance to say anything else to her, but he stepped into her path.

"Hey, you busy tonight?" Blake asked.

No. She, in fact, had no plans.

"Yes," she said.

"Because me and Blake here" — Mil-D came up behind Blake, an Italian soda in his hands — "we were wondering if you wanted to go over to the skate park for some F-U-N."

Blake craned his neck around. "F-U-N? What — dude?"

"What?" Mil-D shrugged. "Some fun, son."

Jordan giggled. "Are you guys always like this?"

"Like what?" Blake said.

"Like brothers?"

"Yes," they both said in unison.

Raven wanted to laugh, too, but that'd ruin her whole I'm-not-affected-by-you act. "I should get back to work," she said instead and made another try for the back door.

"Wait, Raven." Blake blocked her escape yet again. "Come to the skate park with us. It's no fun when I have no one to show off for," he said jokingly.

Do not smile! Raven thought. "I really don't —"

"We'll come," Jordan interrupted. "What time should we meet you there?"

Raven widened her eyes at her little sister, trying to project annoyance. Jordan only grinned.

♥　♥　♥

Raven had never been to the Birch Falls Skate Park before and maybe if she had, she would have recognized her new neighbor the moment she met him. His face had been painted graffiti-style on one of the concrete skate ramps with his name below it in big, bold letters. He was in between Tony Hawk's face and Bam Margera's goofy grinning mug.

"This is so cool!" Jordan said as she and Raven found an open spot on the concrete wall.

Raven had to agree, the atmosphere was a lot more alive and inviting than she'd first thought. Big floodlights lit the half-city-block-size area. Onlookers formed a loose circle around the park. There were a lot of girls watching, chatting; little kids stared in awe, taking note of the bigger kids' moves and skills.

Raven scanned the skaters' faces for Blake. It wasn't hard to spot him. The crowd was thicker near the far end of the park and growing by the second.

Blake was on his board, building speed as he aimed for a ramp in the middle of the park. He bent at the knees, and just before he crested the top of the ramp, jumped, flipping his board. The crowd responded with whistles and hollers.

"That was so cool," Jordan said.

Pretty soon, Blake had the whole park to himself, everyone having gathered on the sidelines to watch. He took more ramps, slid down railings, flipped his board as he sailed over stairways.

And the bigger the trick, the more Raven tensed waiting for him to land perfectly.

By the end of the run, she was cheering along with the crowd.

Blake skated over to her and kicked up his board. "What do you think? Did I do okay?" Sweat covered his face in a shiny veil. He took off his hat and handed it to Mil-D. He flung it into the crowd and a group of girls screeched and fought to pluck it from the air.

Was Blake that *big*?

Apparently he was.

"Wanna try?" he said, running his hand over his close-cropped hair.

Raven raised a brow. "Try what?"

"Skating."

She started to shake her head, but stopped. Why not try? Blake probably thought she was a cold, uptight jerk.

She'd been acting like one, after all. Why not show him she could have fun? That she was adventurous?

"All right."

"Uh, Raven?" Jordan straightened. "You've never even been on a skateboard."

"It can't be that hard."

Mil-D laughed.

"Hey!" Blake yelled across the park, gesturing to a girl to come over. She obliged. "Can my friend here use your pads for a second?"

The girl nodded quickly. "Yeah, no problem." She pulled apart the Velcro on her kneepads and handed everything over to Raven, no questions asked. Either the girl was extremely giving or Blake was like a god to these people.

"Are you sure?" Raven said.

"Yeah," the girl said.

Blake took the helmet from her and stuffed it on Raven's head, clipping the strap beneath her chin. "You're going to need that," he said with a grin.

Raven looked down the concrete ramp. It didn't look that big when she was standing on the sidelines, but right now, it could have been a three-story drop and it would have looked the same.

"Come on, Ray!" Jordan yelled.

"You'll be fine," Blake said behind her.

"You said that every other time and I *fell* every other time."

He shrugged. "You have to fall, that's how you learn." His green eyes watched her and her alone. There were at least thirty other girls at the park, all of them seemingly watching him, but he didn't notice. Or if he did, it didn't affect him.

Raven took a breath and looked out over the ramp. If she didn't go, she would so be dubbed a chicken. And she wasn't. She wanted to show Blake and everyone else watching that she wasn't afraid of anything, most of all embarrassing herself.

She rolled the board over the edge. The front half hung in the air, only her left foot keeping it in place.

Here goes nothing, she thought and put her right foot on the front of the board, her weight propelling her forward, down the ramp. She made it to the bottom, and several people cheered. For her? She didn't know, but she could hear Blake behind her hollering.

"Wooohoo!" he yelled. "You did it, Rave."

Rave? Blake had given her his own nickname. Had he done that on purpose? And did she even like it? Yes, she decided, yes she did.

She flung her arms up victoriously, but lost her balance. The board scooted out from under her and shot forward. The world went up as Raven fell down, landing on her hip. Pain shot down her leg and up her rib cage.

"Raven!"

"Are you okay?" Blake said.

She laughed, rolling over on her back. She was going to be so bruised tomorrow. "I'm fine," she said. Maybe even better than fine.

SIXTEEN ❧

Rule 16: *Be interested in things that interest him!*
Rule 37: *Learn to listen! Do not just talk about yourself!*

"Hey, Sydney?" Quin said from the doorway to the media room. "Can you grab me" — he looked at a sheet of paper in his hands — "*Scooby-Doo Meets the Boo Brothers, Peter Pan,* and anything Care Bears?"

"Sure," she said and went to the movies lined up neatly on the shelves. She scanned the spines of the movie cases and found the Scooby-Doo one quickly. *Peter Pan* was a harder find — it was all the way on the bottom shelf next to the Bob the Builder movies. What was it doing there? Maybe someone needed to alphabetize so the movies were easier to go through.

A project for another day? She'd have to talk to Quin about it. He might think she was a huge dork for enjoying something so methodical, but if it'd help the West Wing, who cared?

Movies in hand, Sydney went to West Two and found Quin in room 412 with the new patient staying overnight after surgery.

"Boo Brothers right here," Quin said, turning on the TV.

The little boy, Seth, clenched his hands into fists and waved them about in the air excitedly. "I love this movie," he said. "It's my favorite," he said to Sydney.

"Oh yeah?" She handed the case to Quin, and he put the disk in the DVD player.

Seth hit the button on the bed to bring his head up. "Yeah. This is the funniest Scooby-Doo one. Probably. Well . . . I like *Zombie Island*, too."

"Cool," Sydney said.

Quin hit the PLAY button and a movie preview came on. "My favorite Scooby-Doo," he said, "is the one with Johnny Bravo."

Seth laughed. "Oh yeah! Johnny is such a dork."

Quin nodded emphatically. "Right on, dude." He dimmed the overhead lights. "Enjoy your movie. If you need anything else, let us know."

"Okay," Seth said, snuggling into his blankets.

In the hallway, Sydney turned to Quin. "You watch Scooby-Doo?"

He cleared his throat. "Well . . . you know . . . Scooby *is* pretty cool."

Sydney grinned.

They passed out the other two movies and officially ended their shift.

"Want to grab something to eat with me in the cafeteria?" Quin asked after they'd punched out.

"Um . . ."

She *was* rather hungry. And she'd been planning on getting something fast-foodish anyway. Her mom was in Hartford for the night, and her dad was going to some dinner for work, leaving Sydney to fend for herself. She'd talked to Drew earlier on her break in hope of making dinner plans with him, but he had already agreed to go to the movies with Todd.

"Sure," she said to Quin. "I'm starving."

The cafeteria at Children's Hospital had the best salad bar ever. Sydney hadn't checked it out before, instead going with something quicker like a pre-made sandwich, but was she going to change that.

She'd gotten a Styrofoam container full of lettuce, grilled chicken pieces, bacon, hard-boiled eggs, sunflower seeds, and croutons. And they had their own brand of ranch dressing that — as Kelly might put it — made it awesome.

Quin had gotten a club sandwich and now sat across from Sydney in one of the booths along the huge floor-to-ceiling windows on the back side of the cafeteria. The sky was dusky outside and smoke-gray clouds covered the sun, turning it into a white glowing orb off in the distance.

"I wish I had my camera on me," Quin said just as Sydney was thinking the same thing.

"You're into photography?"

He looked at her, furrowing his brow. "You are, too?"

"Yeah. I actually won the amateur photo contest that the hospital put on."

"Yeah!" Quin pointed a finger at her and smiled. "I thought my sister said you won, but I was talking to her on my cell at the time and she kept breaking up. Congratulations."

Sydney couldn't help but grin. "Thanks."

"That contest is a huge deal around here," Quin said. "I couldn't enter it because my sister works here. You should be proud of yourself."

Sydney hadn't talked about it much, but she *was* proud of herself. The feeling she'd gotten that day was better than any feeling she'd had from passing an academic test.

"So, how long have you been a photographer?" he asked.

"I just started this year, but I have hundreds of photos already. I haven't yet mastered the art of distinguishing between good and bad, so I've kept them all." She shrugged. "But I think eventually it'll be good to have them around. Then I can see how much I've learned and changed."

Quin nodded. "You're right, there. We are our own worst critics, but after a few years you'll look back and see that you're better than when you started. That should count for something."

Sydney took a bite of salad, then a drink from her Coke. "So, do you do photography on the side or —"

"No." He smiled. "My sister would love for me to go to medical school, but I'd rather be a starving artist than a starving resident. I'm actually going into my sophomore year at the Brooks Institute in California."

Sydney's mouth dropped open. "Serious?"

He nodded. "I know, it's big. Sometimes I think it's bigger than I can handle."

"Yeah, it's only like the best photography school in the country. And also extremely hard to get into."

A blush fanned across his cheeks. "Well . . ."

"Are you into any other art, then? Or just photography? Because I know the Brooks Institute offers degrees in graphics and film, too."

Quin nodded. "They do, but I haven't taken much of them. I'm into almost all kinds of visual art, so I wouldn't close myself off to the idea of something different. I mean, I like all art. Including the less accepted forms."

Sydney frowned. "What does that mean?"

"Let me show you." He unbuttoned his white Oxford shirt. He had on a plain black T-shirt beneath it.

Sydney wondered what he was getting at when he pulled the Oxford shirt off and she gasped.

His arms, from the line of his short sleeve all the way down to his wrists, were covered in black tattoos.

"Oh my god."

Setting the Oxford shirt aside, he said, "I'm not supposed to let my tattoos show here, for obvious reasons."

Sydney grabbed his hand and held it up, turning his arm so that she could see every angle of it.

There was a lotus flower on his forearm and a Buddha above it. There were Latin words and dates, stars and strict linear patterns.

"I never would have guessed."

Well, he did have the long black hair, which was sort of odd coupled with the formal dress he wore to work. Still, Sydney had figured the long hair was something he liked. If he'd never taken his shirt off, she never would have known he was covered in tattoos.

Now that he was in a black T-shirt, several strands of long black hair hanging along his face, Sydney felt she really saw him, that she was looking across the table at the *real* Quin, and she respected him even more.

♥　♥　♥

"How was work tonight?" Drew asked, stooping down to kiss Sydney's forehead.

She stilled, wondering if she should tell Drew about Quin. She felt she should be honest with him. If he was hanging out with someone at work, she'd want to know about it because keeping it a secret made it seem that much worse. Even if the situation wasn't like *that*. Which it wasn't.

Sydney grabbed two spoons out of the dishwasher and handed one to Drew. He slipped it into his bowl of ice cream.

"It was good." Sydney and Drew went into the living room to sit. She went into a big explanation about how she met a young mother who seemed to know everything about the hospital and the machines in her daughter's room and how Sydney was impressed with her. Drew nodded his head at all the right moments, but Sydney could tell he'd started to tune out most of her long-winded explanation.

She ran through the Crush Code in her head, trying to think of a rule to use for this situation. There was one about listening. Maybe she was talking too much, making the conversation only about her.

"So how was the movie?"

Drew shrugged. "It was pretty good, but nothing really that you'd like."

See, she thought, Drew is used to you not giving a crap.

"Tell me about it anyway," she encouraged.

He looked at her oddly, then, "Okay. Well, the main plot point of the movie is that it's set in 2100 A.D., right, and robots have taken over. . . ."

What followed was a fifteen-minute conversation about the difference between robots and alien movies and how CGI was bringing sci-fi into the next generation of movies. Sydney hadn't heard Drew so excited in a conversation since . . . well, since he'd adopted Bear.

Sydney asked questions when she needed to, nodded her head when she was supposed to. For the most part, she just listened, despite the fact that she wasn't, like Drew said, interested in anything sci-fi.

Did that matter, though? She could sacrifice fifteen minutes if it meant making Drew happy.

SEVENTEEN ⤙

Rule 35: *Get to know your crush slowly! (You may discover that you don't like him!)*

Rule 36: *Do not pretend to be a different person when your crush is around!*

"What should I wear?" Kelly said to her closet, wishing she had a personal stylist to tell her the answer.

She decided to go with a pair of American Eagle khaki Bermuda shorts and a smocked puff-sleeve shirt the color of a banana.

She sat down on the edge of her bed to slip on her brown flats, when her brother walked by the open door, their little sister, Monica, hurrying behind.

"Give it back, Todd! Mom!"

Todd held a pad of paper over his head with one hand and his cell phone at his ear with the other.

"Mom's not here," he said. "She went to get some coffee."

Kelly tossed her shoes aside, came up behind her brother, and grabbed Monica's notebook from him. "Quit being such a jerk."

"Thanks," Monica said when she took her notebook off Kelly's hands.

Todd brought his cell up to his mouth. "My sisters are picking on me," he said. He waited for a response and nodded. Then, "Drew says you two should leave me alone."

Kelly rolled her eyes and snatched the cell phone out of Todd's hands.

"Hey!"

"Drew?" Kelly said.

"Yeah?"

"Did you really say that?"

He laughed. "No."

"I didn't think so." Kelly gave the cell back. "Now go away, Todd, please. I have to get ready."

Monica came into Kelly's room and flopped down on the bed, her long, strawberry blond hair sliding along her bare shoulders. "Where are you going?"

"Yeah," Todd said, "where are you going?"

"None of your business."

Kelly sat down next to her little sister and slipped on the pair of brown flats she'd set aside a few minutes ago.

"I'm going out."

Monica raised a brow. "With who?"

Kelly looked from her sister to her brother, both of whom were staring at her expectantly.

"With a friend," Kelly said, checking her reflection in the mirror on the back of her bedroom door.

She sighed to herself. This was the exact reason she'd thought the Crush Code was a bad idea. Adam and she just weren't a good fit. He probably needed someone who could climb Mount Everest while reciting the national anthem backward and skydive without blinking once.

And here she was, little ol' Kelly Waters, clothing aficionado, animal shelter volunteer, going out with the God of Iron Bodies.

It was so ridiculous.

But Adam had asked her out, after all, and she had promised her friends she'd give the Code a try, if only to prove them wrong.

Like Rule 35 said, *Get to know your crush slowly! You may discover that you don't like him!*

And, Rule 36 was an important one for the night: *Do not pretend to be a different person when your crush is around!*

That was exactly what Kelly was going to do. If Adam didn't like her for who she was, then she didn't need him. She'd learned that from going out with Will.

So the plan was, hang out with Adam, get to know him, and then move on when Kelly had all the reasons they were wrong for each other lined up in a neat row to present to Alexia.

Because they were wrong for each other even if Adam had a face that made girls weep. Kelly knew what kind of guy she needed; she needed someone she could get along with. She needed someone like Drew. He was attractive, but not too attractive. Smart, but not arrogant about it. And most importantly? He *got* Kelly. All her little quirks, her obsession with clothing. He didn't seem to mind that Kelly was a girly girl.

Too bad Drew was taken.

♥   ♥   ♥

Jordan Valenti met Kelly and Adam at the front entrance to Bershetti's when they arrived.

"Hey, Kel!" she said. "A table for two?"

"Yes, please."

Jordan grabbed two menus and led them away from the host's podium. Kelly walked alongside her while Adam brought up the rear.

Jordan leaned over to whisper in Kelly's ear as they wound through the restaurant tables. "That guy you're with is really hot."

Kelly nodded. "He is, isn't he? His name is Adam."

They both shot a glance over their shoulder at him. Whereas the other night he'd been in his usual workout clothing — Adidas pants, Under Armour shirt — tonight he was in a pair of faded blue jeans and a blue pinstriped button-up shirt, the top three buttons of which were undone to reveal a white T-shirt.

Jordan sat Kelly and Adam in a booth in the back of the restaurant. They ordered waters and pasta dishes; Adam ordered the spaghetti, Kelly ordered the Italian chicken and couscous.

Surprisingly the conversation came easily and soon their meals arrived. The conversation continued over eating and somehow got onto the topic of Adam's love of poetry and his hobby of writing it himself.

"You have to give me a line or two of something you wrote," Kelly said.

Adam blushed and hung his head. "I told you I was a closet poet and for good reason. I'm not very adept."

"Fine," Kelly teased. "But maybe someday?"

"Sure."

They finished their meal and Kelly excused herself to use the restroom. Finding it empty, she stole a minute to check her cell for any new messages or texts. She'd shut the ringer off since a chirping cell phone over dinner was always rude.

She flipped the phone open and was greeted with an alert that said: *5 New Text Messages.*

"Five?" she said to herself. She'd only had the phone quiet for an hour!

The first one was from Raven: *Ur with the hottie!!*

Jordan must have texted Raven as soon as she had the chance.

There was a message from Alexia that said: *Remember the Code.*

And one from Sydney: *Drew told me u were on a date. good luck.*

Todd: *Dont tell boytoy u eat crayons. he migt think ur weerd.*

Kelly rolled her eyes. Her brother was such an idiot sometimes.

And the last one was from Drew. It said, with perfect punctuation and word usage: *Be yourself and Adam will fall for you. He won't be able to help himself. And if he doesn't see how great you are, Todd and I can beat him up. Just say the word. Later.*

Kelly smiled as she read the message again. Drew had to be the best guy friend ever.

For some stupid reason, tears stung her eyes. She sniffed and laughed at herself. Drew was so good to her, so good that it almost hurt. Why couldn't she be on this date with him instead of Adam?

That wasn't fair to Adam, but it was true.

A few tears escaped from the corner of her eye. She wiped them from her chin.

Get it together, she thought. Drew isn't yours and never will be.

EIGHTEEN ~ꙮꙮ

Alexia hated working the closing shift at Cherry Creek, but at least it was a Tuesday night, which meant it was practically a ghost town.

"Is it always like this?" Alexia asked Jonah as they cleaned up the kitchen.

"Usually. Mondays and Tuesdays are the worst." He shook his head, pushing aside the dirty-blond hair that had fallen in his line of sight.

Alexia quirked a brow. "The worst?"

"I like staying busy. I'd rather be running around with the chaos than sitting with the silence."

"My boyfriend is like that. He likes to stay busy. That's the only way he's like his twin brother. Everything else they're completely separate on."

"How long have you and your boyfriend been together?"

"About four months."

"You guys get along good, then?"

Alexia nodded as she stacked the clean dishes in the

strainer. Jonah threw more dirty dishes in the soapy water and then looked over at Alexia as he scrubbed a deli dish.

"You're nodding your head, but your expression isn't exactly happy-in-love."

Was she that obvious?

She shrugged and took the deli dish from him to rinse it. "We're good, really."

Except for the whole sex thing, of course.

"Alexia?"

"Huh?"

"You sure you're all right?" He nodded at her hand. She clutched the deli dish, her knuckles having gone white.

"Oh." Embarrassment touched her cheeks. She tossed the dish in the hot, clean water. "I'm just . . . well" — she turned to him, leaning against the sink counter — "remember that conversation we had? About your being old-fashioned?" He nodded. "Well, I wish Ben was more old-fashioned, too."

The heat in her cheeks grew. Why was she even talking about this? And to a stranger no less. January of this year, if you'd asked her what she wanted more than anything, it would have been a boyfriend — to actually have a sex life — but now that she had it, she wasn't so sure she wanted it.

"Let me guess," Jonah said, "you guys are talking about the next step?"

Alexia should have known he'd guess the situation. She hadn't exactly been discreet. Anyone could deduce what she was referring to.

"Yes," she said, "and the situation is stressing me out."

Jonah rinsed a dish and set it on the strainer. Alexia grabbed a towel to dry.

"My girlfriend and I had this conversation, too, so I know what you're going through."

Alexia perked up. "Really?"

Jonah nodded. "We decided to wait for sex until marriage."

This Alexia hadn't expected. She widened her eyes. "And you're okay with that?"

"Sure I am. I love my girlfriend. I can wait. And like I told you before, I like to think there is only one great love of your life. If Nina is mine, then it'll all be worth it in the end."

If Jonah and his girlfriend could wait, why couldn't Ben and Alexia? Sex complicated things. Waiting might be better all around.

♥   ♥   ♥

Ben fingered Alexia's hair as they watched a TV show in the den. Alexia's parents were down the hall in their office, planning a new seminar they had coming up in the fall. With her parents home, Alexia steered clear of being alone upstairs with Ben. It wasn't a rule yet, but she did have to keep her bedroom door open. The reason behind that rule made Alexia squeamish. Her parents were worried about her sex life. Ugh. Like she wanted her parents even thinking about her that way.

She'd just as soon stay in the den, which worked in Alexia's favor anyway. If her parents were home, then Alexia didn't have to worry about sexual tension.

"So I've been thinking," Ben said, lowering his voice, "that if you did decide to . . . you know . . . and you wanted it to be special, I could get us a hotel room or plan something else special. . . .

He continued playing with her hair, his fingers brushing against her neck every few seconds, causing her to tremble. She wanted to close her eyes and feel his fingers elsewhere, but no, they couldn't. Not with her parents down the hall and her hormones going wonky.

"Actually," she began, "I was wondering, what would you say if I decided to stay a virgin?"

Ben clutched his heart. He grunted and groaned. "Oh god, I think I feel my heart breaking!"

"Ha. Ha. Ha." She poked him in the ribs.

"I swear, Alexia, I'll die if I don't share myself with your heavenly body." He smiled, letting her know he was kidding. But was he?

Nothing made perfect sense anymore. It was nice to know Ben wanted her that bad. It almost turned her on, but fear of making the decision burrowed deep into her chest.

Ben shifted so he could look her straight in the face. "If you want to wait, then I'll support you, but I am not going to like it."

"Well, it's not going to be particularly easy for me either. And besides, I'm not saying that's my final decision, it's just a thought."

He leaned over and kissed her forehead. "It's kind of cute, you know that? You waiting until marriage."

"Thanks, I guess?"

"It's a compliment. I swear it." He shifted, kissing her this time on the lips. "I have to go."

Alexia groaned, glancing at the clock on the cable box. It was just after two in the afternoon and Ben was supposed to meet his brother and father at the golf course at two thirty.

"I don't want you to go," she said.

"Oh, I don't want to go. Trust me." He stood from the couch, his khaki shorts slouching on his hips. He stretched, his T-shirt inching up, exposing a triangle of stomach and hair running below his boxers.

Something fluttered in Alexia's stomach. She quickly moved her eyes back up to his face. "I could kidnap you," she said, standing next to him.

"Yes, please do that. And promise me you'll do naughty things to my body while you hold me hostage."

Alexia snorted, and they both laughed.

"How did I ever get lucky enough to have you?"

She cast her gaze aside, grinning like crazy. Ben could still manage to make her feel like the world's coolest girl.

"Well, I wouldn't say lucky exactly . . . you know . . . since we haven't . . . you know . . ."

"Hey." He put a finger beneath her chin and pulled up so she had to look at him. "Stop thinking about it for now, okay? Just take a week and don't think about it once. We can talk about it later. Okay?"

That was easy for him to say. She'd been trying not to think about it for weeks.

"I don't want to pressure you. I love you too much," he said.

"I love you, too."

Alexia walked him to his car, where they shared another long kiss before Ben left.

Inside, Alexia went to the kitchen to grab a bottle of water. She found her parents there sitting at the island, their voices low. When they noticed Alexia, they went silent.

"Hi, honey," her dad said.

"Hi." Alexia went to the refrigerator and grabbed a bottle of Smartwater. "What are you guys doing?"

Her parents shared a knowing look.

"We've been discussing something." Her mother got off the stool and came around the island. She pushed aside Alexia's hair, letting it fall down her shoulder. "We wanted to talk to you about Ben."

Alexia stepped back, suddenly feeling the tension in the room. How had she missed it walking in?

"Oh? What about Ben?"

"Well," her mother began, "we like Ben, don't get us wrong, but we feel like perhaps you two are moving too fast. You are only seventeen, after all, honey."

Dr. Bass swiveled in the stool, leaned back into it, and crossed one leg over the other knee. Alexia knew that look. He was analyzing her, trying to get a read on her expression and body language.

Alexia went stone still.

"We think it would behoove you to spend a little more time with your girl friends," he said.

"I do." Alexia tried to keep her voice level.

Her mother busied herself at the counter, filling her teacup with more milk. "We're not trying to butt into your life, Alexia. We're just trying to guide you. Your father and I waited until we were married to have . . . sex" — Alexia's mouth dropped open as her mother went on, oblivious to the discomfort she was causing her daughter — "and I think our relationship as adults is much more successful than it would have been had we prematurely shared ourselves."

Alexia blinked. Both her parents stared at her.

"You did *not* just say that," Alexia breathed.

"Honey." Dr. Bass readjusted. "We love you. We just want to see you make good decisions, and peer pressure is a very potent inhibitor."

Alexia closed her eyes and inhaled deeply. Her parents were driving her insane. When were they going to get out of the house and leave her alone like they had been for the last three years?

Suddenly, they were home all the time and, yes, they were butting into her business. *All the time.*

"Thanks, Mom and Dad," Alexia said, moving around them slowly as if they might pounce on her. "I'll take into consideration everything you've said."

As soon as she reached the doorway to the living room, she bolted.

NINETEEN ∽

Rule 4: *Find out what your crush likes — hobbies, sports, music! Then immerse yourself in it!*

Sydney picked up her digital camera and turned it on, checking the battery. Full charge. Good. She threw the camera in her messenger bag and looped the bag over her shoulder.

In the hallway, she knocked on the bathroom door. Her mother had come home late last night and Sydney hadn't had a chance to talk to her.

"Mom?"

"Yeah?"

"I'm going to the park. Just wanted to say hi. I'll be home in a few hours. Maybe we could go get lunch together or something?"

There was a long pause. Sydney pressed her fingers into the door, strained to hear her mother on the other side.

"Mom?"

"Um . . . how about we talk more when you get home, okay?"

"Sure. If you need me or anything, just call my cell."

"Okay. And, honey?"

"Yeah?"

"I love you."

"Love you, too. Bye."

Sydney left, driving straight to the park. It was just after eleven when she arrived. Mothers were still there with their children. People were beginning to arrive to enjoy the outdoors on their lunch breaks. This was Drew's favorite place to come and his favorite time of the year. She thought she'd surprise him by taking some photos and framing them; that way he would always have a piece of summer.

This was Rule 4, the way she interpreted it.

Sydney already knew what Drew liked and hated, so the first part of the rule didn't pertain to her. She could, however, immerse herself in something Drew enjoyed.

She found an open picnic table beneath one of the younger maple trees the city had planted about five years ago. It allowed her a little bit of cover while also keeping her shot somewhat in the sunlight. She didn't want to have to turn on the flash.

Getting comfortable on the table, Sydney opened her messenger bag and pulled out her camera. She turned it on and checked through the viewfinder.

Off in the distance, a mother plucked her baby from a stroller. She rubbed her nose against the little boy, giving Eskimo kisses. Sydney zoomed in and snapped off three shots. She resisted the urge to check the results on the digital screen. She wanted to leave them as a surprise for when she got home.

Sydney moved on, finding a mother and daughter near

the pond. The mother pointed at the swans and the little girl crept next to her mother, moving slowly, afraid to scare the swans away.

The mom produced a bag of stale bread and the two threw bits into the water.

Sydney clicked off several shots. The little girl giggled as her mother smiled, watching her daughter and nothing else.

A long time ago, Sydney and her mother were like that. Before Mrs. Howard became focused on work, they'd come down to the park together to feed the ducks. Afterward, they'd get ice cream at Dairy Scoop. Sydney always got the strawberry cheesecake, and her mother went with plain chocolate. They'd share, though, so Sydney got the best of both bowls.

That seemed eons away now. As if they weren't her memories, but perhaps someone else's from a past life.

Mrs. Howard had promised to cut back her hours, to be home more, but lately, she'd been slipping into her old routine, staying overnight in Hartford. Sydney hadn't seen her since Wednesday morning and even that meeting had been brief.

At least she was home for the weekend. Hopefully, they'd get to hang out.

♥　♥　♥

"Mom?" Sydney set her bag down on the dining room table. "Mom?"

The TV was off in the living room. That stupid fish clock ticked its tail behind Sydney.

"Mom?"

Still no answer.

Sydney checked the living room and the den. Then the bathroom and all three bedrooms.

Her mother was nowhere.

In the kitchen, Sydney went to grab a Coke, when something on the refrigerator door caught her eye. It was a note in her mother's handwriting.

At first Sydney thought her mom had left to go to the store or something, but the note was longer than that, a full page of slanted cursive handwriting.

Dear John and Sydney,

I wanted very much to make this work. I wanted to be a wife, to be a good mother. I used to be, once upon a time. Remember, Sydney? Sometimes I wonder whatever happened to that woman. Work took over my life, I don't deny that. But I like working. I like working hard. I like the responsibility. I like being important.

You guys take care of yourselves without me. These last few months, I've felt like an imposter in my own home. I don't feel like I belong here, and I don't know why. I don't know how to fix that. At work, that's what I do, I fix things, organize, make important decisions to make the company run smoothly, but at home, I'm lost, and I don't like that feeling.

There's a huge prospective client we've been working with in Italy, and I was asked to go. I don't know when I'll be home. Or if I'll be home.

Sometimes I think you're better off without me anyway.

Remember that I love you guys with all my heart.
Mom

Sydney gritted her teeth as she stared at the note tacked up on the refrigerator door with a plastic pineapple magnet as if it were a grocery list or something even less important.

Tears blurred her vision, and she clenched her jaw harder.

Her mother left? For good?

Just like that?

Sydney grabbed her phone from her bag and hit number two on speed dial. Voice mail picked up right away.

"This is Anita. Leave a message, and I'll call you back."

BEEP.

"Mom! How could you!" Sydney screamed. "I hope I never have to see your face again!"

Sydney slammed her thumb against the END button on her phone and slumped against the kitchen counter, the sobs taking over.

♥   ♥   ♥

"Just, could you sit down for a second?" Drew said, resting a hand gently against Sydney's shoulder.

She whirled on him. "I don't want to sit down!"

He pulled back, put his hands up. "All right."

It'd been two hours since Sydney came home and found her mother's note. Since then, Sydney had called her mom's cell six more times and gotten voice mail.

And when her dad came home and read the note, instead of going into a rage and calling his wife's phone, too, he just nodded his head and disappeared into the den.

Sydney hadn't seen him since.

What the hell was wrong with her parents? Were they aliens? Incapable of feeling emotion? Why wasn't her dad angry? Why wasn't he slamming doors and throwing things? Any normal husband would be stomping around the house in a rage, but no, Sydney's dad went to the den and probably started alphabetizing his history books.

And her mother . . .

Did she not care about her family? Had she not considered what leaving would do to Sydney or her husband? Instead, she just traipsed off to Italy. Working there was probably a treat. She apparently didn't love her family enough to stick around to work things out.

What had Sydney done wrong? Should she have talked to her mother more? Made more time for them to hang out?

Sydney plopped down on the bed and set her head in her hands. Maybe she was the reason her mother left. Maybe she'd driven her mother away because she wasn't cute and bubbly and warm like Kelly was. Maybe she should have tried harder, tried harder to be a good daughter. She had to admit, she didn't relate to her mother as well as she had when she was a kid.

When she was in elementary school, her mother was her hero. She wanted to spend every waking moment with her. And now, Sydney could feel the distance widening, even before her mother invested much of her time in her work. And maybe that was why she'd focused more on SunBery Vitamins than on her family.

If Sydney had needed her a little more, maybe her mother wouldn't have turned to her job.

"Syd?" Drew said, taking her hand in his. "Is there anything I can do to help?"

She shook her head, kept her eyes squeezed tightly shut. "Just go," she muttered. "I just want to be alone."

His hand slipped away. He got up, walked to the door. "If you need me, I'll be at Todd's."

"Fine," she managed to say as his footsteps faded down the hallway.

July

TWENTY ✎

Rule 17: *Always look your best in the company of your crush!*

Kelly grabbed her cell as it rang on her dresser. She saw a picture of Alexia on the front screen, her tongue sticking out. Kelly always giggled whenever Alexia called and that picture popped up.

"Hey!" she said once she answered.

"Hi, Kel." Alexia didn't sound as upbeat as Kelly thought she should be. It was Fourth of July! The day of parties and celebrations of independence! And most importantly, fireworks!

"What are you doing tonight?" Kelly asked.

"Going to the park. I'm meeting Ben there later."

Kelly sat on her bed and resumed flipping through her new copy of *Teen Vogue*. She scanned the outfits looking for ideas for tonight's party. Not that she had, or could ever afford, the kind of stuff within the glossy pages. Still, it was pretty easy to find cheaper versions. You just needed to know where to look.

"What are you doing?" Alexia asked.

"Meeting Adam at the park."

"Yeah?" Alexia finally sounded upbeat. "What are you wearing? Are you doing your hair or anything? I told you that you guys were perfect for each other. It's the Crush Code at work."

Kelly rolled her eyes. Okay, so she was thankful for her friend's help and enthusiasm, but technically the outing tonight was just as friends, and Kelly wasn't even one hundred percent sure she dug Adam.

He was hot and super nice and had a sweet, sentimental side, but . . .

He just wasn't Drew. And she was having a hard time getting past that. It wasn't that she was madly in love with Drew, it was just . . . oh, she couldn't even explain it to herself if she tried. It was too complicated for words.

"Do you need help getting ready?" Alexia asked before Kelly even had a chance to answer her last billion questions.

Kelly was about to say no, she was fine, but Alexia cut her off.

"You know what? I'm bored anyway. Why don't I come over and help you fulfill rule seventeen: *Always look your best in the company of your crush!*" She pulled in a breath. "I'll be there in five."

"Wait, Lexy!"

The line went silent. Kelly pulled the phone away from her ear and hit the END button. She sighed, setting the phone and her magazine aside. Suddenly, she felt like stuffing her face with chocolate. Preferably chocolate chip cookies. Out in the hallway, she heard the familiar sound of video games blaring from Todd's room. Todd shouted something about turbo boosts and eating dust, and Drew replied with a retort involving a boot in the head.

Kelly looked in Todd's room.

"Hey," she said.

Todd ignored her, but Drew looked up and said, "Hey," back, which prompted Todd to cheer. Drew turned back to the TV screen and groaned.

"You're done, dude," Todd said. "Shouldn't have taken your eyes off the screen."

"Whatever." Drew tossed the controller on the bed. He rubbed his face, then his hair, leaving a trail of mussed black spikes. He looked so cute right now. Kelly sometimes wished she could squeeze her eyes shut and make him disappear. That way, she wouldn't have to see him looking all gorgeous and Drew-like.

"I gotta take a piss." Todd got up and squeezed past Kelly, poking her in the ribs as he went.

Ignoring her brother, Kelly went into his room and pushed aside dirty clothes on the bed to sit next to Drew.

"You and Sydney going to the park tonight?" She told herself she didn't care whether or not he went, but really she did.

Drew reached over to the desk to grab his bottle of water. "Yeah." He took a swig and twisted the cap back on. "About eight o'clock, I guess. You going?"

Kelly nodded. "With Adam."

Drew leaned back on the bed, propping himself up with his elbows. "He seems like a nice guy."

"Yeah." Kelly turned sideways, crossing her legs Indian-style. "He's great and everything, but . . ."

"But what?"

"I don't know. It's just . . . I don't get the click, you know? Maybe that doesn't make sense."

Drew sat up and turned, too, his knee brushing up against Kelly's bare chin. She shivered.

"Yeah, it does," he said. "It makes total sense."

"I want to like him."

Drew shrugged. "You can't force that stuff, Kel."

"Yeah. I know."

"Maybe you should tell him . . . you know . . . before he gets too involved?"

Kelly looked up finally and met Drew's neon blue eyes hiding behind his black-framed glasses. He'd been wearing them more lately. As pretty as his eyes were, Kelly thought he looked just as good with the glasses on as off and had told him so.

"Yeah," she said, swallowing, "maybe."

Todd clapped his hands in the doorway. "Ready for some ass kickin'?"

"I should go anyway." Kelly got up quickly. "Alexia is coming over."

At the doorway, she glanced over her shoulder and caught Drew's gaze. He blinked and looked away.

Heat crept up Kelly's neck and spread into her cheeks. Suddenly butterflies were flapping excited wings in her stomach.

She hurried out of the room.

♥　　♥　　♥

Alexia grabbed a green-and-gray striped tank top out of Kelly's closet and handed it to her. "Try that."

Kelly sighed and turned around to change.

"I think I like the jean shorts better than the kha-kis," Raven said from her perch on the corner of Kelly's desk.

Sydney shook her head. "The khakis."

When Alexia decided to head over to Kelly's to help her get ready for the Fourth of July party in the park, Alexia thought it would be fun to grab Sydney and Raven, too, and get all the girls together.

And it was helping Alexia get her mind off sex and Ben. At least she knew tonight was safe. They were hanging out at the park. The park meant no bedroom and no bed, which meant definitely no sex.

At least Alexia knew she could breathe tonight and just have fun.

Kelly turned around and spread her arms out. "What do you think?"

Raven shrugged. "I still like the jean shorts better."

"I like what you have on," Sydney said.

A knock sounded on the bedroom door. Kelly pulled it open and Drew sauntered in. He sat down next to Sydney, planting a kiss on her lips.

Even he seemed uneasy around Sydney, as if she'd snap at any moment.

Everyone knew about Mrs. Howard taking off for Italy, leaving nothing but a note behind, but Sydney wasn't talking about it, just like she wouldn't talk about Drew breaking up with her earlier in the year.

She seemed fine right now, but they all knew her bottled-up emotions could pop on a moment's notice. Alexia tried not to be the trigger, making sure not to mention Mrs.

Howard or ask Sydney how she was *really* doing. Sydney would talk when she was ready and if she didn't, well . . . then . . . they'd witness the breakdown, which would serve as therapy in its own way.

"You guys almost ready?" Drew said, wrapping his arm around Sydney's shoulders.

Kelly glanced at him, then his arm on Sydney. She quickly looked away, focusing on the shoes in the bottom of her closet.

"I'm ready," Alexia said.

"Me, too." Raven got up, checking her cell phone for messages. "I'm meeting someone there anyway."

Sydney frowned. "Who are you meeting?"

"Um, my neighbor."

"Great." Kelly slipped into a pair of flip-flops. "Let's go, then."

Parking was always brutal at city functions, especially during Fourth of July. Instead of driving the four blocks to the park and scrambling to find a parking spot, the group walked from Kelly's house.

The sun was beginning to set and the day's hot temps were disappearing with it. Clouds dotted the sky like wispy paint strokes and the moon was barely a sliver.

Alexia kept up with Raven, who was practically jogging to the park while Kelly, Todd, Sydney, and Drew hung farther back.

"So who's this neighbor you're meeting?" Alexia asked more out of curiosity than anything.

"Just someone who recently moved into the neighborhood. My mom asked me to show him around."

Alexia quirked an eyebrow. "Him?"

Raven pursed her lips and gave Alexia an exasperated look. "He's cool. Just a friend."

Two blocks from the park, cars packed the curbs along every side street. People walked in groups toward the city center, their hands and arms overloaded with coolers and picnic baskets and folded lawn chairs.

Alexia was going to bring lawn chairs, but she wasn't sure what Ben's plans were. She decided to show up empty-handed, since Ben was all about spur-of-the-moment adventures. Maybe he'd want to leave the main city park and drive out to the state park, then hike the Sky Trail so they could watch the fireworks from a hill. Or maybe he'd borrow his parents' boat and take it out on Garver Lake.

When the group reached the park, they wound through the lawn chairs and blankets spread out on the grass. Children ran around the playground, screaming and laughing, the parents following closely behind.

The air smelled like barbecue and hot dogs and spent fireworks.

"So where are we going exactly?" Sydney asked, catching up to Raven and Alexia.

Kelly came up, too, leaving Drew and Todd behind.

"I told Blake I'd meet him near the fountain," Raven said.

"I'll call Adam and tell him to meet me there." Kelly pulled out her cell. "Hey," she said when Adam picked up, "are you here right now?" She nodded, then, "Okay, meet me at the fountain."

Alexia gave Kelly's shoulder a squeeze. "You're so lucky."

"Why?" Kelly frowned.

"I bet every girl here is checking Adam out at this very minute."

"Yeah," Kelly said distantly, shooting a glance over her shoulder, away from the fountain where Adam would have been.

What was her deal anyway? She had the hottest guy on this coast, but she was barely excited about meeting him. Was the Crush Code failing her? Maybe Adam wasn't responding to the Code like Alexia had hoped? Maybe the Crush Code was missing a few rules.

"There's Blake," Raven said, pointing at a short guy standing next to a really big guy.

"Which one's Blake?" Sydney asked.

"The one with the black hat on."

Blake looked about their age, maybe a year older. Along with the black hat, he had on white board shoes and loose-fitting jeans. There was a black bracelet around his wrist.

Sydney slowed, eyeing the really big guy. "What about him?"

"Oh," Raven said, "that's Blake's bo — uh, uncle."

Raven introduced everyone. Blake and his uncle, Mil-D, shook everyone's hand.

"It's cool to meet you all," Blake said, sticking close to Mil-D's side.

"Kel?" Adam came up behind Kelly, running his fingers over the small of her back.

She turned and gave him a friendly smile. "Hey."

"You look nice tonight." Adam bent down to kiss Kelly's cheek, which made Drew scowl and look away.

What was up with that? Kelly wondered.

"I have something to show you," Adam said to Kelly, then turned to the group. "Can I steal her? If you guys don't mind?"

"Go ahead," Alexia said. To Kelly she whispered, "Good luck."

The two sauntered off, everyone watching them leave. Alexia wished she and Ben were like that again, a new couple just getting to know each other, no pressure about sex.

"Drew?" Sydney grabbed his hand, and he blinked.

"Huh?"

"Let's go find something to drink."

"All right," he said.

They left, too, leaving Alexia and Raven with Blake, Mil-D, and Todd. The latter two got into a conversation about video games. Blake and Raven were in their own conversation about skateboarding.

Raven was smiling, batting her eyelashes as she looked up at Blake. How she could see him beneath the brim of that hat, Alexia didn't know. When Blake disappeared in search of a bottle of water, Alexia pulled Raven aside.

"I don't know if you even realize you're doing it, but you're kind of flirting with Blake," Alexia said. "What about Horace?"

Raven's smile quickly faded into a scowl. "I am not flirting with him. We're just friends."

"Well, it doesn't seem like you're just friends."

Raven set her hands on her hips, straightened her shoulders. Big, silver hoop earrings swung from her ears.

"You know what, Alexia? You can butt out of my business any time now." With that, she stalked off, leaving Alexia alone by the fountain, the roar of the water sounding suddenly too loud in her ears.

Was she being too nosy? She just wanted Raven to remember Horace and think of how he'd feel if he saw Raven right now. Could *Raven* even see Raven right now? Because no matter what she said, she *was* flirting with Blake, and Blake could barely keep his eyes off her.

TWENTY-ONE ～ॐ

Rule 14: *Make him notice you! Get his attention! Draw him into you!*

Rule 26: *Do not feel you have to tell your friends who you are crushing on!*

Rule 30: *Do not tell anyone that you have a crush on someone unless you know you can trust them not to tell your crush!*

Excitement floated on the air like the fire sparks, but Sydney just couldn't catch it. Rule 14 of the Crush Code said, *Make him notice you! Get his attention!* But Sydney didn't feel like being here, let alone smiling and flirting and pretending everything was okay. She just wanted to be home right now, curled in bed, reading a book with a bowl of popcorn by her side.

And more importantly, she wanted to be alone. It wasn't anything against Drew or her friends. She just needed some Sydney time while she tried to sort some things out. Maybe she'd get that time tomorrow, go out somewhere with her camera.

"Need anything?" Drew said, holding her hand tightly as if he were afraid that he'd lose her if he let go.

"Actually," — she plopped down on one of the swings, abandoned by the little kids now that darkness had settled in — "could you see if you could find an elephant ear? I smell them, but I don't see them."

Drew nodded, raked his fingers over her back. "I thought I saw someone selling them by the back entrance. I'll head over there."

"Thanks."

He disappeared into the crowd and Sydney clutched the swing, resting her head against one of the chains and closing her eyes. The noise of the park was nearly deafening. Conversation mixed with the sound of fireworks screeching and popping. Kids screamed, parents hollered. A headache blossomed at the base of her skull. She groaned.

Within minutes, Drew returned, a large elephant ear in his hand. "Found one," he said, handing it over.

"Thanks." She took a bite. It was warm and soft and sweet. Her bad mood almost lessened. At least food would never let her down.

"Is there anything else?" Drew asked, sitting in the swing next to her.

She wanted her camera, but she wouldn't ask Drew to run home and get that. She should have thought to bring it herself.

"Can we just sit and watch?"

More children screeched as a fountain sprung a cascade of golden sparks into the semidarkness. A few dogs barked at the sound and light.

"Sure," Drew answered, toeing at the wood chips spread out in the sand.

And that's how they spent the rest of the night, sitting there in silence until the fireworks ended.

♥ ♥ ♥

Kelly leaned back on her elbows on the blanket Adam had spread out for them. It was fleece, blue, at least a queen-size. He'd also packed a cooler of Pepsi and water with some brownies on the side. He was so darn perfect that Kelly could have married him that very second if it hadn't been for the whole lack-of-chemistry thing.

"You good?" Adam asked, leaning back on his side.

Kelly nodded. "You did great."

"Really? Because you seem . . . I don't know . . . somewhere else."

Kelly finally looked at him. The cotton material of his T-shirt strained against his biceps, hugged his toned chest. His shirt crept up just a little bit so that Kelly could see a sliver of his *extremely* hard stomach and the waistband of his Calvin Klein boxers.

She really was somewhere else mentally, but she could have kicked herself for it.

She wanted to be there, focused on nothing but Adam.

But all she could think about was Drew.

Why had he made that face when Adam said she looked good tonight? Drew had commented earlier that he thought Adam seemed like a good guy, yet that expression had said something else.

Did he think Adam was playing Kelly? *Was* Adam playing Kelly?

Kelly scoffed at herself. Technically, one might say Kelly was playing Adam. She had admitted to herself *and* to Drew that she wasn't feeling Adam. Now she was just leading him on.

Someone tall and dark-haired swung slowly on a swing just twenty feet from where Kelly sat. A red burst of fireworks lit his face, and Kelly's stomach tingled.

Drew.

Next to Kelly, Adam sighed. She tore her eyes away from Drew.

"What?" she said.

Adam sat up. "You are somewhere else, aren't you?" He nodded in Drew's direction.

"Oh . . ." It was a good thing darkness had begun to set in. Kelly's face felt hot as embers. "Drew . . . he's just a friend."

"Kelly." Adam turned to her. "I like to pretend I'm a writer, remember?" He grinned. "If I didn't know people or the way they look when they're angry, annoyed . . . in love . . . then I shouldn't be a writer." He gave her a playful nudge. "I know that look."

She started to shake her head but instead looked at the blanket, ran her fingers over the soft material. It would be so easy to stay here, to stay with Adam and force herself to like him.

That would be the easy route.

But she didn't want to.

What she wanted to do was get up and run over to Drew and then . . .

Well, she didn't really know what she'd do after that. And what about Sydney? And Adam?

It was all wrong.

"I came here with you," she said to Adam. "And I like hanging out with you."

As a friend, she thought.

More fireworks boomed in the sky, lighting Adam's face now that the darkness was thicker. He grabbed her, pulling her closer. Her heart panicked in her chest. Was he trying to kiss her now?

He whispered in her ear.

"There's this poem," he said, "that my grandmother used to quote all the time. 'Love is the wild that runs through the forests.' She used to say, 'You see the wild, Adam, you run after it. Don't let it get away.'" He pulled back, looking Kelly straight on.

A purple firework blossomed in the darkness. Kelly looked up, seeing Drew off in the distance. He leaned against the swing chain, watching the fireworks half-heartedly.

"He's my best friend's boyfriend," Kelly heard herself say. "I just can't."

Drew caught her staring then. He straightened, lifted a few fingers in an almost imperceptible wave.

It was wrong. Wrong. Wrong. Wrong.

She couldn't. Ever.

She looked away. "I'll stay here with you," she said to Adam, deciding that the safest route was here with him.

TWENTY-TWO

Rule 7: *Be adventurous and daring! See life as an adventure!*

Rule 18: *Respect yourself! Demand that your crush respects you as well!*

Rule 19: *Do not allow your crush to pressure you to do something you do not want to do! Do only things that you and only you want to do and are comfortable with!*

Alexia's cell phone rang in her bag. She fished it out and smiled when she saw it was Ben. She broke away from Raven and Blake. "Hey," she answered.

"Hey. Where are you?"

"I'm by the fountain. Are you here?"

Alexia waited for a response, but when none came, she thought maybe the line had disconnected. "Ben?" Still nothing.

Fireworks popped behind Alexia. Several kids ran past her screaming and laughing. She plugged her other ear. "Ben, are you there?"

"Raa!" Someone poked her in the ribs. She screeched and whirled around.

"Got you," Ben said.

"Oh my god, you!" She put her phone away and reached out to swat him, but he grabbed her wrist, twirled her around and dipped her.

"Ben!" Alexia laughed while she held onto his arms with white knuckles. "Bring me back up!"

He did, wrapping his arms around her and pulling her in for a long kiss.

"I'm so frickin' happy I'm here with you and not out on the boat with my parents." He sighed, scratching his overgrown hair. It curled at the nape of his neck and around his ears. It probably drove his parents nuts and that was probably one of the reasons he kept it long.

"So the barbecue didn't go so well?" Alexia asked.

"As well as the French Revolution. But I did finally get my graduation present, which sort of made up for the debacle that was a family gathering."

"What did you get?"

"Come on." He grabbed her hand and pulled her through the park, dodging more fireworks, weaving around blankets and lawn chairs until they reached the street.

"Where are we going? We're going to miss the fireworks!"

They walked a block and then turned right into the parking lot behind Wendell Bakery. Ben pulled Alexia over to a forest green Jeep Wrangler and stopped.

"What are we doing here?" she asked, looking around. "Where —"

It finally dawned on her. She looked at the Jeep again

and then at Ben. His pearl-white teeth shone bright in a big smile.

"You got a new Jeep?"

"Yeah. This is my graduation present."

"Oh my god, Ben! This is awesome." Alexia ran her fingers over the slick, shiny hood. She made a circle around the whole vehicle. The roof was off, as were the doors.

"Want to go for a ride?" Ben jangled the keys in his hand and waggled his eyebrows.

"But the fireworks?"

"If we hurry up, we can head over to the state park and catch the end of the show."

Alexia raked her teeth over her bottom lip. "Yeah. Let's go."

♥　　♥　　♥

Ben downshifted as they turned into the state park. The wind ruffled Alexia's hair, and she pulled it to the side out of her face.

"This is awesome," she said, imagining them spending the rest of the summer cruising around Birch Falls in the new Jeep. It would be perfect.

"I know," Ben said. "I love it. Best thing I ever got."

They found a parking spot and got out. The fireworks boomed off in the distance, their sparks lighting the sky red. There were no other cars here, which meant they had the entire park to themselves.

"We should go up to the Sky Trail," Ben said, grabbing Alexia's hand, threading his fingers through hers. "Oh, wait. I brought a blanket." He pulled it out of the Jeep and they headed up the stairs that would take them to the top of the Sky Trail.

By the time they reached the top, Alexia was out of breath, but the fireworks were blazing through the sky and she wanted to see at least *some* of them. They hurried along the dirt trail to the far side of the hill near Garver Lake.

Finding a good break in the trees, they laid the blanket out and sat.

A purple and then orange firework went off in the distance. Ben lay back, putting his hands behind his head. Alexia lay next to him, curling into the crook of his arm.

"It's beautiful," Alexia breathed. They might have been some five miles away from the city park, but the fireworks were still spectacular, the color brighter than ever. And Alexia liked the quiet.

She sat up, looked Ben in the eyes.

"Hi," he said.

"Hi." She leaned over, kissing him gently. Everything felt perfect, and she wanted to share it with Ben.

He sat up and Alexia leaned back on the blanket. Ben ran his fingers through her hair, then along the nape of her neck. She shivered, pulling him down closer as he ran his tongue softly over her lips.

Every nerve in Alexia's body came alive. Her stomach knotted in excited butterflies, and she couldn't seem to think straight.

The kiss went from soft and innocent to urgent and intense. Alexia could feel Ben's heart drumming against her chest.

"We should stop," Ben said against her lips.

Yes. Yes, we should stop, she thought, but she didn't want to.

Ben pulled his hand down to touch the bare skin peeking out from beneath Alexia's tank top. His fingers were warm, smooth on her skin. Alexia breathed in sharply.

Stop, Alexia thought again, but then Ben's hand crept farther up her shirt and all she could think was, Keep going. Keep going. His fingers caressed her ribs and then went beneath her bra.

Oh my god.

Ben's lips pulled away from Alexia's mouth and ran down her neck.

"Do you want me to stop?" he asked.

Say something, Alexia thought, but she couldn't seem to connect her brain to her mouth, and her hand grabbed Ben by the back of the head, keeping him close to her. She didn't want to stop.

TWENTY-THREE ～◦

Rule 6: *Make him feel special, like he is the only guy in the world!*

Raven turned her Nissan Sentra into the airport parking lot and navigated through the maze to find a parking spot. She finally found one about five minutes away from the building, but she still had twenty minutes before Horace was due to arrive. She'd wanted to get here as soon as possible so she wouldn't make him wait any longer than he needed to.

Shutting the car off, Raven threw her keys in her bag and then checked her reflection in the tiny mirror behind the visor.

Clean teeth? Check.

Glossy lips? Check.

No makeup smudges? Check.

She ran her hand through her hair once, then twice, wanting to make it look perfect. She'd blown it out with a hair dryer so that it was pin straight. She'd been going for the volume effect, but instead it just hung along her face like a dark curtain. Maybe she should have used that Giovanni Vacell wave-enhancing gel instead and gone with the messy look.

Why are you worrying so much? Horace will love you no matter what.

Raven reached for the door handle when her cell went off in her bag. She smiled to herself, thinking it must be Horace and that he must have gotten in early!

The screen on the outside of the phone said it was Kelly.

Raven's shoulders sank as she flipped the phone open. "Hey," she said.

"Hey. Have you talked to Alexia since the Fourth?"

Raven got out of the car and locked the doors. "No, why?"

"Because I haven't either. She's gone hermit on me."

"She and Ben have been getting more serious. They barely come up for air. She's probably hanging out with him."

"Yeah."

"Anyway," Raven said as she stepped up to the sidewalk running in front of the airport, "I'm picking up Horace right now. Can I call you later?"

"Oh, I forgot Horace was coming home! Tell him I said hi."

"I will."

"Later!"

Raven said good-bye and hung up.

The glass doors to the airport whooshed open. Raven walked through as she went to baggage claim, where Horace had said he'd meet her.

She still had fifteen minutes. Now she just had to sit and wait.

She bumped shoulders with someone.

"Raven?"

Spine rigid, she shot a backward glance and saw Blake. "What are you doing here?" Panic turned her voice squeaky, which made her blush like some silly schoolgirl.

Blake pointed at Mil-D in line at the airport McDonald's. "We're going to L.A. for a few days. Mil just had to get his McCrack before we boarded."

Raven found herself laughing at the McDonald's joke, but quickly squashed it as a new stream of people winded through the airport. Horace appeared, cheeks sun darkened, hair a few inches longer, waving at her over the heads of other passengers.

She swallowed. Hard.

"Who's that?" Blake said, watching Horace navigate through the crowd.

"My boyfriend," she muttered, and the perpetual grin on Blake's face faded.

He shoved his hands in his jeans pockets. "So this is the boyfriend, huh?"

Horace came over, wrapped his hand around Raven's. "Hey," he said, his husky voice hitting all the right notes in her stomach and making the butterflies dance.

He was in a pair of ripped jeans, white strings hanging from the knees. A white band T-shirt peeked out from beneath a red, white, and yellow plaid Western shirt. There was a necklace around his neck with some sort of animal tooth strung on it.

Raven loved Horace, but suddenly her cheeks warmed as she watched Blake watch Horace. She wondered what he thought and for some reason she cared.

Did he think Horace was a dork like the rest of the jocks at school?

"Hey," Blake said, holding out his hand. "I'm Blake. Raven's new neighbor."

Horace shook because he was a gentleman like that. "Horace. It's nice to meet you."

"Likewise."

Mil-D sauntered over. The Big Mac in his hands looked tiny compared to his overall size. "Almost ready, son?" he asked around a mouthful of food. "Ray-ray!"

"Hi, Mil," she said, tightening her grip on Horace's hand. She wanted out of here. Like now.

This whole situation felt wrong. She had nothing to feel guilty over — it wasn't like she cheated on Horace — but the butterflies in her stomach were suddenly warring.

"We should go," she said to Horace. "Have fun in L.A.," she said to Blake, thankful that, after this awkward encounter, she would be Blake-free for a few days. It would give her a good amount of time to forget about how fun it was to hang with him. Or how cute he was when people bragged about him.

He pulled his hat down more, hiding his eyes. "See you guys later."

"Later, kids," Mil-D said, flashing the peace sign before he ambled off after Blake.

Horace leaned over and kissed Raven on the lips. "I missed you," he said, that secretive smile lighting his face.

He didn't even pause to ask about Blake or Mil-D or why Raven had failed to mention her new neighbor was a guy their age.

She loved him for that, for his unflinching trust in her.

She just hoped she could live up to his expectations.

♥ ♥ ♥

Raven parked outside Bershetti's. "Hungry?" she asked, arching a brow at Horace.

"As a matter of fact, I'm starving. Airplane peanuts aren't very filling."

They got out and Raven went straight to Horace's side, taking his hand again in hers. She hadn't been able to let him go since the airport.

"It's my treat." She held the door of the restaurant open so Horace could go in ahead of her.

"Ray, you don't have to do that."

She shook her head. "I already made reservations for lunch. Besides, I want to make you feel special today."

Rule 6 of the Crush Code said: *Make him feel special, like he is the only guy in the world!*

For her, Horace was.

They went inside and were seated near the windows, sunlight playing over the table. It was so bright that Horace left on his aviator sunglasses, and Raven put on her white oversize ones.

"I bet everyone is looking at us like we're insane," she said, laughing.

Horace shrugged. "So what. Celebrities do it all the time."

"Yeah, but we're not celebrities."

He sat forward, folding his arms on the tabletop. "Speaking of celebrities. Did you check out that contest I told you about? With Kay-J?"

Raven made an apologetic face. "Umm . . . no."

"Ray." Horace sighed. "Why not?"

"I don't want to win some *American Idol*-like contest. I want to stay with you guys. I want to stay with October."

"October will always be there. You can come back to us whenever. If you got this job, think of the experience you'd get. It's an opportunity that you'd be stupid to pass up."

Raven's expression softened, seeing the seriousness on Horace's face. He wasn't usually so . . . well, persistent. Or blunt.

"It almost sounds like you want me to leave October."

His Adam's apple bobbed in his throat. She wished she could see his eyes now. "I just don't want you waiting around here for something that might not happen. October might not ever go farther than Birch Falls, Connecticut, and I don't want you stuck here because of me."

Raven frowned. He was starting to sound like her mother. "What's this about?"

He sighed again, ran his fingers through his hair. "Just promise me you'll at least check the Web site out."

"Okay," she said quickly because she didn't like seeing him so agitated. "I'll check it out when I get home."

He leaned over the table and kissed her. "Thanks."

With that, he picked up his menu, commenting on how he missed the food in Birch Falls.

Raven put on a cheery face because she wanted to enjoy the afternoon, but in the back of her mind, she couldn't help but wonder if Horace was keeping something from her.

Did he want to break up with her? Was that why he was pushing her to try out for the contest? This was his easy way of getting rid of her?

No, that didn't seem like something Horace would do. She trusted that if he ever had doubts about their relationship, he'd talk with her about it first before making any crazy decisions on his own.

So what was this all about, exactly?

TWENTY-FOUR

Rule 3: *Wear raspberry body splash — it drives boys wild!*

Rule 26: *Do not feel you have to tell your friends who you are crushing on!*

Friday morning, on her way to work, Sydney pulled into the drugstore on the corner of Mulberry and Danner streets to grab some lip balm. She couldn't find hers, and she liked having it at work because it was cold in the hospital. Her lips were always dry.

Inside the store, the assistant manager, Tammy, waved to Sydney from a display of new body sprays.

"How are you today?" Tammy asked, ripping open a cardboard box at her feet.

"Fine, thanks." Sydney went straight to the lip balms and took a package of two vanilla tubes off the rack. Better to have a backup. She decided she'd grab a bottle of water, too, while she was here and went over to the coolers on the far wall.

When she passed Tammy at the front of the store, Sydney paused, her nose picking up the scent of something sweet. "What's that smell?"

Tammy straightened and pushed up the sleeves of her floral blouse. "Raspberry body splash. One of the bottles was leaking in the box. Smells nice, though, doesn't it?"

Sydney nodded, eyeing the display Tammy was putting together. There were bottles of cucumber melon spray and McIntosh apple, something called Hawaiian ginger and another called Japanese cherries.

Raspberry body splash . . . why was that setting off bells in her head?

The Crush Code. There was a rule about raspberry body splash driving the boys wild. That was one of Kelly's additions to the new code. She had an entire shelf of body sprays in her bedroom. Sydney typically didn't use sprays or perfumes or anything really, for that matter.

Did raspberry body splash really drive boys wild or had Kelly made up a useless rule because she hadn't wanted the Crush Code in the first place?

Well, the spray *did* smell good, either way. And Sydney wasn't adverse to trying something new. Would Drew like it? Would it drive him "crazy"? Despite her best efforts, Sydney had yet to reignite the spark in their relationship, and she was almost frustrated with trying at this point.

Trying to save a relationship with body splash was such a dumb idea, but there she was, grabbing a bottle off the shelf anyway.

After paying, Sydney went out to the car and sprayed the raspberry body splash on the underside of her wrist. She didn't want it too strong. She didn't want to choke out the kids at the hospital, but a little bit couldn't hurt, right?

♥   ♥   ♥

"Hello, Carl," Sydney said as she entered the boy's room in West Two. "How are you today?"

Carl, an eleven-year-old who'd just had surgery on his heel, shrugged and flipped through the meager fifteen cable channels on the TV.

"I'm bored. Like really, really bored."

"Where's your mom?"

"Getting lunch."

Sydney thought for a second, then, "How about I bring in an Xbox?"

Carl stopped flipping through the channels to look over at Sydney wide-eyed. "There's an Xbox here?"

Sydney nodded. "With lots of games, too."

"Do you have Madden?"

"I don't know. But I'll check."

"Cool! Thanks."

Sydney went to the media room and stopped just inside the doorway. Quin was there organizing the movies.

He looked up at her through his glasses. His hair was down today around his face and wavy, too, as if he'd washed it and let it air dry.

"Hey," he said, straightening.

"Hi." She entered the room, going to the video game shelf. She scanned the titles, running her finger along the spine of each game box. There were so many, more than any video store she'd ever seen.

"Looking for something?" Quin asked.

"Umm . . . Madden something?"

Quin went to the third shelf, pulling out a football game. "Here you go."

"You know where everything is, don't you?"

He shrugged. "Oh, hey, by the way, I've been meaning to tell you I saw your picture the other day in the art hall. I was really impressed."

A smile spread rapidly over her face. "Yeah?"

Quin nodded. "The light composition was great, and I loved the fluid motion of the runner."

Sydney didn't even pretend to know what he was talking about. "I'm afraid I don't know much of the technical side of photography."

"Well, you have a good start on instinct. You can learn techniques. If you want, I can take you out sometime. My schooling has to be good for something, right?"

"Really? You wouldn't mind?"

"No. I love photography, and people like talking about the things they love."

Sydney laughed. "That's true."

But what would Drew say if she hung out with another guy? There was nothing romantic about Quin's invitation, but that wouldn't matter to Drew. Guys didn't think like girls did. It wasn't okay for a girl to hang out with a guy she wasn't romantically linked with.

It was such a double standard because Drew hung out with Kelly all the time and Sydney never said anything about *that*.

"I'll keep the invitation in mind," Sydney said to Quin. "It's just, I have a boyfriend and I don't know if he'd . . . you know, be okay with it. But I appreciate the offer."

"Oh, yeah, sure."

She grabbed the TV cart and headed back to room 412, regret and disappointment settling in her stomach. She didn't want to hurt Drew, but she really wanted to go with Quin on a photo excursion. Was that so wrong of her? She hated that she had to decide between her boyfriend and a hobby that she loved. The fact was, she could learn something from Quin. He was enrolled at the Brooks Institute!

It just disappointed her that she had to miss such a great opportunity.

TWENTY-FIVE

Rule 10: *Have a sense of humor! Guys like to laugh!*

"God, I love you," Ben said, squeezing Alexia to his side as they hung out on her bed. "You're the best thing that's happened to me since my brother peed his pants in that carnival fun house six years ago."

Alexia laughed because Ben's twin brother, Will, often held himself as if he were above everyone else. And Alexia had gone into that fun house. She hadn't peed her pants.

Ben kissed her forehead, his fingers running over her ribs through her T-shirt. An excited shiver teased her back. She bolted upright. "I think I'm going to check my Email." She went to her desk and shook the computer mouse.

She, Alexia Bass, was no longer a virgin, but she'd only had sex that one time and it'd been over a week now. She was still a little freaked out by what had happened.

Ben sat on the corner of her desk. He was wearing his usual cargo shorts and a blue T-shirt. The only skin Alexia could see was his legs and his arms, but her brain filled in the rest using the night of the Fourth as reference.

"Alexia? What are you doing?"

A blush spread across her cheeks, and she looked back at the computer screen. "I'm just checking my Email."

"Except you've been staring at the screen for about five minutes. Are you trying to check your Email using mind control?"

She shook her head, barely cracked a smile.

"What is it, Lexy?"

She sighed and rubbed at her forehead. Could she tell him what she was thinking? Of course she could. He would never make fun of her.

"The other night," she began.

"Are you regretting it?"

"No." But that wasn't entirely the truth. Still, that's not what she'd wanted to talk about. And besides, she couldn't go back and change her mind. It was done. What she could control was what happened from here on out.

"I know we used something," she muttered, looking at her hands in her lap, "but . . ."

"I know. Look." Ben pulled his wallet from his back pocket and showed her two condoms slipped inside. "Take one. So you always know you have it."

She shook her head.

"Take it." He put it in her hand, closing her fingers around it. He leaned over, put his finger beneath her chin and kissed her. "I love you, Lexy. All I want is for you to be happy."

She nodded, butterflies flapping satisfied wings in her belly.

Despite everything with the sex issue, she loved him, too. And she felt like the luckiest girl in the world to have

167 —

him. She knew he cared for her, that sex hadn't been his goal right from the start.

She was just happy that the stress of making the decision was over. Now she just had to deal with the aftermath of having *made* that decision.

It would be okay, she thought. As long as she had Ben, it'd be okay.

♥   ♥   ♥

Later that night, after Ben left, Alexia called Raven to hang out. Alexia wanted to talk to one of her friends about the sex thing because she needed to tell *someone*, and Raven seemed the obvious choice. Alexia and Raven had always been closer than the other girls. Not to mention, Raven wasn't a virgin, and Alexia hoped Raven would make her feel not so stupid for having lost her virginity.

When she got no answer on Raven's cell, she decided to drive over.

Pulling up to the curb, she noticed Raven across the street at her neighbor's house hanging out on the front porch.

Alexia parked and walked over. Blake was in the middle of a story about his visit to L.A. last week. Raven, head back, laughed at a joke about Hollywood "Bimbinos." Blake smiled, clearly pleased with Raven's reaction.

Rule 10 said to have a sense of humor. *Guys like to laugh!*

Was Raven using the Crush Code on Blake?

"Hey," Alexia called, waving from the bottom of the porch steps.

"Alexia, right?" Blake said, nodding his head just once in a greeting. He waved her up. "Come hang. I just got back from L.A., and I'm starving for conversation with chill people."

Raven went quiet, the smile having left her lips.

"Actually, I just wanted to talk to Raven for a second," Alexia said.

Raven got up and tugged down her tank top. "I'll be right back," she said to Blake and followed Alexia to the street, out of Blake's hearing range.

"What's up?" Raven asked, crossing her arms defensively over her chest.

"Well." Alexia swallowed, licked her lips. Suddenly her problems vanished, and she said, "Are you cheating on Horace with Blake?"

Raven widened her eyes, hung her mouth open in disbelief. "No. How could you even ask me that?"

Alexia shifted her weight from one foot to the other. "It just seems . . . I don't know . . . like you're hanging out with him a lot, and I thought maybe you'd decided to use the Crush Code on him. I know how you are, Raven. You like the thrill of the hunt."

Brow furrowed, Raven straightened, putting herself an inch taller than Alexia. "You make it sound like I'm some . . . cougar or something. God, Alexia. I'm not a slut."

"I didn't say that —"

"But you implied it."

"No." Alexia shook her head, feeling the situation spiraling out of control. She didn't know how to fix it. Or how to calm Raven down. Blake and Mil-D were suddenly quiet on the porch.

Alexia leaned closer to Raven and lowered her voice. "I just don't want to see Horace get hurt and then have you calling me because you're upset that you screwed up the relationship. You love Horace, Raven."

"Yeah, Alexia, I know." Raven's shoulders went rigid. "And I'm not cheating on him, so why don't you butt out of my business and go psychoanalyze someone else."

Raven stomped across the street to her own house, opened the front door and slammed it shut behind her. Alexia stood frozen by Mr. Kailing's mailbox, wondering what had just happened.

Her face was hot, her throat felt ready to close.

She glanced up at Blake's house, and he and Mil-D quickly looked away. Alexia shot them a scowl before getting in her car and leaving.

TWENTY-SIX

Rule 7: *Be adventurous and daring! See life as an adventure!*

Rule 31: *Do not send your friend to tell your crush you like him!*

On Sunday afternoon, Kelly sat on one side of the living room in the cushy reclining chair and her brother on the other side on the couch. There was a bag of popcorn in Todd's lap and a bowl in Kelly's. The TV blared music videos. It was literally the only thing on right now.

"Ready?" Todd said, a piece of popcorn in his hands.

Kelly opened her mouth into an O, and Todd chucked the piece of popcorn at her. She leaned forward, eyeing the popcorn sailing through the air. She caught it.

"Yes!" she said, clenching her hands into victorious fists. "Now my turn."

She threw a piece at Todd, but it sailed right over his head and disappeared behind the couch.

"Nice throw," he said sarcastically.

"Ha. Ha. Let me try another one." She tossed another piece to him and this time he snatched it from the air.

She clapped her hands. "Yeah! You were like a dog catching a Frisbee."

Todd narrowed his eyes. "Aren't you HIL-arious."

Kelly set her bowl of popcorn on the coffee table and went over to the couch, flopping down next to her brother. "I'm bored!"

"Let's build a castle out of cheese."

"You are such an idiot."

Kelly closed her eyes and instantly she thought of Drew. She'd been thinking of him all day. And all day yesterday while she worked at the shelter. And all day the day before that, too.

It didn't help that he was best friends with her brother and at the house all the time. Something had changed between them. She couldn't tell what. Maybe it was the fact that she'd admitted out loud to Adam that she liked Drew.

Drew didn't know that, of course, but that had to change the way Kelly acted around him and maybe he'd picked up on it.

"Let's go do something, then," Todd said, chomping on a mouthful of popcorn.

"Like what?" Kelly sat up.

"Something fun."

The Crush Code came to mind. Despite the idea behind it (forcing Kelly to go after Adam) some of the rules were fun to follow. Maybe there was an idea in the code.

"I'll be right back," she said and went to her room to grab her list of rules.

Rule 1: *Be playful, fun, and flirty!*

Nope.

Rule 6: *Make him feel special* —

No.

Rule 7: *Be adventurous and daring!*

Hmm . . . that had potential, but what could they do in Birch Falls that was adventurous and daring?

When she was a kid, she, Todd and Drew, and some other kids from the neighborhood would get a group together to play capture the flag.

That used to be her favorite game.

Tucking the Code back in her desk, she went out to the living room.

"I have an idea," she said. "Let's play capture the flag."

Todd spit out a popcorn kernel. "Hell, yeah. I'm in."

"Cool." Kelly grabbed his cell phone off the coffee table and tossed it to him. "Call Drew and see if he can come."

♥　　♥　　♥

Kelly bent over, sweeping all her hair forward so she could tie it in a high ponytail. Drew and Todd were in front of her, Adam next to her. She'd invited him because, despite the realization that they were not going to be dating each other, they did make good friends.

Kelly liked Adam, just not *like that*.

With her hair tamed, Kelly took the pink rubber band off her wrist and tied it up.

Someone whistled behind her. "Nice view."

She straightened, shooting Craig Theriot an eat-rocks-for-breakfast look. He only grinned at her.

"Who invited you?" she asked.

Todd and Craig shared a guy handshake.

"I invited him," Todd said. "Why?"

Kelly rolled her eyes. Craig and her brother were the perfect duo; they'd make a good sideshow act at the idiot circus.

A few other people showed as the group waited in the parking lot of Eagle Park. Kelly had called her friends, but Sydney said she just wanted to hang out at home. Raven had asked if Alexia was going to be there and when Kelly said she wasn't sure, Raven suddenly had chores to take care of. Kelly wasn't sure what that was all about. When she called Alexia to get the scoop, her brother said she was working.

Now, looking around at the group of twelve, Kelly realized she was the only girl.

Great.

"Let's break into teams," Todd said. "Draw names? Captain picks the teams? How do you guys want to do it?"

"Who are the captains?" Matt asked.

"Let's draw names for captains," Drew said, shaking hair from his eyes. "And then captain picks."

Kelly stuck close to Adam, trying not to look at Drew. She didn't want him catching her staring, but suddenly she couldn't take her eyes off him.

He was in a pair of faded, boot-cut jeans and vintage brown leather boots. It was mid-sixty degrees now that the sun had set, but he had on a white long-sleeve shirt and a blue T-shirt over that.

Craig said something to him and Drew shook his head, laughed, flashed those pretty white teeth, and when he looked away from his friend, he turned his neon blue eyes directly on Kelly.

A week ago, she might have smiled or made a face at him. Instead, she turned to Adam, her cheeks most likely flushed. There was an odd weakness in her knees. She hadn't felt this way since last winter when Will flirted with her in their American government class and later asked her out.

"Blue team on the south end," Todd said, throwing Matt the blue flag. "Red team has the north end."

"I'll call Drew when we're set," Matt said. "Deal?"

Drew nodded.

"Are we ready, then?" Todd rubbed his hands together. "You're all going down."

"Whatever," Kelly countered. "They have *you* as a captain."

Todd rolled his eyes. "I'm the capture-the-flag master."

"Master of losing." Kelly laughed, giving her brother a shove as she passed him and Drew.

"Good luck," Drew said to Kelly, grinning, "'cause you're going to need it."

♥   ♥   ♥

"Have you told him yet?" Adam whispered as he and Kelly slinked through the trees.

Darkness had settled through the park. Kelly could see the trees in front of her, but little else. She tugged down the hat she'd put on at the start of the game. That's what they used as their individual "flags." To take out someone from the other team, you had to get their hat.

"Told who what?" she said.

Adam stopped. "Drew. Have you told Drew?"

Kelly pursed her lips and went ahead of Adam, keeping close to the trees.

"I can't tell him," she finally said.

"Should I, then?"

Kelly whirled around. "No! Don't you dare."

Adam laughed. "All right. Fine."

She relaxed and continued walking. "He can't ever know. He's going out with one of my best friends. That's like one of the mortal sins of friendship."

"Yeah, but you can't help who you like." Adam hurried to match her pace.

"But I can help whether or not I ruin another relationship."

A twig snapped somewhere off to their left. Adam grabbed Kelly's arm and dragged her down. They used a thick tree trunk as cover, poking their heads around it to watch the surrounding forest.

"You see anyone?" Kelly whispered.

"Shh."

A few minutes later, Kelly saw a flash of white shirt. Who had worn a white shirt to play capture the flag?

Drew had, she remembered.

He and Mike Renze crept through the thickening shadows.

"There's the wild," Adam said directly in Kelly's ear.

She narrowed her eyes at him, remembering the line of poetry he'd quoted the night of the Fourth. That love was the wild that ran through the forests.

"Go get it," he said, grinning, and then stood up, running off in the other direction.

Mike and Drew froze.

"I'll get him," Mike said, darting after Adam.

Alone now, Drew surveyed the area. Kelly clung to the tree in front of her, the bark digging into her forearm. She held her breath, afraid that Drew would hear it. Her heart hammered loudly in her ears.

When Drew passed her hiding spot, Kelly went around her tree to came up behind him. She lunged, but he grabbed her arm and tackled her to the ground.

She burst out laughing as Drew wrestled her hat off.

"I told you that you were going to need luck."

Kelly met his eyes. Even in the darkness, she could see the vibrant blue color.

"I let you take it," she countered.

Drew was practically on top of her, his face just inches from hers.

I could kiss him, she thought, they were that close.

He was warm next to her, his breath hot against her cheek. She could feel his heart beating through his shirt.

He wasn't laughing anymore and neither was she. She was pretty sure she wasn't breathing either.

Drew bent down. Every nerve in Kelly's body sizzled. His lips brushed hers, and she inhaled sharply. Her fingers trembled at her sides.

Drew breathed roughly, licked his lips. He leaned down as if to kiss her again, real and aggressive this time, when his cell rang in his pocket.

He bolted up, startled by the sound.

Kelly lay there in the old, crisp leaves among acorn caps and green moss.

Drew answered his phone. "Hey, Syd," he said, eyeing Kelly.

Kelly's stomach churned. She swallowed down the heat rising in her throat. There was no way Sydney could know what had just happened, but Kelly felt as guilty as if Sydney were standing right there looking down at her.

Kelly scrambled to her feet, fixed her hair, and wiped the dirt from her pants. She headed off down the trail that would take her out of the woods.

Footsteps hurried behind her. "Wait," Drew said, holding his hand over his cell.

"I have to go," Kelly said, keeping her eyes straight ahead.

"Kelly." He ran in front of her. "Just two seconds." He went back to his cell phone and said to Sydney, "What? No. I'm with Mike."

Kelly widened her eyes at the blatant lie. Drew cocked his head to the side, apologetic. She wasn't the one he should be apologizing to.

"I'm leaving," she whispered and hurried out of the woods.

This time, Drew didn't follow.

TWENTY-SEVEN

Rule 13: *Do not be bossy! Do not tell your crush what to do!*

Rule 19: *Do not allow your crush to pressure you to do something you do not want to do! Do only things that you and only you want to do and are comfortable with!*

Rule 25: *Compliment your crush two times a week!*

Sydney poked her head inside the den. "Dad?"

He looked up from whatever he'd been doing at his desk. "Yes?"

Gray stubble covered his chin. He was still in his pajamas — a pair of blue flannel pants and a white T-shirt — and there were bags beneath his eyes.

"You're not going to work today?" Sydney asked.

"I took a leave of absence." He pushed his glasses back to the bridge of his nose.

"Well, I have to work today, and then after work, I think we're all going to the carnival."

He nodded, picked up a pen. "Have fun, then."

The clock on the wall behind him ticked each second. It was the only sound in the house, and it'd been like that for days.

There'd been no word from Sydney's mother. Not a phone call, a voice mail, not even a postcard.

Anger made Sydney clench her jaw. It was like they didn't even exist. Like her mother flew off to Italy and forgot that she had a husband and a daughter.

Did she not care what her sudden departure had done to her family?

Apparently not.

Which made Sydney even angrier.

"Okay," she said to the silence. "I'm leaving," she added, before closing the door and looking out at the empty living room. The bare coffee table. The darkened TV screen. The couch that looked brand-new because it was hardly ever used.

Sydney lived in a movie set.

Or at least that's what it felt like.

There were things around the living room — books, pictures, a Roman statue — but they looked like props against a fake setting, a place portrayed as a family room but without the family.

Tears bit at her eyes. She clenched her jaw again, took in a steadying breath through her nose.

No crying.

I need to dwell less on my mother and focus more on myself, because that's what she'd do.

♥　　♥　　♥

Sydney pulled into the Children's Hospital parking lot and found a spot. She shut the car off and quickly called Drew while she had a few extra minutes. "Are we doing anything tonight? Like maybe going to the carnival?"

"Did you want to?" he asked.

Sydney rolled her eyes. Drew had been acting weird the last few days. She supposed it had a lot to do with her attitude. She hadn't exactly been in a good mood since her mother left. There'd only been two things that'd put a smile on her face. Work at the hospital and photography.

She brushed clear lip gloss over her lips and smacked them together.

Don't be bossy, a voice in her head warned, the voice that was in charge of remembering the rules from the Crush Code.

"I'd like to go to the carnival," she said softly, "but if you have something else in mind, that's fine, too."

"It might be fun. I hear they have a new ride this year. It's called the Zipper."

Sydney had heard about that ride. They locked you inside a cage shaped like a teardrop and then the "zipper" ran the cage around and around at hysteria-inducing speeds.

That kind of ride was not Sydney's kind of ride. She much preferred something that stayed closer to the ground.

Don't be bossy, that stupid voice said again.

When they got to the carnival, she'd nicely tell Drew they weren't going on any crazy rides like the Zipper.

"Let's plan to go after I get out of work," she said, getting out of the SUV and locking it up. "I'll come over to your house about seven?"

"Sounds good. Love you," Drew said.

"Love you, too."

♥   ♥   ♥

The Birch Falls Carnival came into town every year in mid-July. When Sydney was a kid, her parents would bring her, send her on the little kiddie rides while her mother stood back, her camera in hand, snapping pictures of a laughing Sydney. Those pictures were stuffed in a tote somewhere in the attic, forgotten like the rest of her mother's life, apparently.

"How was work today?" Drew asked, offering the woman at the ticket counter a twenty-dollar bill.

Sydney looked around the carnival, a massive affair set up in the middle of a field on the north side of town. Red and yellow and green lights shone brightly against the darkening sky. A smooth, excited voice sounded through a speaker system, "Welcome to the twenty-sixth annual Birch Falls Carnival. Carnival bracelets can be purchased at every entrance at the ticket booths." The message went on, announcing a chain-saw-carving exhibit near the west entrance and a magic show later that night. A group of young girls ran past Sydney, headed for the roller coaster ride shaped like an alligator.

"Work was fine," Sydney answered absently, scanning the faces for someone familiar. Her friends were supposed to be meeting her here. Raven said to meet by this entrance, but Sydney didn't see her, or anyone for that matter.

"Sydney?" Drew called. "You have to get your bracelet."

Sydney went to the ticket booth and stuck her arm inside the little opening at the bottom of the Plexiglas window. The large woman on the other side wound a pink plastic bracelet around Sydney's wrist and tightened it into place, snipping off the excess with a pair of scissors.

"Enjoy the carnival," the woman said.

"Thanks." Sydney twirled the bracelet around. "What color did you get?"

Drew held up his, frowning. "Same color."

Sydney laughed. "It looks good on you."

The frown disappeared and Drew smiled. "Thanks." He put his arm around Sydney's shoulders and pulled her into him. "I haven't heard you laugh in a while. I missed it."

Sydney shrugged. "It's just been . . . rough, you know, at home. My dad seems barely able to function and . . ." She trailed off. She wanted to be able to vent to Drew, but she just didn't have the energy. She'd rather push it to the back of her mind and not deal with it. At least not now. "Let's just try to have fun tonight, okay?"

"Sure. I can't wait to try the Zipper."

Sydney cringed. "About that — I don't think I'm getting on."

Drew groaned. "Oh, come on. You have to try."

"I don't know."

They walked a while, silent, passing several kiddie rides and games.

"Sydney!"

Sydney looked over toward a game booth dominated by teddy bears the size of a St. Bernard. Raven, Alexia, and Kelly waved. Horace grabbed a teddy bear from the man behind the booth front. Ben congratulated Horace on his "exceptional squirt gun skills" while Todd laughed at the very small difference in size between Horace and his new toy.

The group converged in the center of the midway.

"That shirt looks cute on you," Kelly said, nodding at Sydney's new shirt. It was the white one with the red hearts down the front. She'd worn it to work with a pair of black pants, but changed at the end of the day into a distressed jean miniskirt and threw on a black beaded necklace, too.

"Thanks," Sydney said. "It's comfy."

Kelly smiled, but it came off awkward for some reason. She shifted, the smile fading when she glanced next at Drew. He shuffled his weight around and looked at the ground.

Sydney wasn't allowed a moment to dwell on their weird behavior because Drew grabbed her by the arm and dragged her away. "Let's do the Zipper first." He nodded in the ride's direction.

It was the tallest ride at the carnival. The teardrop cages whipped around the ride, some cages spinning uncontrollably. Screams sounded from the top, carrying all the way down the midway to Sydney. She wasn't going anywhere near that ride.

"Whoever screams first is a sissy," Ben said.

"Ohh," Kelly said. "I've been wanting to ride that one."

"If you cry, I'll never let you forget it," Todd said.

"I'm not going to cry!" Kelly gave him a shove. "Besides, who was the one crying at the end of *Brother Bear*?"

"I was seven years old!" he said.

"You were thirteen!"

"Stop fighting, you two," Drew said, stepping between Kelly and Todd. "Come on, let's go get on the Zipper." Drew motioned for Kelly to follow him, but Kelly shook her head and fell back by Raven, who was avoiding everyone but Horace.

Sydney sensed tension in the group, but she couldn't quite figure out where it was coming from. Alexia and Raven maybe? They hadn't said one word to each other since Sydney arrived. There was something odd going on with Kelly, too.

"Hey, Syd?" Drew said. "Are you coming?"

"I told you I didn't want to," she answered quietly, hoping no one made fun of her for being a "chicken." Todd would make fun of her because he was an idiot.

"I'll be with you," Drew said. "It's not that bad. I swear."

How would he know? The ride was new this year. He'd never ridden it before. The group had pulled ahead of Sydney and Drew, making their way to the Zipper.

"Just try this one ride for me," Drew said, "and then we'll do whatever you want."

Sydney looked over at the Zipper again, at the cages whipping around. Her heart hammered in her chest just thinking about climbing on there, but she wanted to please Drew. She wanted to show him that she was open to new things.

"All right," she said. "Just one ride."

♥   ♥   ♥

The door on the cage slammed shut. The ride operator pulled down the latch, locking Sydney and Drew inside.

Sydney pulled in a deep breath, sweat beading on the nape of her neck and below her nose.

Oh god, she wanted out so bad. She wanted to plant her feet on the ground and stay there.

Their cage moved up one level so Raven and Horace could pile in the next cage. It went on like that for another five minutes or so as the ride operator filled the rest of the cages with new riders. Sydney and Drew's cage inched up to the sky. When they reached the highest point of the ride, Sydney clutched the handle on the door, squeezing her eyes shut.

"I wish you hadn't talked me into this," she muttered, swallowing hard against the lump in her throat.

"You'll be fine." Drew put his arm around her shoulders and squeezed. "Oh, here it goes."

Their cage moved and kept moving. Through the metal door, Sydney saw the ground rush up to them and then disappear, replaced with the sky as the "zipper" ran around and around. The faster the ride went, the more unstable Sydney and Drew's cage became. It rocked back and forth, so that at one point Sydney was parallel with the ground and then a second later completely upside down.

Her stomach rolled, her heart quickening.

"I think I'm going to be sick!" she screamed as Drew screeched with delight.

Sydney wiped her mouth with a wet paper towel. She flushed the toilet, her lunch swirling down the drain with the disappearing water.

"You okay?" Alexia asked, pulling Sydney's hair back.

"I think so." Sydney stood up. Her head was still woozy, the world rocking back and forth like it had on the ride. She shuffled out of the bathroom with Alexia, Raven, and Kelly behind her. Drew rushed up, offering a bottle of water.

"I'm so sorry, Syd," he said. "I really didn't think it'd affect you that badly."

"I told you I don't like those kinds of rides," she said, taking the water and drinking quickly, hoping to get the vomit taste out of her mouth.

"I know. Again, I'm sorry. Really." Drew pulled her into a hug and kissed her atop the head. "I love you. Do you still love me?" he asked, laughing lightly.

Sydney sighed. "Yes, of course I love you."

She just wished he'd listen to her more. And it wouldn't be so bad if they both liked the same stupid carnival rides.

TWENTY-EIGHT ～❧

Rule 11: *Act distant but interested! Guys love a challenge!*

Raven typed in the Web address Horace had given her earlier at Scrappe and hit ENTER. She sipped from the hot chai Horace had made her while she waited for the screen to load.

The audio played before the graphics popped up on the hot-pink background. Kay-J's soft, syrupy sweet voice accompanied quick pop beats. A second later, a picture of her loaded, her wide, ultra-white smile matching her white tunic tank top.

Raven read the front-page text.

Hey! It's Kay-J! Thanks for stopping by. If you're here on the site, I assume you've heard about the new show I'm doing called Back Up Kay-J. *We're looking for one backup singer to accompany me on next summer's tour.*

Not only will the lucky winner get to travel the world, but she/he will also record one song for my new album, Rockin' the Pink.

I'm excited to meet everyone and hear your voices!
Check out the auditions page for details!
XOXO
Kay-J

Raven turned down the volume on the computer to quiet the up-tempo beats.

So, okay, Kay-J was pretty good, and her music had that weird, infectious vibe to it that made even the laziest people get up and dance.

But that wasn't Raven's kind of music. Couldn't Horace understand that?

Sighing, she clicked on the AUDITIONS link and brought up a new page.

She scanned the dates and locations. There was an audition next week in California. Way too far away. One week later, auditions were in New York. That was like a two-hour drive from Birch Falls. That was manageable.

If Raven even decided she wanted to try out, that is.

In the meantime, just in case she did go to the city and audition, Raven figured she'd better know the songs she would be asked to sing. She downloaded a few Kay-J tracks to her iPod and went for a walk.

As she headed down her driveway, sunglasses in place, she scanned Blake's house, looking for any sign of life. She hadn't seen him in the five days since she'd had the argument with Alexia out in front of his house.

The front windows of his house were dark now. The large upstairs window — the one Raven guessed had to be Blake's room — was covered with dark curtains.

Had he jetted off to somewhere else? What if he didn't come back?

Who cares? she thought. Not me.

She turned up the volume on her iPod when a few kids down the block screamed as they ran through a sprinkler.

Raven tried to focus on the music.

Kay-J's music was undeniably pop commercial. There wasn't a lot of depth to her lyrics. Probably she didn't even write them herself. The first track Raven listened to was about a breakup that Kay-J blamed herself for.

The second track, with a speedier tempo, was about a beach party, if Raven was hearing the lyrics right.

She listened to the second track over and over again, memorizing the lyrics. The chorus was quick and catchy and Raven was singing it quietly by the third listen.

As she ambled down the sidewalk, a large, black SUV rolled to a stop at the curb. The passenger-side window came down and Raven glanced inside.

It was Blake.

She sucked in a breath. The corners of her mouth curved into a relieved smile. He was still around. He wasn't leaving Birch Falls for some big city.

Pausing the iPod, Raven popped the earbuds from her ears and walked over to the SUV.

"Hey," she said, trying to act uninterested. "You're home."

"I got in two days ago but . . ." He rubbed his puffy bottom lip with his index finger. "Well, let's just say I was under the weather."

Raven arched a brow. "Party too hard?"

"Something like that."

Had he been out there hooking up with random girls? Jealousy wedged in her gut, and she scrambled for the Crush Code instinctively.

The only rule she could remember said to act distant but interested.

Who came up with that rule anyway?

How could you be distant but interested? Seriously.

Probably it was best for her just to act distant.

Especially after Alexia accused her of cheating on Horace with Blake. Keeping her distance would prove to Alexia that Raven was faithful, and then Raven could rub it in her face.

Raven pushed away from the SUV's gleaming black body and blacked-out wheels. "Well, I'm sorta busy, so I'll catch you later?"

He cleared his throat, pulled down his hat an inch. "Yeah. Okay."

"Bye." She waggled her fingers and smiled triumphantly.

Uh-oh, she thought as Blake grinned and waved back. I just acted distant but then threw him an interested departing gesture.

Great.

TWENTY-NINE

After a terrible day at work (a chaotic lunch rush, a batch of burned bread, and a plugged sink drain), all Alexia wanted to do was relax. She'd take a shower, get into some comfy clothes, and hang out in her bedroom watching *Romeo and Juliet*.

But as soon as she opened the front door and kicked off her shoes, her parents appeared out of nowhere, their mouths set in a grim line. Alexia knew "relax" wasn't going to be possible.

"We need to talk," Dr. Bass said. "Come into the office."

They disappeared down the hallway.

Alexia just stood there for a second trying to calculate her chances for escape. And if she succeeded with escape, how far would she get before her parents called the cops?

Sighing, she went to the office slowly. Whatever this was, it wasn't good. This just smelled like trouble.

When she entered the office, her mother shut the door. Her dad sat behind his desk in his large leather chair. He pulled off his glasses and set them on the clean desktop.

Alexia's mom, perched now on the edge of the desk, folded her hands, setting them on her knee. Alexia sat across from her parents. Every nerve in her body snapped and her brain yelled, *Run!*

"Tell me," Dr. Bass said, grabbing something from his desk drawer, "what this is."

The blood pooled in Alexia's cheeks when she saw what was in her father's hand.

A condom.

More specifically, the condom Ben had given her, the one in the shiny red wrapper that said RIBBED FOR HER PLEASURE! right across the front.

Crap.

"Um . . ."

If she pretended not to know, would they buy it?

"I'm really disappointed in you, Alexia," her mom said. She took in a breath. "I thought we had discussed waiting."

Alexia shifted, bit her lip. She already felt conflicted enough about losing her virginity and now her parents were lecturing her about it? Tears welled behind her lids. A burning sensation filled her throat.

"I . . ."

"I suspected you and Benjamin were getting too serious." Dr. Bass shook his head. "I should have put my foot down. But I will now before it's too late."

Alexia shook when her breath faltered with the tears.

"You're grounded," Dr. Bass said, "and I think you need to be spending a little more time with your friends and a little less time with your boyfriend."

She just stared at them, her teeth clenched, tears streaming down her face. She didn't know what to say.

"Is there anything you have to say?" her mom asked, furrowing her brow.

Alexia shook her head and swiped at the tears.

"You're excused, then," her dad said.

Alexia got up and left.

♥　　♥　　♥

When her phone rang around eleven that night, Alexia dove for it before her parents heard the ring and took the phone from her. They hadn't exactly gone over the terms of the grounding, and she wasn't sure if she was supposed to be using the cell or not.

A picture of Ben popped up on the screen. Alexia answered, "Hello?"

"Hey! What are you doing? I thought you were going to call me when you got home from work."

"I was. I just got sidetracked."

Should she tell him about the condom and the grounding? It was almost too embarrassing. And what was he going to think about her parents' advice to break away from him?

It'd be just like him to drive over here and confront her parents. He'd try to charm his way back into their good graces.

No, Alexia thought, better to wait.

"Is it too late to come over?" he asked.

"Probably." She listened to the sounds coming from downstairs. Her parents and her brother were watching a new movie. It didn't sound like anyone had noticed the phone ringing.

Ben sighed. "I guess I'll just go ahead and tell you over the phone, then."

Alexia froze. "Tell me what?" What was he talking about?

"I finally decided what I'm doing this fall."

"What?" He'd already received a handful of acceptances from colleges in the area. He'd been adamant about choosing. Alexia wouldn't say so out loud, but she'd wanted him to choose something closer to home so they could see each other.

"I've decided," he began, "that I'm going with Will to Pepperdine University."

Alexia's mouth dropped open. She blinked. Furrowed her brow. Had she just heard him right?

"Pepperdine? Like Pepperdine in California?"

"I know it's far, but I've been thinking about it for a long time. I just didn't want to say anything and scare you."

It felt like her heart had stopped beating.

The air in her lungs felt stale and cold.

"Lexy?"

California?

"Lexy, you're mad, aren't you?"

"No," she said, maybe a bit too quickly. "I'm just . . ."

"In shock. That's why I wanted to tell you face-to-face, but I just couldn't wait."

Pulling in a breath, she sat up straighter and tried to organize her thoughts. "So, you're for sure going? Or you're just thinking about it?"

Maybe there was still time to talk him out of it!

"I already decided. Will and I signed up for classes. We leave August twenty-ninth."

Oh.

"That's . . . really soon."

"Yeah."

"Ben."

"I know."

Alexia sat down on her bed and held her head in her hands. She'd just lost her virginity to someone who was moving to the other side of the country. It might as well be Iceland!

She'd already cried a billion times today but suddenly felt on the verge again. Hadn't she completely drained her tear well? Apparently not. They slipped from the corners of her eyes. Her breath shuddered down her throat.

"Are you crying?" Ben asked, his voice soft and concerned.

"No." She swallowed. She had to get off the phone before she really started balling. "I have to go."

"Lexy."

"Just call me tomorrow, okay?"

"Lexy."

"I love you," she said and hung up.

She shut her phone off, tossed it in the corner chair, and then laid back on her bed, curling into her pillow. It still smelled like Ben from the last time he'd been over when her parents had gone out of town.

Alexia took in a big breath of his scent, and the tears fell harder.

Why had he chosen Pepperdine? Why couldn't he have just gone to college somewhere in Connecticut? And she'd thought him being an hour away was going to be torture.

Their relationship was over. Maybe he wouldn't break up with her and maybe he'd promise to be the best long-distance boyfriend in the world, but how was she going to survive without him?

They only had five weeks to spend together.

That wasn't long enough.

How had Alexia gone from single to having a boyfriend to losing her virginity and her boyfriend all in the same year? It was too much. Having a boyfriend was too much.

She closed her eyes against the tears. All she wanted to do was fall asleep now and forget this day ever happened.

THIRTY ✺

Rule 21: *Be mysterious! Show him there is some mystery about you!*

Rule 25: *Compliment your crush two times a week!*

Rule 17: *Always look your best in the company of your crush!*

When the doorbell rang at the front of Kelly's house, unease and excitement mixed in her chest, making her heart quicken.

It was Wednesday night — poker night — which meant that doorbell might very well be Drew.

Matt and Kenny had already shown up. They were in the basement with Todd eating the oatmeal chocolate chip cookies Kelly had made earlier. They'd also invited Adam over, but he wasn't there yet.

Kelly practically ran to the front door, hoping to beat Todd there. She ran into her little sister, Monica, and gently pushed her aside.

"Jeez," Monica breathed. "What are you in a hurry for?"

"Oh . . . uh . . . I don't want to make anyone wait at the door," Kelly answered.

When she reached the foyer, she stopped, checked her blue shirt to be sure she wasn't revealing too much cleavage, and then pulled the door open.

"Oh," she said, seeing Adam standing there.

"You were expecting someone else?" He arched a brow, shot her a teasing grin.

"No . . . I just —"

Drew pulled his truck up to the curb in front of Kelly's house and parked. She looked past Adam.

Adam followed her gaze. "Yup, you were expecting someone else." He sighed and stepped aside as Drew came up the front steps.

"Hey, Kels," Drew said. "Adam. What's up?"

"Came to kick your ass in poker, that's all."

Drew chuckled. "Yeah. Sure. I'm master champ."

Kelly held open the door as the two boys sauntered inside. Monica turned down the TV, inconspicuously watching Drew and Adam as she picked a few crackers from the box on the coffee table. Her eyes got wide when she saw Adam, and she stopped chewing for a fraction of a second.

"Hey, Monica," Drew called, but she barely shot him an acknowledgment.

Kelly didn't blame her little sister. Adam was, after all, extremely gorgeous. If only she felt that chemistry with him on a personal level. It was still tempting to force the relationship, but she couldn't, and Adam probably wouldn't even let her now that he knew how she felt about Drew.

"Come on," Drew said to Adam, "let's head downstairs."

"All right." Adam nodded a parting greeting to Kelly.

"Wow." Monica paused the movie when the boys were out of hearing range. "Who was that? Is he your new boyfriend?"

"No. We're just friends."

"Why?" Monica sounded horrified by this idea.

"Because . . ." Kelly went to the kitchen for her second snack, the one she'd use to get herself downstairs without seeming obvious.

"Because why? Have you looked at him? I mean, really looked at him? He's so cute."

"I know, Mon. I'm not blind."

"Then he doesn't like you?"

Kelly took out the big plastic bowl of black bean salsa she'd made earlier and popped the top. "I don't know if he likes me or not. But we're just friends. I like someone else."

Monica pulled herself up on the kitchen counter and pushed her strawberry blonde ponytail off her shoulder. For a thirteen-year-old, she was entirely too boy-crazy. At least that's what Kelly thought.

Monica licked cracker cheese from her lips. "Who do you like, then?"

"Like I'm going to tell you!"

"I won't tell anyone."

Kelly rolled her eyes. "Like the time you promised you wouldn't tell Todd about how I broke his Playstation?"

Monica shrugged innocently. "That was an accident. I thought he wouldn't be mad."

"I'm not telling you," Kelly said again, because her sister would tell Todd and then Todd would bug her about it and possibly make her life hell until she promised never to crush on his friends again.

But worst of all, what if Drew found out?

It was one thing to admit to yourself that you were in love with your best friend's boyfriend, but once it started getting around, it would become real and embarrassing and shameful.

Monica grew bored eventually and went back to her movie. Kelly filled a bowl with tortilla chips and grabbed her homemade salsa, then headed downstairs.

Alternative music blared from a stereo on the small entertainment center. Todd had pushed the couch farther back to make extra room for the metal folding chairs that sat around the red felt poker table.

Drew threw down his cards, flashing three jacks. The guys burst into shouts of surprise and awe.

"Master champ," Drew said breezily, sliding the red, white, and blue chips into his pile.

Kelly set down the snacks and looked over Adam's shoulder at the new hand he'd been dealt. He had two nines, a ten, a jack, and an ace. Not a very good hand, that one.

"What do you think?" Adam asked her.

She pointed to the ten and jack. "Get rid of those."

"Hey, hey!" Todd yelled.

Adam said, "What?"

"No asking your girlfriend for help," Todd said.

Kelly grunted. "We're not —"

"We're just friends, dude," Adam said.

Drew stilled and looked from Adam to Kelly. "Just friends?"

Adam nodded.

Drew's lips twitched as if he were going to smile but decided to bury it.

"Oh," he said, his eyes lingering on Kelly, "that's cool."

"Yeah," she said, realizing all too late that Drew hadn't really been *talking* to her, just *looking* at her.

The tension was almost palpable. Kelly shifted when the guys hollered again about something else, but Drew, he didn't say or do anything but look at Kelly.

I'm losing this battle, she thought. How am I ever going to stop liking him when he looks at me like that?

Sighing, she turned away, escaping quickly upstairs.

"Hey," Drew said from Kelly's open bedroom door.

She looked up from her *CosmoGirl!* magazine. "Hey." She sat up on the bed, tucking her feet beneath her. "Game all done?"

He nodded. "Everyone ran out of chips."

"And who was the one who had all the chips when the game was over?"

"Well, me, of course."

"Were you counting cards again?"

He gave her an impish grin. "I'll never tell." He came farther into the room and, with every step, his good mood seemed to slip away. "Have you talked to Sydney at all?"

"No. Not much. She's been kinda distant lately."

Drew plopped down next to Kelly. She tensed, her emotions conflicting. She wanted to be close to him, but felt guilty for it. She scooted a few inches to the left, away from him. If he noticed, he didn't say anything about it.

"I haven't been able to talk to her much. She isn't opening up about her mom leaving."

"Yeah. That was crazy, wasn't it?"

"Yeah. Who does that? Just ups and leaves their family?"

Kelly shook her head. "I don't get it. That's for sure."

A short silence spread between them. Kelly repositioned herself on the bed, trying to get comfortable. If she'd known Drew was going to come into her room, she would have put something else on. Instead, she was in a pair of green-and-purple-striped shorts made to resemble men's boxers.

As if reading her unease, Drew looked over at her, then down at her legs right next to him. "I wanted to tell you," he looked at the floor, folded his hands together, "that you look good today."

A blush instantly pinked Kelly's cheeks. She pulled hair down in front of her eyes, hiding herself and the pleased look on her face. How could she follow Rule 21 (be mysterious!) when she could barely keep herself together around Drew?

"You look good, too," she mumbled. "Those are my favorite jeans, by the way."

His eye contact was sudden and intense. "Yeah?"

"Yeah."

This bout of silence felt, not uncomfortable, but dangerous. As if it were prefacing something forbidden between them.

Kelly quickly looked away.

"So," Drew said, rubbing his hands together, "you and Adam? I thought you guys were together."

"No. We're just good friends. I like someone else."

Drew raised a brow. "Who?"

"Secret," she said with a smile.

"I have a secret, too," he said softly.

"Yeah?"

He nodded. "I like someone else, too."

Kelly raked her teeth over her bottom lip once, twice, then once again.

"Drew, I —"

"Dude, let's go." Todd burst in the room, his car keys jingling from his fingers. "We're supposed to meet Heather in five minutes."

Drew stood up abruptly. "I'm coming." He glanced at Kelly over his shoulder. "I'll talk to you later."

"Yeah," she said.

When the front door slammed shut, Kelly collapsed back on her bed. She hadn't done anything remotely physical, but her breathing was quicker, her heart beating excitedly in her chest.

Had Drew almost admitted liking her?

An hour later, Drew called.

"Hey," she answered.

"This might sound insane, Kels," he began, ignoring a greeting altogether, "but I have to say it. So just listen, okay?"

Kelly's heart was a fervent drum in her chest. "Okay."

Drew took in a breath. "I had a crush on you when we were kids, and I never said anything because I didn't think you felt the same way, you know, because I was a huge dork back then, and then Sydney . . ." He sighed. "I'm in love with you, Kelly. I've been in love with you for as long as I can remember."

It felt like the blood in Kelly's veins froze over, like her heart stopped beating altogether. She didn't even blink.

"Say something, Kel."

She wanted to laugh, to cry, to scream at the top of her lungs. This was right and wrong all at the same time.

"I'm sorry," she said. "I have to go."

She hung up before he could object.

She closed her eyes, tears biting beneath her lids.

This was easily the best and worst thing that had ever happened to her.

THIRTY-ONE

Rule 34: *Do not get depressed and listen to sad love songs if your crush does not notice you!*

Raven's decision to act distant toward Blake was working well. Maybe *too* well.

She grabbed a wet cloth and came out from behind the counter at Scrappe. Blake and Mil-D were there sitting on the two pumpkin-colored chairs near the front window. Blake had said no more than two words to Raven since he came in and it was starting to drive her nuts.

Was he playing games with her now? Served her right. She had, after all, used the Crush Code on him, which really, in its truest form, was a game. Especially when one of the rules specifically said to *act distant but interested*.

Cloth in hand, Raven went over to the round café tables and started washing them, hoping she wasn't too obvious.

Had she done something to piss Blake off? Why was he ignoring her?

With every table she washed, she got closer to the front windows and closer to Blake. He had his cell open, texting someone.

"Andrea wants us to come out to Vegas," he told Mil-D. "She's having her birthday party at PURE."

"Dude," Mil-D shook his head, "that ain't our scene. I don't know."

Yes, good thought, Mil-D. Keep Blake away from those scary Hollywood starlets who hop cities just to celebrate their birthdays.

Was that the kind of girl Blake liked? Because if that was the case, he was way out of Raven's league. She couldn't compete with Hollywood girls with their pearly white veneers and bleached blond hair and stick-thin figures.

Not that she needed to compete with them anyway. She didn't like Blake like that.

Blake flipped his phone closed and took a sip from his frappé. "Who cares where it's at? Andrea always throws the best parties."

Mil-D shrugged. "All right. Whatever you want."

When Blake looked over at her, Raven suddenly realized she'd stopped washing the tables and was now staring at him. She went ill with embarrassment and disappeared in the back room before she did something really stupid.

At home later that night, Raven put on one of the quieter, more angsty songs by the alternative band, Gray Door.

She was in no mood for peppy, upbeat songs. Most of all Kay-J's songs were poppy tracks, no matter how badly Horace wanted her to learn the lyrics.

"But you've thought about the contest, right?" he asked, twirling in half circles in her computer chair.

"Yes, I've thought about it." She flopped back on the bed and spread out. She knew she was being dramatic, but she didn't care.

Horace stopped twirling. "Have you talked to your mom yet?"

Raven rolled her eyes. "Yeah, right. She'd never let me go."

"So what are you going to do?"

"I don't know. I probably shouldn't even go."

"No. You need to go."

She sat up. "Why? Why do you want me to do this so badly?"

He sighed, scrubbing his face with his hands. "I've already told you."

"Yeah and you've never been one to think the band was pointless or a dead end. I mean, seriously. What is going on?"

He shook his head. "It's nothing, okay?" He got up and came over to kiss her. "I just want to see you succeed. Is that so bad?"

"Well . . . no." She grabbed her throw pillow and picked at the fuzz sticking to the fleece material. "I guess I can probably get to the city without my mom finding out."

Horace thought about it before answering. "I hate to see you lie to your mom, but once you win that contest, she can't really say much about it. And you'll only be there one day."

She nodded. "Now I just need to figure out how I'm getting there without her noticing I'm gone."

Horace kissed her forehead. "We'll figure it out, okay?"

"Okay."

"I gotta go. But I'll see you tomorrow. Think about practicing those Kay-J tracks."

"I will."

He waved to her before leaving, and she begrudgingly turned on her iPod to the first Kay-J track.

August

THIRTY-TWO ～❀

Rule 29: *Do not write your crush an anonymous Email or letter, because he might think someone else sent it!*

"Just tell him already," Adam said, holding up his padded hands for Kelly to punch.

Kelly unleashed a right hook and then a double left. Kickboxing was good for venting frustration.

"Just call him up and say, 'Hey, Drew, I'm in love with you, too.' It's really not that hard."

Kelly pushed forward with a wild right hook. "Yes, it is hard because he's going out with my best friend!" She landed another right and then bent over, resting her gloves on her knees. Her breath came fast, sweat rolling down her temples.

Why? Why? Why?

Why her? Why Drew? It was like the Fates had conspired against her. Or maybe it was her own idiotic fault for not telling Drew how she really felt three years ago before he started going out with Sydney.

If she had, maybe it would be her with Drew right now, not Sydney. Maybe they'd be planning their senior years together, trying to decide which college to go to together.

"You all right?" Adam asked, ripping apart the Velcro on his pads. He tossed them to the side. They thudded against the wall, the sound echoing through the room.

Kelly straightened and wiped the sweat from her forehead with the back of her arm. "You really think I should tell him how I feel?"

Adam nodded. "He deserves that much. He came out and told you what he was feeling and you practically hung up on the poor guy."

Kelly winced. She had done that, hadn't she? That was seven days ago now. Drew hadn't called her since. He also hadn't made one single appearance at the house. Todd even commented on how Drew had flaked on him Tuesday night. Apparently, a new video game had come out, and they were supposed to check it out together.

Drew must hate her. He must think of her as a huge jerk.

"I should call him," she mused, holding out her hands so Adam could remove the boxing gloves.

"You should talk to him in person, though."

Kelly paled, picturing it in her head. How was she supposed to tell Drew she loved him straight to his face without stuttering or passing out or something else equally embarrassing?

Adam was right about one thing, she needed to be honest with Drew because he'd been honest with her.

Unfortunately, so much time had passed since his phone call that Kelly worried he wouldn't want to see her now.

She had to get him to her without him *knowing* it was her.

An hour later at home, she plopped down at her desk and the Crush Code caught her eye. She flipped through the printed pages. Anonymous Email, she thought. That was blatantly breaking one of the rules, but it was all she had. Plus, the whole point of sending an anonymous Email was so Drew *would* think she was someone else. She was afraid a meeting with her would scare him away if he knew ahead of time.

She logged into an email account she'd set up forever ago so she could surf a fashion message board. Her name wouldn't come up on the email anywhere because she'd set it up using the name Trisha Keller.

Drew, she typed, *meet me at Eagle Park at the fountain at ten. We need to talk.*

She clicked the SEND button before she changed her mind.

♥ ♥ ♥

Drew's computer dinged with a new email message alert. Sydney set her book aside on his bed and got up. She poked her head down the hall and heard the rushing of the showerhead coming from the bathroom.

She opened the email program and checked the new message.

Trisha Keller? Who was that?

Drew, meet me at Eagle Park at the fountain at ten. We need to talk.

There was no name, no nothing. But whoever Trisha was, she obviously knew Birch Falls if she knew Eagle Park. Was this a secret meeting? Was Drew seeing someone else behind Sydney's back? Her stomach knotted into a mixture of emotions: anger, betrayal, curiosity. Curiosity because Drew wasn't an outgoing person. How would he meet a girl, someone who didn't even go to their school?

It just didn't make sense.

Sydney deleted the Email, shut the program down, and went back to her book. She was going to find out what was going on.

♥   ♥   ♥

"I'm going to the store," Sydney called through the house. "Anyone need anything?"

Drew and his mom were at the kitchen table playing an intense game of chess. Sydney had hung out at the house all day because her house was too quiet and gloomy.

"No," Drew said, barely looking up from the chessboard.

"I'm fine," his mom said, her game face on. A headband held back her long, black bangs. She'd tied the rest of her hair into a loose knot.

When those two got into a game, the rest of the world was a haze they paid little attention to. And they'd probably be playing for another hour. It was plenty of time for Sydney to sneak off to the park, find out who'd

Emailed Drew, and get back home before he realized she was gone.

Plus, Drew had been downright irritable lately. The game of chess would do him some good.

Sydney's watch said it was just after nine forty-five. The sky was pale with the impending darkness. Sydney turned on the headlights once she got inside her SUV.

A men's baseball game was playing over on the first ball diamond at Eagle Park. Cars lined the front parking lot. Sydney found an open spot farther down and got out. She hurried over to the fountain with fifteen minutes to spare.

It was darker over here without the lights from the baseball game. Sydney found a good hiding spot behind a large chestnut tree.

The wait seemed to spread out into an hour. Her heart beat at the back of her throat, her knees felt weak.

What if Drew really was cheating on her? Maybe that's why he'd been in such a bad mood lately. He didn't love Sydney, he wanted someone else, and he didn't know how to break up with her a second time.

A darkened figure cut through the trees. The gurgling of the fountain quieted the footsteps. Sydney held her breath.

The person walked into a sliver of moonlight slicing through the thick canopy of trees.

It was Kelly.

Sydney took in a breath, clenched her jaw, and stalked out from her hiding spot.

"Why were you meeting Drew?" she said.

Kelly's eyes grew wide, her mouth dropped open. "I . . . uh . . ."

"And why did you send an Email as Trisha something-or-other?"

Kelly raked her teeth over her bottom lip. "It's . . . well . . . Drew and I were meeting because we're worried about you."

"Me?"

"Yeah, I mean . . ." Kelly shifted her gaze to the mossy forest floor. "You've been distant lately. He's noticed it and I noticed it and we were trying to come up with a way to cheer you up."

Hands on her hips, Sydney steeled her spine. "What, were you planning an intervention?"

"No! No way. We're just worried is all. You know, with your mom . . ."

The tension in Sydney's shoulders slipped away. She wasn't sure if she should be angry or relieved. Drew wasn't cheating on her with some girl named Trisha. He was just worried about her.

She'd wanted to kick him in the groin when she found out he was supposed to meet a girl in the park. And why had she automatically assumed he was cheating on her? Maybe because she didn't trust people in general anymore. She blamed that on her mother.

How could you have faith in other people when your own parent promised to be there for you and instead took off for another country?

Sydney leaned over and set her elbows on her knees, put her face in her hands.

Kelly hesitantly sat next to her and crossed one leg over the other. "Are you okay?"

Sydney sighed and shook her head. She was just so tired — tired of her life spiraling down the drain. Why couldn't things work out for her? Why couldn't her mother come back and bring the family together?

"Do you want to talk about it?" Kelly asked.

"There's nothing to talk about," Sydney answered. "My mother left us, and I don't think she's coming back. There's nothing else to say about it."

The sounds of the baseball crowd cheering filtered through the trees, reaching the girls in the darkness. Sydney straightened, dragging her fingers through the fountain water behind her.

"I'm sure it'll get better," Kelly said, "eventually."

Sydney stood, dried her fingers on her black yoga pants. She didn't want a pep talk, she didn't want anything. "Don't tell Drew about this, please?"

"Of course." Kelly got up, too, and tugged on the hem of her tunic top.

"Thanks." Sydney barely managed a wave as she hurried from the park.

THIRTY-THREE ⬿

Rule 28: *Do not spend more than two months trying to find out if your crush likes you!*

Being grounded sucked.

Alexia flipped through the TV channels for the third time, knowing the search was futile. It was the middle of summer; the only thing on right now was reality TV.

Getting up, she went to her bedroom and grabbed her notebook. The Crush Code had been on her mind the last few days, and she'd wanted to go over the rules again.

Kelly and Adam were hanging out, from what Alexia heard, but they weren't *together*-together, which meant something with the Code wasn't working right.

Alexia had wondered a few weeks ago if perhaps they were missing a few rules. And like any work of creativity, the true work came through revising.

Alexia called her friends and asked them to come over. Thank god, her parents hadn't grounded her from them.

Kelly was the first to arrive. It looked like she'd been hanging out around the house, too. She wore a pair of red terry-cloth shorts with a number nine printed on the thigh and a white halter top. Her arms and legs looked tanner, so maybe she'd been lying out in the sun.

"So what's up?" Kelly asked as she breezed past Alexia, her strawberry-blond ponytail swinging behind her.

"I wanted to talk about the Crush Code."

Both girls headed for the kitchen, and Kelly took a seat at the breakfast nook, folding her arms over the glossy cedar table. She rolled her eyes before digging her cell from her bag.

"We aren't adding more rules, are we?"

Alexia leaned back against the kitchen island. "Well, I thought about it. I really want to help you get Adam."

Kelly clicked through a few things on her phone and then slipped it into her bag. "We're not right for each other."

The front door opened. Alexia looked down the short hall and saw Raven and Sydney. Raven looked stunning as usual. She was in a jean skirt, a black vintage Ferrari T-shirt, and black boots that reached her calves. Her hair flowed around her shoulders in loose waves. Her eyes were hidden behind chunky white sunglasses.

Sydney usually looked pristine, but today she wore a simple white T-shirt and bleached blue jeans. And . . .

Alexia pointed at Sydney's feet. "You're wearing flip-flops?"

"That's what I said." Raven plopped down across the table from Kelly. "Sydney has gone over the deep end."

"Who cares what kind of shoes I wear?" Sydney said, shoving her hands inside her jeans pockets.

"That's just it," Alexia said. "*You* usually care what kind of shoes you wear."

Kelly nodded. "Yeah, I specifically remember you saying you wouldn't wear flip-flops if they were the last pair of shoes on earth."

Sydney took a seat on one of the barstools at the island. "Can we not discuss my footwear please?"

Alexia grabbed her notebook and sat down at the table, leaving Sydney alone at the island. "So," she began, flipping to her handwritten notes, "I was thinking maybe we'd add a few more rules to help Kelly out."

"Oh, and I needed to be here for it?" Raven said. "I mean, it's not like the rules are for me anyway, right?"

Alexia took in a breath. Apparently Raven was still mad about the accusations Alexia had made about Blake. Well, that was just fine, Raven would get over it eventually.

Alexia uncapped her pen and without looking over at Raven said, "When we made the Code, you said you were going to follow it so you *didn't* develop a crush. These new rules might benefit you, too."

"I'm really not sure if we need more rules," Kelly said.

Sydney sauntered over from the barstool and plopped down next to Raven. "We can still add the rules, can't we? And then if Kelly decides she doesn't need them, fine."

"What about you?" Alexia asked Sydney. "Are you still using it for your relationship with Drew?"

Sydney shrugged. "I'm taking a Code break right now."

"Oh," Alexia said, wishing Sydney would explain more.

"All right." Kelly sighed. "What are the new rules?"

Alexia read the rules out loud without interruption.

"Rule 39: *Do not be indecisive. Once you make up your mind stick to it.*

"Rule 40: *Do not be needy, clingy, or possessive!*

"Rule 41: *Do not crush on a boy who has a girlfriend!*"

When Alexia glanced up from her notebook, she noticed Kelly looked three shades lighter than she had when she arrived at the house.

"What's wrong, Kel?"

She swallowed, gave a diminutive shake of her head. "Nothing."

Raven fished her cell from her pocket as it went off. She read the text message and said, "I gotta go. Lexy, why don't you Email me the new rules." She paused, seemed to consider what she should say next. "Unless, of course, you think I will use them on someone else."

"What's up with her?" Sydney said when the front door slammed shut.

"I made her mad," Alexia replied.

"How?"

Honestly, Alexia was kind of embarrassed that she'd accused Raven so blatantly of cheating on Horace. It might have been a bit inconsiderate on her part, and she didn't want to admit it to her other friends.

"It was nothing, really," she said and moved on to another subject. "So, how's work at the hospital going?"

"Fine," Sydney said.

"Just fine?" Alexia leaned forward. "Have you met any hot guys?"

Sydney grabbed the saltshaker from the middle of the table and spun it between her fingers. "No. No one."

"I was there the other day with my brother." Alexia sat back against the padded chair. "And there was this one guy with long black hair and glasses. Who's he? He reminded me of Drew. Except with long hair."

Sydney stood up. "Speaking of work, I have to go home and get ready. I have to be in soon. I'll talk to you guys later." She threw an afterthought of a wave over her shoulder before leaving.

Alexia looked at Kelly. She was on her cell again, punching in a text message. She'd been aloof since she got to Alexia's. Kelly used to get that way whenever she had a fight with Will, her ex-boyfriend. Boy troubles always made her quiet.

"So how is it *really* going with Adam?"

Kelly glanced up. "Like I said, I don't think we're meant for each other."

"Yeah, but if you just use the rules —"

"I don't want to use the rules on Adam." She blinked and looked away. "I just . . ."

"What?"

She got up and slung her bag over her shoulder. "I just wish you'd stop trying to fix my love life, Lexy. I mean . . ." She threw up her hands and shook her head. "I just can't right now."

She disappeared from the kitchen, and a few seconds later, shut the front door behind her.

Alexia watched through the kitchen window as Kelly pulled her car out of the driveway.

What was going on with her friends? Suddenly, they felt further apart than they'd ever been, and The Crush Code was supposed to make them feel closer.

Or at least that's what she'd told herself. The Breakup Code had brought them back together; she just automatically assumed The Crush Code would do the same.

Had she been wrong? Had the Code somehow gone awry?

Her whole life felt awry right now, because of losing It and Ben leaving soon. She tried not to think too hard on the latter. He was leaving — going to another state — in just three and a half weeks.

Her chest ached thinking of it. It didn't help that she was grounded and the time she had left to spend with Ben was quickly dwindling.

A tension headache bloomed behind her eyes. She set her head down on the tabletop and tried to breathe in deeply. This was supposed to be The Summer. So far it'd been a summer of hell and how was she supposed to enjoy her upcoming senior year when her boyfriend was leaving?

THIRTY-FOUR ∼

Rule 24: *Become his friend! Talk to him but do not become one of his boys!*

Kelly grabbed two braided leashes from the hook near the back door.

She clipped a leash to Reba and then one to Nimmi, leading both dogs out the back door.

The animal shelter was at the front of a wooded five-acre lot. Trails had been worn away in the forest where the workers at the shelter took dogs on walks.

"Come on, you two," Kelly said.

The sun beat down on Kelly's bare shoulders as she walked across the lawn to the perimeter of the woods. As soon as they entered the dense growth of trees, the temperature instantly cooled.

The dogs, too, seemed happier. Reba surged ahead, but Kelly tugged her back. Nimmi was content to trot along Kelly's right side, keeping with her pace.

They turned a corner in the woods and walked through sun-dappled leaves. A squirrel scampered across branches overhead, the leaves rustling. For the most part, the woods were quiet until Kelly's cell went off in her pocket.

She checked the new text.

Her heart leaped into her throat when she saw the message was from Drew.

Are we still friends?

She shifted her weight. Were they friends? Technically, they were more than friends if they both liked each other, weren't they? You can't be friends with someone you're in love with.

You just can't.

But Drew didn't know how she felt yet. After that whole fiasco with Sydney, Kelly was afraid to admit her feelings to anyone, let alone the one guy who mattered. What if Sydney found out? She'd done something sneaky in order to intercept Kelly's email and then hid in the park until Kelly showed up. What if she, like, bugged Drew's phone or something?

It was ridiculous, but still . . .

And it would just further complicate everything if Kelly told Drew. He wasn't likely to forget her confession and go on his merry way with Sydney.

No, admitting would only make things worse.

I dont know if we can b friends, she texted back, feeling all the blood drain from her cheeks. Losing Drew felt akin to losing her foot. She just couldn't live without him, could she? He'd been a best friend for forever now. Could she really cut him out of her life?

And would he even let her?

I'm sorry I ever said anything, he replied.

Dont be sorry!

I just. I thought you and me. there was something there.

Ur with Sydney, Kelly punched in on her cell while also trying to manage the dogs, *even if there was something. we cant.*

What are you saying, Kel? he sent back. *you either like me or you don't. forget Sydney. forget everyone for one minute and give me a straight answer.*

Kelly stopped again, clenched a hand into a fist. She growled at the silence. Why did this have to be so hard?

Why did she have to like Drew? Like, seriously, what made her like him so much? What was it about him? And why couldn't it have been someone else?

"Anyone else!" she screeched.

The dogs barked.

What was she supposed to say to Drew?

Either she was honest with him and herself and told him the truth. Or she gave him an answer that was better for everyone involved. If she and Drew got together, the effects would ripple through Kelly's entire group of friends.

She felt the first stinging of tears as she typed in the new message. She didn't want to do this, but it was the right thing to do.

I dont think we should talk anymore. and thats the truth.

She hit the SEND button and turned off her phone.

"So what movie do you want to watch?" Sydney held up *10 Things I Hate About You* and *The Perfect Potion.* "Comedy or mystery and intrigue?"

Drew grabbed one of the velveteen throw pillows and propped it between his head and the arm of the couch. "I don't care."

"But there's a huge difference between a comedy and a mystery. What do you feel like watching? Light or serious?"

He looked over at her. "I don't care, Sydney." He enunciated each syllable as if he thought she were slow today or something. He'd been like this since she got off work. He'd barely spoken at all and when he did, he was extremely cold.

"God," she muttered, "you don't have to be such a jerk."

She stood up.

Drew spread out his arms. "And I told you I didn't care which movie we watched!" He stood, too. "I don't even want to watch a movie. So there. I made my decision. Neither."

"What is with you today?" Sydney put her clenched hands on her hips. "Did I do something wrong?"

He sighed. "I just really . . . don't want to watch a movie."

Sydney was really trying to make an effort to make Drew happy. It was her idea to have a movie night tonight, just her and Drew. She wanted to forget about everything else for just one night. Instead, Drew showed up in a bad mood and nothing Sydney did seemed to matter.

She was tired of this . . . tired of everything. Tired of Drew's mood swings. Tired of her mother making promises and breaking them. Tired of her friends judging her on everything from her footwear to how she expressed her feelings.

Tired.

"You know what"— she pointed a finger at Drew, narrowed her eyes —"I changed because of you, Drew. I made an effort to be a different person. The person you wanted me to be. I tried to be the person my mother wanted me to be, and I took all the AP classes and was on the student council. Nothing seems to be good enough! For anyone! I'm in this house all alone every single day! Why do I strive to make so many other people happy when no one is even looking to see what I'm doing?"

She took in a breath.

Drew's shoulders visibly sunk. His expression went soft.

But Sydney wasn't going to give him a chance to apologize. Not now. It was too late.

"I'm done pleasing everyone! Starting now. I think we need to break up."

Drew stilled. It took him a few seconds to blink and shift. "Syd."

She shook her head. "Just go."

He parted his lips as if he were going to object but instead exhaled. He didn't say anything as he scooped up his car keys from the coffee table and left out the back door.

Sydney sunk to the couch. She didn't even feel sad. As a matter of fact, she felt like a huge burden had been lifted off her shoulders.

She picked up her cell from the kitchen counter and dialed a number.

Weeks ago, Quin had invited her out to learn a few photography techniques. At the time, she'd never considered accepting the invitation, but she needed this, she needed something new, something just for her.

"Quin?" she said when he picked up. "If the invitation still stands, I'd like to take you up on that offer to learn some photography techniques."

He didn't even pause before answering. "Sure. When would you like to go?"

"Um . . . now?"

"Well, sure, I guess. I'm not doing anything."

Sydney gave him directions to her house, and they said good-bye. As she hung up, Sydney couldn't help but smile to herself. She felt better already.

THIRTY-FIVE

Rule 15: *Have an outside interest that you can talk to him about!*

Rule 40: *Do not be needy, clingy, or possessive!*

Sydney was sitting on the front porch when Quin pulled up along the curb. She'd expected a four-door sedan, probably silver or white, something plain, nondescript.

She'd never really thought of a car as a reflection of the driver, but this car, it looked like it should belong in the pages of a history book, and Sydney realized that that car was *Quin*.

It was like a piece of art with four wheels.

With her bag slung over a shoulder, Sydney headed down the front walk to the curb just as Quin got out. He was in a plain white T-shirt, his hair tied back, partially hidden beneath a gray fedora.

"What kind of a car is that?" she asked.

"It's a 1962 Chevy Impala." He leaned against the car, crossing his arms over the roof. "It was my grandfather's and then my dad's and now mine."

There was not a single spot of rust on the gleaming black body. The chrome rims reflected the green grass of Sydney's front lawn.

"It's so . . . cool," she said, frowning at her own fascination with a vehicle.

Quin came around to the passenger side. "I like it"— he held the door open for her —"because no one else in town has one."

Sydney slid inside on the bright-red leather bench seat and looked at the interior of the car. There was no trash on the floorboards, no open ashtray stuffed with safety pins and nail clippers. As Quin went around to the driver's side, Sydney glanced in the backseat. There was a camera bag, a tripod, and a worn copy of *Alice in Wonderland*.

Quin got in behind the wheel and started the car. A local radio station played soft jazz music across the speakers. He put the car in drive and took off.

Sydney couldn't help but watch him, her eyes roaming over the tattoos. If she saw him every day for the next six months, she was pretty sure she'd discover something new in his tattoos every single one of those days.

"So where are we going?" she asked.

"Surprise."

"Really? So you're not even going to give me a hint?"

"Nope."

It'd been a long time since she'd embarked on an adventure. With Drew, it was all about plans. Sydney had missed spontaneity.

Sydney fell quiet, letting the jazz music fill the space between them. It was a good fifteen minutes before either of them spoke.

"You look good today," Quin said.

Sydney glanced down at her black yoga pants and plain white T-shirt. She considered them pajamas more than public attire, but Quin had said to dress comfortably. This seemed like the perfect outfit.

Instead of washing her hair and then blow-drying it pin straight, she'd pulled it back in a haphazard ponytail, then pushed her bangs away from her face with a stretchy white headband.

"Umm . . . I do?"

Quin nodded. "Beauty is more than explicit glamour or perfection."

A smile curved her lips. "As an aspiring photographer, I should probably know that, huh?"

"Yup. I wasn't sure what kind of a camera you had, so I brought an extra one in case you wanted to try something new."

"I just have a simple digital camera my mom bought at Wal-Mart. It's, like, a six megapixel."

"Then you'll love the camera I brought you. You'll have fun with it."

They reached the next town, Wesarck, in thirty minutes because they took the scenic route. Wesarck was half the size of Birch Falls, with one main street you could travel just one way down. Each intersection on the main strip was done in red and white cobblestones. There was a large clock, where the road curved, that rang the hour as they passed. It was already six in the evening.

Quin turned left off the one-way street and the road curved around an overgrown railroad track. A field spread out from there, the grass taller than Sydney's knees. Farther, in the distance, the leaves of an English elm tree seemed to glitter as they shuddered in the breeze.

Just a few minutes later, Quin pulled up in front of a large redbrick building with a tower in the center and a curving balcony on the second floor held up by four gray Ionic columns.

"This is beautiful," Sydney breathed as she walked up the four steps to the front entrance. On closer inspection, she noticed paint peeling from the columns, concrete crumbling from the steps, crunching beneath her tennis shoes.

"I think so, too," Quin said, coming up behind her. "It's the Ramsey Theater House."

"Is it abandoned? I mean, it doesn't look abandoned. Will we . . ."

"Get in trouble?" He quirked an eyebrow. "Not if I have the key to get in." He held out his hand, one key ring and key dangling from his index finger. "It's not as exciting as breaking in for the sake of art, but I know the owner and he lets me come in here whenever I want."

Sydney smiled, a bit relieved and disappointed all at the same time.

He unlocked one of the doors — there were two sets — and pushed in. The door creaked on old hinges. Cobwebs clung to the doorframe, and Quin swiped them away before Sydney went in.

More crumbled concrete covered the floor. It might have once been marble or maybe something else equally exquisite, but it was hard to see. They'd come in on the lobby, which was wide open but not quite as tall as the building was outside.

Stairs curved up to Sydney's left. The railing hung from just a few screws. Hand-carved crown molding was covered in dust and dirt.

"The really amazing part," Quin said, "is the theater itself. Come on."

He led her around the stairway and to several sets of doors. Some were closed, some wide open. Beyond the doorways, Sydney could see one enormous room, sunlight spilling in through a hole in the ceiling.

She went ahead of Quin and the breath faltered in her throat.

It was like she stood at the top of a mountain looking down on a town crumbling and forgotten. There were several chairs missing from the rows of the audience section. Foam spilled from tears in the cushions. The gold wallpaper peeled back from the wall, exposing holes in the plaster beneath.

But, miraculously, the deep crimson stage curtain was still intact, still hanging from its hooks. And jutting out from the east and west walls were eight private balconies.

"Quin," Sydney said, "this is more than amazing. It's —"

"I know."

And that was all he had to say because Sydney knew that he understood exactly what she couldn't put into words.

That's why they had cameras, why they were photographers — because sometimes even words couldn't do a scene justice.

♥   ♥   ♥

They spent two hours taking pictures. The camera Quin had given Sydney — an Olympus E-510 — with a memory card inserted, had two hundred and fourteen pictures. Quin's had even more. He was undoubtedly better at seeing the perfect shot and Sydney couldn't help but watch him as he worked.

She could learn a lot from him.

As Quin went to the car for something, Sydney sat on the stage looking out. The decay of the building was sad, but it was beautiful all the same. She suspected she could search for another place like this for fifty years and never find one quite as amazing.

When Quin came back, he had several shopping bags in his hands and a blanket folded beneath his arm.

"I thought we'd have a picnic," he said, swiping away dust and debris with his foot. He spread the blanket out on the stage and Sydney sat on it despite the fact that her butt was already filthy from sitting and wandering in the building.

Quin had packed a mix of veggies and bottles of water. There were also whole-wheat turkey wraps with cream cheese, lettuce, and sliced tomatoes. Sydney grabbed a slice off one wrap and took a bite. "I love these."

"Me, too."

"So," she said before licking cream cheese off her finger, "what made you decide to go to school for photography? I mean, aren't you afraid of graduating but not being able to find a job?"

"The whole starving artist thing?" he clarified.

"Yeah."

"I guess I've never really thought about it, but I love photography so much that I'd rather starve then get stuck in a corporate job I hate." He shrugged. "I'm hopeful that if I'm good enough, I'll get a job eventually. I just have to work hard for it."

Sydney took a drink of water. "I was raised to strive for the best grades. To do the things that would help me score an Ivy League university acceptance. I never questioned any of that. I thought that's what I'd wanted."

"And now?"

She lifted a shoulder, took another bite off her wrap. "I don't know. My mom . . . she'd probably think going to school for photography would be a waste of time."

"And do you respect your mother's opinion?"

She used to, but now that her mother was gone . . .

"No," she said. "Not really."

Quin finished his wrap and wiped his hands on a napkin. He leaned back, propping himself up with one hand. "You really have to do what makes you happy, you know? Not your mother. Your father. Your friends."

"Or my boyfriend," she muttered.

"What?"

"Drew," she said. "My boy — well, my ex-boyfriend now. He was always the same way. He takes all the AP classes. He's into sports. He wants to go to a good school. I think that's why we were such a good couple because we'd rather stay home and study than go out."

"Ex-boyfriend, huh?" Quin pushed a stray lock of hair behind his ear. "Are you okay with that? Did he break it off?"

"No, I did. And yeah." She nodded. "I'm okay with it."

"Some breakups are good things." He sat up. "I was with this one girl in high school, Hillary. This was before I'd gotten my first tattoo. I must've been, like, fifteen. I got my first tattoo when I was sixteen. Anyway, I was that jock, you know, the jerk that everyone liked for no good reason." He picked up a piece of crumbled concrete and rolled it between his fingers. "Then my parents died. And things changed."

Sydney faltered. She'd never asked Quin about his parents, but she'd just assumed they were around like his sister was. "I'm so sorry."

He shrugged and tossed the pebble of concrete into the recess of the stage. It bounced off the wall and skittered across the stage. "As you can imagine, being a jerk, I started rebelling and being an all-around ass and Hillary . . . she just made it worse. I remember when I got my first tattoo she said it was hideous, and I broke up with her right there." He laughed. "Of course, my sister wasn't very happy about the tattoo either, but she wasn't as verbal about it. She was the one that got me into art. Hillary always thought art was for 'losers who have no social life.'"

"Hillary sounds like a real winner."

"Oh, she was."

"I've been going through some stuff with my parents." Sydney halted when she realized what she'd just said. Did she really want to get into how messed up her life was? Probably not. "It's nowhere near as intense as what you went through, I'm sure. . . ."

"Tell me about it," Quin prompted, seeming genuinely interested.

So she told him. Everything from her mother's work-aholic tendencies to her promise to be there more. And then her sudden disappearance and how sometimes the only thing keeping Sydney from not exploding was writing all her frustrations down on paper in her journal.

"I'd say that's intense," Quin said, "in a different vein, maybe, but still intense. Most parents don't just walk out on their children." He paused, then, "I kept a journal with photographs after my parents died. I realized we didn't have very many pictures of them, and then they were gone. I became obsessed with capturing moments."

It occurred to Sydney that she wanted to capture this moment because she felt better right now than she'd felt in a long time. She grabbed the camera, turned it on, and got in close to Quin's shoulder, holding the camera up with her right hand.

"Good idea," he said, clearly having read her mind.

She readied her finger on the button. "Say cheese." She snapped the shot.

THIRTY-SIX

Kelly looked out the kitchen window to the driveway, where the sounds of a bouncing basketball made her heart literally leap into her throat. Todd hardly ever played basketball by himself, which meant . . .

Drew.

Knees bent, arms raised, he tossed a free throw at the hoop. It didn't even hit the rim as it fell through the net.

Kelly wanted to be out there. She wanted to joke around with him. She wanted to tell him that she was crazy in love with him, too.

But she couldn't.

Even if Sydney had broken up with him and he was now a single man.

Kelly closed her eyes and sucked in a weary breath. She liked Drew so much that sometimes it hurt just thinking about him. Longing was definitely an unpleasant emotion.

When she opened her eyes, the boys were gone and the basketball was silent. The back door opened and their voices carried down the hallway from the mudroom to the kitchen.

Kelly went rigid.

Todd was the first one into the kitchen. He gave her a brotherly shove. "What's up?"

She parted her lips to respond but suddenly Drew was there, looking at her, his hair slick and disorderly from sweat. He wore a sleeveless T-shirt, black gym shorts. His biceps looked even more toned close up.

It was like the buttery yellow kitchen walls blurred and there was only her and Drew. She wanted to say so many things to him right now and her heart beat frantically as her mind thought about the hundred different confessions.

I can't, she thought and turned away.

"Hey," Todd said, pulling open the fridge, "did I tell you me and Drew are throwing you a birthday party?"

Kelly glanced over at her brother. "Umm . . . no."

Her birthday — August 23 — was on a Saturday this year. Usually her parents got cake and ice cream and pizza, and she invited her friends over. But Todd had been talking about an end-of-summer bash/birthday party for Kelly for the last three years. Now he was going away to college, so evidently he wanted to throw that party before it was too late.

But maybe even more surprising — Todd had said Drew was helping him throw the party. Was that because he'd volunteered? Or because Todd had roped him into it?

It'd been a week since Drew had texted Kelly and she'd told him they couldn't be friends. He hadn't called her since. He'd shown up at the house Tuesday and then Thursday, but he'd barely looked at her, let alone spoken.

Now he was helping plan her birthday party? Yeah, right. Todd had definitely forced him.

Todd threw Drew a cold bottle of water and then turned back to Kelly. "The party will be awesome. I promise. We'll make it great, huh, Drew?"

"Yeah," was all he said.

"We're out." Todd waved at Drew to follow him out of the kitchen.

Drew didn't hesitate. He surged forward, passing Kelly. She watched him go and couldn't help but notice his scent lingering just behind him as he left.

The smell was that familiar Drew smell — no cologne, no laundry detergent, just Drew. It was like clean water and home-baked food. Or something. She just knew it by smelling it, describing it wasn't quite so easy.

She wished she could curl into him and stay there for hours, his arms wrapped around her. She hadn't had a guy hold her since Will. That was like seven months ago now. She was practically a nun.

Of course, if she really wanted a guy, she could probably go out and find one. She could probably talk Adam into holding her at the very least. But she knew, deep down, it wouldn't be the same. Not if it wasn't Drew.

Later that night, as her parents watched the evening news, Alexia said she was going out for a walk but called Ben before she left and told him to meet her at the park.

This was officially the sneakiest thing she'd ever done.

It took her a good twenty minutes to walk to the park from her house. Seeing Ben there, she wanted to burst into tears and scream with giddiness all at the same time.

It seemed like it'd been forever since she had seen him last.

She ran across the parking lot and over to the bench he sat on beneath a huge oak. He got up, held his arms out, and she jumped into him.

"Umph," he said, tightening his hold on her. "I missed you, too." He kissed both her cheeks and then her lips. It started out as a peck and then grew into something more heated.

Soon Alexia was tingling all over.

Ben was the one to pull away. His lids were heavy with contentedness. He dropped down to the bench and pulled Alexia down with him.

"So, Houdini, what's with the Great Escape? Your parents know where you're at?"

She giggled. It felt good to laugh.

"I told them I was going out for a walk," she explained.

"Impressive." Ben propped a foot up on the bench and rested his arm on his knee. "So how've you been? Your parents letting you out enough? Getting you some sunlight? I hope they're feeding you."

Alexia playfully shoved him. "Yes, they're feeding me. And I'm fine."

"Really?"

She licked her lips, tried to squash the weak feeling in her chest.

"Okay," she said. "I'm not fine, exactly."

Truth was, she was miserable. She couldn't understand why Ben had chosen Pepperdine out of all the colleges that had accepted him. Did he want to get rid of her? Maybe this was his easy way out?

"Come here," he said softly, pulling her on his lap. She nestled into the crook of his neck, liking his arms wrapped around her tightly.

"It'll be okay," he said. "I promise."

He'd read into her emotions without her saying a word. That's how close they'd become. Did it have to end already? Because it would probably end no matter what Ben said.

Long-distance relationships just didn't work.

THIRTY-SEVEN

Rule 27: *Do not keep crushing on a guy if it turns into an obsession! His loss if he can't see the jewel that you are!*

Rule 41: *Do not crush on a boy who has a girlfriend!*

Raven's shift at Scrappe started in thirty minutes. It would only take her five to drive from home to the shop, but as soon as she saw Blake outside on Mr. Kailing's porch with Mil-D, she put on her shoes, grabbed her bag, and headed out.

She made sure to slam the door loudly so Blake would hear. And then she descended the stairs slowly and practically went at a snail's pace down the driveway to the curb where her car was parked.

When she reached the car, she even made a show of dropping her keys, hoping to stall. She sighed dramatically and scooped down to pick them up. She straightened, shooting a glance across the street.

Mil-D waved to her. The magazine in Blake's hands fell just an inch and his eyes flicked across the street for one brief second.

He didn't wave, however. He didn't even smile.

Raven sighed and got in her car.

What was his deal? Had she gone too far with the cold shoulder? Whose stupid idea was it anyway to use that rule?

Uhh, yours, she thought. It was your stupid idea to use the rule when really you shouldn't have been using the Code at all.

She started up the car and pulled away from the house, checking across the street just once more.

And this time . . . she was almost certain she caught Blake watching her.

♥   ♥   ♥

Rain pelted the front windows of the coffee shop. Thunder rolled off to the west just seconds after a flash of lightning streaked across the darkened sky. It was only six o'clock, but looking outside, Raven could have easily mistaken it for ten.

Because of the weather, the coffee shop was buzzing with activity. Most of the tables and comfy chairs were taken. Conversation mixed with the soft jazz music playing on the stereo. Raven brewed a few shots of espresso while Horace threw ingredients for a frappé in the blender. He turned it on, and the ice crunched loudly.

When he turned it off, Raven realized the latest Kay-J hit was playing on the radio. Horace shot Raven a look.

She tried to ignore him as she stirred the freshly made latte. She handed it to the waiting customer and took the next order. As she poured two shots of French vanilla syrup into the cappuccino, Horace came over and nudged her.

"What?" she said.

"You're singing along." He smiled and shook the reddish-blond hair from his eyes. "You sound good. You've been practicing."

She blushed. "Yeah, well, it's not nearly as much fun as singing for the band."

The band hadn't played in almost three months now. First Horace was gone visiting his father in Detroit, then in July, Hobbs's family went on vacation out west, and now Dean was grounded for getting caught drinking.

It'd been so long since Raven played with October that she was beginning to think it had all been a dream.

"The band will play again soon," Horace said, keeping his voice low so only she could hear. Her mother wasn't at the shop, but it was habit to keep band talk low-key.

"Yeah, but what if I win the contest, then what? Not that I even think I have a chance. . . ."

"I think you do and if you did win and you went away for two months or whatever, the band would still be here when you got back." He popped a cinnamon candy in his mouth and grinned at her. If they were alone and not in the middle of a coffee shop with fifty billion eyes on them, Horace would have kissed her just then. He had that look in his eyes. Raven's stomach fluttered thinking about it.

They went back to making their coffees, the conversation on hold for now.

As the rain relented and the thunder dissipated, the coffee shop crowd thinned out. Raven finally had a chance to sweep and clean up. She was emptying out the garbage cans when the front door opened and Blake walked in.

With A Girl.

Raven faltered and Blake caught her.

He didn't smile or grin wickedly. Or any of that male chauvinistic stuff.

Instead, his eyes swept swiftly over her as if he didn't see her at all.

The girl looked at Raven, too, but her eye contact lasted a bit longer. She was extremely pretty in a sweet girl kind of way. She had long blonde hair with honey blond highlights and chestnut lowlights.

She wore a cute pair of khaki shorts and a white T-shirt with a pink silhouette of a hummingbird just above her chest.

When Blake set his hand at the small of her back, her face instantly glowed and the smile that echoed would have put any dental commercial to shame.

Blake said something to her and she laughed. It was light and airy, musical.

Even Raven was charmed.

Horace took their orders, and they sat at the table off in the corner.

Privacy, Raven thought. Blake wanted privacy.

Raven scooped up the garbage bags, and embarrassment colored her cheeks. She felt like the world's lowliest time-clock slave. The bags were suddenly cumbersome in her hands, banging against her legs. She wrestled them to the back room and then the Dumpster outside.

The cool air left over from the storm felt good on her hot cheeks.

Was Blake trying to make her jealous? Because he was doing a good job of it.

Or maybe Raven had read the signals wrong. Maybe Blake had never liked her in the first place. Maybe he'd always intended to keep their relationship on a strictly friends basis.

And why did she care anyway? She was freaking out and they weren't even boyfriend and girlfriend!

It was like she was an obsessed fan or something.

Back inside, wanting to keep herself busy, she grabbed a lint roller and went around to the upholstered furniture. When Horace was finished waiting on his last customer, he came over.

"Have you thought about New York yet?" he asked.

Raven peeled a sticky layer off the roller and ran it over the cushion of the pumpkin-colored chairs in front. "No. I mean, I could drive myself if I really —"

"No," he said quickly. "You're not going to the city by yourself."

She warmed at Horace's obvious protectiveness. She didn't deserve someone so good to her.

"Could Sydney or Alexia or Kelly go with you?" he asked.

"Syd could probably get away without her dad noticing, but she's working at the hospital a lot."

Horace plopped down on the couch as Raven moved onto the next chair. "I wish I could take you, but that'd be too noticeable if I asked for time off around the same time you did."

"Yeah."

"Maybe . . ."

Horace looked up. Raven turned around.

Blake stood just behind her.

"You need to get to New York?" He pushed up the brim of his hat so that Raven could see his eyes better.

"Yeah." Horace got up. "There's a contest there that Ray wants to enter."

"Well, I don't want to enter. . . ."

Blake cut her off. "I can take her."

"Yeah?" Horace raised a brow.

"Yeah. I was supposed to be in New York on the four-teenth, but I can switch the schedule if I want."

"The auditions are the fifteenth," Horace replied.

Raven set the lint roller down. "Look, I really don't need a ride —"

"Cool," Blake said. "I'll just reschedule, and we can go together."

"This is great, Ray," Horace said, finally letting her in on the conversation.

"We'll leave early the fifteenth, then," Blake added.

His girl friend (not officially *girlfriend* until Blake said so!) came up behind him.

"Ready?" he said to her. She nodded, a lock of hair fall-ing in front of her eyes. She was so shy it was almost cute.

"I'll call you later, Rave," Blake said. He held out his hand to Horace. "Later, man."

"Yeah." Horace shook. "Thanks, by the way. This means a lot to us."

"No problem." He waved and led his girl friend out the door.

"This is great," Horace said, leaning over quickly to peck Raven's cheek. "Everything is working out."

Raven watched Blake out the front windows of the coffee shop. He held the passenger-side door of his SUV open as his friend climbed in.

This was great? Hardly great at all. Raven was going to spend several hours in the car with Blake driving to New York. That was great for all the wrong reasons.

THIRTY-EIGHT ∽

After a hard day at the animal shelter, Kelly came home, took a shower, and plopped down on the couch. Her mother was in the kitchen baking cookies for some charity event she was going to. Her dad and little sister were in the den playing a heated game of Uno.

Kelly flipped on the TV and clicked through the channels. MTV played reruns of yet another season of *Real World*. Snooze. VH1 played some stupid "celebrity" show. Bravo had on their popular cooking competition, but it was an episode Kelly had already seen.

Since there was nothing else on, she left it on Bravo and slumped against the cushions. It was hard to focus, though, when she could hear her brother and Drew down the hall in Todd's bedroom.

Kelly tried to tune out the boys, focusing on the TV instead, when she noticed new picture albums lined up on the entertainment center shelf. Her mom had been talking about buying matching albums all summer.

Evidently, she'd stopped talking about it and actually did it.

Kelly grabbed two off the shelf — there were a total of five — and propped her feet up on the coffee table. She opened the first one and was greeted by a family photo from Christmas several years ago. Kelly looked about eleven or twelve. The pictures went on for a few pages and then pictures of spring and summer popped up.

She stopped on a picture of Drew and Todd when Drew sauntered out of the hallway. He hesitated there, looking from her to the kitchen, obviously weighing the safer option. Hang out with Kelly's mom in the kitchen? Or risk sitting with Kelly?

She wanted to tell him to sit, but they were still on shaky terms. After all, Kelly had told him they couldn't be friends. She'd been bluffing, of course, and Drew probably knew that, but the situation was still awkward.

This whole thing was an elaborate dance Kelly knew none of the steps to.

"Hey," she finally said, trying to smooth out some of the discomfort.

"Hey." He sat down beside her, glancing over her shoulder at the photo album on her lap. He laughed when he saw the picture of him and Todd. "I remember that. That was the day we played a huge prank on Kenny."

"The one where we all waited around the corner of his house and then pelted him with flour bombs?"

"His face . . ." Drew shook his head and chuckled. "The look on his face was awesome."

"Yeah." Kelly turned the page and the entire spread was of the neighborhood kids covered in flour and dirt. Kenny got it the worst. Flour turned his black hair white; it stuck to his eyelashes.

"That was my idea, you know," Kelly said.

Drew snorted. "It was my idea."

"No, I just let you think it was your idea."

He hung his head back. "You always were manipulative back then."

Kelly dropped her jaw. "I was not!"

"Then how do you explain talking me into marrying you when we were eleven? I didn't feel I had much choice, you were so pushy."

Rolling her eyes, Kelly tried to remember the year they were eleven. Had she pretended they were married?

She vaguely remembered something about it.

"Well," she began, "maybe I did talk you into an early marriage, but back then, I had the biggest crush on you. And I remember telling my mom that I wanted to marry you when we were older."

Drew grinned. "Really?"

"Yeah." She nervously tugged on a hunk of blond hair. "I mean, it wasn't a crazy obsession or anything. . . ."

"Sure."

He paused then and ran his fingers through his unruly hair. He still hadn't gotten it cut. It now hung in layers over his forehead and along his temples. Kelly thought it fit him well.

"You want to hear a crazy confession?" he said.

Kelly raked her teeth over her lip. No, she thought. This is dangerous territory again.

"Yeah," she said.

"I had a crush on you the moment I first met you." He tapped one of the photos of them, their arms around each other's shoulders. "I still remember that first day we met. You and Todd were playing in the driveway with sidewalk chalk and he kept writing *Kelly smells* over and over again. He spelled *smell* wrong."

They both laughed.

"And then I came over," he continued, "and you were the first one to say hi. I remember thinking your voice was squeaky."

"That's because I was nervous," she replied.

"So was I."

Somehow, the distance between them had lessened and Kelly could feel the heat of Drew's breath on her cheek, could smell his familiar smell.

Excitement, nervousness, and apprehension mixed in her belly. She leaned forward, cleared her mind, and tried to feel the moment.

Drew leaned in, too, and kissed her.

The contact was like an electric shock to Kelly's body. Every nerve seemed to tingle with the after effects.

When she didn't pull away, Drew threaded his fingers through her hair, along the back of her neck. A shiver went up her spine as his tongue slid softly over her lips.

Butterfly wings in her stomach beat to a fervent drum in her chest. And when Drew pulled away, she was actually breathless.

Drew's eyes were heavy-lidded. "Kel," he said.

God, she'd been dreaming of that kiss for years.

"Kel?"

She reined in her focus. "Yeah?"

"You okay?"

"More than okay."

For now anyway. Later she might be a mess when she realized what they'd just done.

But for now she just wanted to enjoy it. Enjoy everything.

"I'm ready," Todd called from his bedroom. "We're going to Bershetti's before poker, right? Cause I'm friggin' starving."

Drew looked from Kelly to the hallway. "Yeah," he answered Todd. To Kelly he said, "You want to come?"

"To Bershetti's?"

Drew nodded.

"Would I be . . . I mean, I don't want to interrupt guys' night out."

"You won't." He took her hand in his and squeezed. "Besides, I want you to come."

"All right."

Drew dropped Kelly's hand when Todd came out of the bedroom.

"Kelly's coming with," Drew said as he scooped up the keys to his truck.

"What? Dude!"

"Dude," Drew said, "I want her to come."

Kelly couldn't help but grin. She was so used to her older brother getting his way. It was nice to see someone else telling him how it was.

They piled in Drew's truck. Kelly sat in the middle, which put her very close to Drew. Their knees touched the entire time. Kelly had to curl her hands into fists so that she didn't grab Drew's hand. She wanted to, but she didn't want Todd to see.

When they reached Bershetti's and Todd got out, Drew quickly leaned over and pecked Kelly on the lips. He smiled.

At the entrance to Bershetti's, Drew held the door open for her and she hurried past. It took a minute for her eyes to adjust to the softer lighting inside the restaurant and when it did, she froze, noticing the person standing in front of her.

Drew froze, too.

It was Sydney.

THIRTY-NINE ∾

Sydney looked from Drew to Todd and then to Kelly. The tension was instantaneous. Even Todd must have felt it. His shoulders tensed as he stood just behind his sister and Drew, his eyes sweeping over Sydney and Quin standing behind her.

Quin, for the most part, was oblivious. He might have felt a change in the energy, but he didn't know why as plainly as everyone else did. He kept close to Sydney, which might have made the whole situation worse.

"Hey, Syd," Kelly said. She smiled at Quin. "I'm Kelly."

He shook her hand. "Quin."

Todd and Drew said nothing and made no move to introduce themselves. Drew had barely looked at Sydney since he entered the restaurant.

Sydney shifted, wondering where the hostess was. Was she lost?

"Hey, guys!" Jordan, Raven's sister, called, hurrying up to the host podium. "I'm sorry about the wait. Are you guys all together?"

"No," they all said in unison.

If the situation weren't so strained, Sydney might have laughed.

"Just two, please," Sydney said, putting her back to Drew and the perpetual scowl on his face.

Maybe she should have felt guilty for being out with Quin, but technically, they were just friends and Drew was hanging out with Kelly, after all.

Well, okay, so Todd was with them, too, but there was something about Drew and Kelly together that got under Sydney's skin. Maybe it was the way they stood closely together, almost touching shoulders. Or the way Drew glanced at Kelly every few seconds as if double-checking her very existence.

"A table for two, then," Jordan said, scooping up two menus. "Right this way."

She sat them in a booth along the back wall, which gave Sydney a good view of the entire restaurant. Drew came in a few seconds later with Todd and Kelly. They were given a table in the middle.

"So," Quin began, "was there something I missed just now?"

"What do you mean?" Sydney wasn't sure she wanted to discuss what had just happened. Did Quin really want to hear her complain about her ex-boyfriend?

"At the front." Quin tipped his head back toward the entrance. "With your friends."

Sydney sighed. She leaned over the table and lowered her voice. "That guy with the dark hair, that's Drew."

Quin arched a brow. "Oh. That explains it."

"And the blonde . . ." she paused, realizing both Kelly and her brother were blond. "The girl, that's Kelly. One of my best friends."

Quin widened his eyes. "And she's with Drew because . . ."

"Well, the blond *guy*, that's Kelly's older brother and Drew's best friend. And Kelly and Drew have been friends for a long time. That's how I met Drew, through her. But now . . ."

She trailed off, glancing inconspicuously across the room. Kelly laughed at something Drew said. Todd shook his head, clearly annoyed about something.

"But now?" Quin prompted.

"I don't know." She pursed her lips. There was something there she was missing. She just didn't know what. Maybe Drew liked Kelly? Or maybe Kelly liked Drew? Or maybe Sydney was just jealous that Kelly and Drew got along so well. They always had. For friends, they rarely fought.

"Did you want to go to another restaurant?" Quin asked. "We could go to Gorsh's. The food there is good."

"No. It's okay. I just . . ."

The ringing of her phone cut her off. It was her dad calling.

"Hello?"

"Sydney. It's Dad."

Like she didn't know that. Then again, when was the last time her father called her cell phone?

"Could you come home?" he said.

"Why?"

"Because your mother is here."

Sydney's mouth dropped open. If she hadn't been clutching the phone so hard, she probably would have dropped that, too.

"Mom?"

Quin straightened, clearly getting the gist of the conversation.

"Yeah," her dad said. "She wants to talk to us."

"All right."

Sydney hung up. "I have to go."

"Your mom?" Quin said. "Is she back?"

"Yeah."

Quin reached over and grabbed her hand. He squeezed. That's all he had to do. He didn't have to say anything.

Sydney smiled, thankful that she had him as a friend.

♥ ♥ ♥

Kelly watched as Sydney left Bershetti's with her friend Quin.

Who was he anyway? A friend? A boyfriend?

Kelly hadn't heard Sydney mention him. Was she keeping things from Kelly? Maybe Sydney didn't trust her anymore, maybe it had something to do with that meeting in the park the night Kelly had conspired to see Drew.

What had she been thinking anyway? This couldn't work.

Drew caught her eye, gave her an encouraging wink. Kelly managed a weak smile.

After they'd eaten, Todd went to the bathroom and Kelly took the opportunity to say everything that had built in her head since Sydney left.

"This is insane!" was the first thing out of her mouth. "She probably hates me now. We can't do this, Drew. I mean, really. We can't!" She flailed her arms in the air. "Why do I have to like you so much?"

He smiled. "You like me 'so much'?"

Kelly cocked her head to the side. "I'm being serious."

"So am I."

"We can't do this, Drew."

He leaned over suddenly, raking his fingers through her hair and kissed her. Right there in the middle of the restaurant. It was enough to leave her breathless.

"We already are doing it, Kel. And nothing you say is going to make me go away."

For some reason, all the dread and doubt melted away. She smiled.

Todd came back from the restroom, making Kelly and Drew separate. But beneath the tablecloth, Drew took Kelly's hand in his, his thumb rubbing circles on her hand. It was that small act of encouragement and the way Drew looked over at her now that made Kelly want to forget that their relationship was possibly going to cost her a friend.

FORTY

Alexia picked up a box of old-fashioned chocolates and stacked it on top of the Tootsie Rolls in the back room at Cherry Creek Specialty Store. Out front, the store was chaotic, but Alexia had been given the task of "organization" so she could thankfully hide back here where it was quiet.

Of course, being alone in a small stockroom gave her a lot of time with her thoughts. Too much time. She couldn't stop dwelling on the fact that Ben was leaving or that she'd lost her virginity to him. Had he planned on going to Pepperdine before they'd done it?

If she'd known then that he was moving to California, she might have done things differently.

"Hey, Alexia."

She shrieked when Jonah came into the room.

"You scared me!"

He laughed. "Sorry. I just came back to see if you needed any help. It's dead out front now."

With a rapidly beating heart, she nodded. "Maybe you could go through the deli containers? I think we could combine several open boxes and get rid of the rest."

"All right." Jonah passed her and opened a box of one-pound containers.

What would Jonah do if his girlfriend was leaving him? She decided to ask him.

"Hey, Jonah?"

"Yeah?"

"Hypothetically speaking . . . what would you do if your girlfriend decided to go to school on the other side of the country? Would you be okay with that? Or would you be mad?"

He stopped doing what he was doing to look over at her.

Maybe the "hypothetical" route had been a bad choice. Too obvious, maybe?

Straightening, he took in a thoughtful breath and said, "Well, I don't think I'd be mad, not if the school she'd chosen was a school she really loved. College is a big thing in everyone's life. It has to be the right school if you're going to spend four or more years there and thousands of dollars."

Alexia nodded. "That makes sense."

He swiped sweat from his forehead. "Is there . . . I mean . . . are you okay? Is your boyfriend moving somewhere far?"

She licked her lips. Bit the corner of her mouth. "Yeah," she said. "I just, I don't know how to deal with it."

"I suspect if your relationship is strong enough, you guys will survive just fine. Talk to him about it."

"Yeah," Alexia said, but there was more to it than that. Alexia had to factor in the whole sex thing, and she couldn't talk to a guy about that. She might have to turn to one of her friends instead.

♥   ♥   ♥

After work and a hot shower, Alexia called Raven. They hadn't talked since Alexia had invited everyone over to add on a few rules. Raven was probably still mad at Alexia. She had every right to be.

Thankfully, Raven wasn't mad enough to avoid Alexia's call altogether.

"Hello?" she said after picking up on the fourth ring.

"Hi." Alexia draped her legs over the arm of her father's reclining chair. She wiggled her toes as she clutched the phone, her fingers slick with sweat. What if Raven hated her?

"I was calling," Alexia began, "to tell you how sorry I am that I butted into your business. I didn't mean to make you mad. Obviously, I did, and I had no right to accuse you of something like cheating on Horace."

Raven was silent for a minute and then, "It's all right." She sighed. "I know why you did what you did, but it still annoyed me that you didn't trust me. I mean, if my best friend didn't trust me, then why did my boyfriend?"

"Well, maybe Horace knows you better than I do."

Raven snorted. "Doubtful. I don't think he knows me well enough and the scary thing . . . ?" She paused again. "I can't stop scoping out other guys. Like, why can't I just focus on Horace?"

"It's okay to check out other guys as long as you don't touch them. You know? Look, but don't touch?"

"Yeah."

"Hey," Alexia hung her head back and looked at the ceiling in the living room, "why don't you come over? We can talk more. I have some stuff going on, too. . . . I . . . I don't know, I just want someone to talk to."

"Sure. I'll be there in a few minutes."

They hung up and Raven pulled in the driveway some twenty minutes later. They went to Alexia's room. Alexia sat at the head of the bed while Raven spread out at the foot, her finger twirling a lock of her luscious hair.

"So how are you and Ben?"

Alexia stiffened. She'd wanted to invite Raven over to confess everything, but now the idea frightened her. What if Raven thought Alexia was crazy or something?

Raven is the least likely person to judge you, Alexia thought.

So Alexia told her everything, from losing her virginity on the Fourth of July to Ben's decision to go to Pepperdine, to Alexia's fears of losing Ben altogether.

"I can't believe you've kept all this bottled up," Raven said when Alexia finished. "Why didn't you call me?"

Alexia shrugged as she picked at the lint on her black cotton shorts. "You were mad at me."

"So."

"So. I . . . I don't know. I guess I should have."

"Yeah." Raven scooted up on the bed and gave Alexia a hug. "It doesn't matter what we're fighting about; you can call me whenever with whatever. Got that?"

"I got it."

"So, wow," Raven said, "this is a lot."

Alexia grunted. "I know. I've been so frustrated over this whole thing."

"Well, I don't blame you."

"What am I going to do?"

"Honestly? I don't know. On the one hand, you can't really ask him to stay here because that would be selfish, but if it's bothering you that much, you can't keep it locked up longer. It'll ruin your relationship."

Raven bit at her nail, brainstorming. Finally she said, "This might sound really bad, and I know it's tough to think about, considering you lost your virginity to the boy, but have you ever thought about breaking it off with him when he leaves? California is a really long way away."

Alexia closed her eyes. She had considered breaking it off, but didn't want to voice it because the idea scared her. She loved Ben, she'd given her virginity to him, she didn't want to lose him, not now.

But how could they work, being so far apart?

FORTY-ONE

Rule 39: *Do not be indecisive. Once you make up your mind, stick to it.*

Going to New York with Blake had seemed like a bad idea when Horace had agreed to it for Raven and it was even worse now that Raven was in the SUV. Especially with Blake and his girlfriend, Lana, in the backseat, Lana giggling with that sweet voice of hers. It turned out, the girl at Scrappe *was* his girlfriend. She was due back in Newport Harbor that evening and was taking a flight out of New York. At least the ride home to Birch Falls would be quiet. Not that Raven disliked Lana, it was just . . . awkward having her here because Raven wasn't exactly sure what was going on between her and Blake. Did Blake like Raven? Was he trying to hook up with other girls while Lana was at home?

Just thinking about it made Raven's head hurt.

Raven pulled out her cell phone and flipped through her contact list. Who could she text to pass the time? Horace was working. Jordan was probably still sleeping.

"What kind of music do you want to listen to?" Mil-D asked.

Raven looked over at him. At least she had Mil-D. At least she wasn't the odd third wheel.

"I don't care," she said. "I like almost everything except for country."

Mil-D chuckled as he flipped through the channels on the Sirius Satellite Radio. He stopped on a channel called Hit List, and Kanye West's latest track blared through the expensive sound system. Mil-D bobbed his head to the beat.

"Oh, I like this song!" Lana said and started singing along.

Raven glanced at her watch. It was just after nine in the morning, which meant they'd been on the road less than half an hour. The sun shone brightly as it rose in a clear, blue sky, but the windows on the SUV were so darkly tinted, Raven didn't even need her sunglasses.

She shifted in her seat, the leather squeaking beneath her.

"Hey, Rave?" Blake said.

She turned to glance back at him. His hat sat crooked on his head. It almost annoyed Raven how cute he looked right now.

Why couldn't her across-the-street neighbor be ugly? It would have saved her a lot of trouble.

"Yeah?" she said.

"You doing okay?"

She furrowed her brow. "I'm fine," she said and straightened in her seat.

Two seconds later, her cell phone chirped with a new text message.

Thank god, she thought. Someone to talk to.

She hit the OK button and checked the name. It was from Blake. She shot him a scowl over her shoulder. He couldn't just talk to her face-to-face?

She read the message.

What's up with u? uve been so chill lately.

Sometimes it was hard to translate Blake's language. Did he mean chill as in "laid back" or chill as in "cold"?

Maybe she'd better ask.

Cold, he typed back.

Lana sat forward and poked her head between the front seats, her French manicured nails scratching against the leather as she said, "I love this song, too! Who is this?"

Raven tuned into the new track. "This is Nickelback."

"Oh yeah. I like them."

Raven smiled. "Yeah. Me, too."

Lana sat back in her seat just as Raven's cell went off again.

Ur not going 2 answer?

I haven't been cold, she typed back, then quickly shut off her text alerts so the phone wouldn't constantly go off.

Liar, Blake said.

She scowled at him. He grinned back.

I'm not lying, she said.

Yes u r.

She chewed on her lip as she tried to decide on her response. Tell him to shove it? Tell him he was delusional? Or tell him the truth?

And what was the truth, exactly?

She liked him. Or at least had a tiny crush on him and she'd been cold because the crush scared her.

There, she'd admitted it. She liked Blake.

The hair on the nape of her neck stood up. She rubbed at it, trying to force the chill from her skin.

It didn't work.

All right, she typed, *truth is, i sorta like u. i mean, not like that . . . i luv Horace and i wont ever hurt him . . . but i'm still attracted 2 u and that scares the hell outta me.*

He got the message, read it, and smiled to himself as he responded.

While Raven waited, her stomach twisted into knots. The sixty or so seconds it took him to reply seemed more like a thousand. What if he wasn't attracted to her? What if he thought she was an idiot?

The screen on Raven's phone lit up when she got a new message. She took a deep breath and opened it.

U like me?

That was his reply? She furrowed her brow and punched in a new message.

Yes u idiot!

He laughed to himself.

"Who are you talking to?" Lana asked.

He looked up, shot her a smile. "Cedric. He met a new girl last night."

Raven widened her eyes at him. Thankfully, Lana couldn't see Raven because she was hiding behind the passenger seat.

He was blatantly lying to his girlfriend! Raven felt ill with guilt.

"Tell Cedric I said hi," Lana said.

"I will."

Lana reached between the seats and switched the station again.

"Hey now!" Mil-D said. "I was listening to that."

"Yeah, but I don't like that song."

Mil-D sighed and shook his head.

U lied 2 her, Raven texted.

It was a white lie.

No, a BIG lie.

Listen, he texted, *thing is, i like u 2 and i know exactly what ur going thru. trust me. i'm on the road all the time. screaming girls, die-hard fans. its crazy and its easy 2 get swept up in the excitement. but i luv lana and i try very hard 2 b good 2 her.*

Raven looked back at him now. The smile, the sarcasm, was gone, leaving his expression incredibly serious.

R u good 2 her? she asked.

Ive been for the 6 months we've been 2gether.

Raven shut her phone off.

She hadn't mistaken the attraction she'd felt between her and Blake, but she'd definitely misread his intentions. She was a friend he kept at arm's length to keep himself safe from destroying his relationship.

He did seem to understand exactly what Raven was going through. That, and the way Alexia had put it — that it was okay to be attracted to someone else as long as you were faithful — made Raven feel a lot better.

Blake was right; you had to work hard to have a good relationship. That kind of thing didn't come easy. It *shouldn't* be easy. But was Raven working hard enough?

FORTY-TWO ~

Rule 33: *Do not stalk or stare at your crush!*

They arrived in New York sometime around one P.M.
Auditions didn't start until five, but Raven wanted to find a
good spot in the line.

First, they had to drop Lana at JFK Airport. What a
mess that was. Raven had never flown before and if the
maze of roadways and traffic and different terminals at JFK
were any indication, Raven could wait several more years
before tackling it. She closed her eyes against the chaos,
pulling out her iPod, slipping the earbuds in her ear. One of
Kay-J's faster, poppier songs played close to Raven's ears,
the bass beats almost drowning out the noise of the airport.
She sang the lyrics over and over in her head, slumping
against the car door for comfort.

"Hey, Rave!" Someone shook her.

Raven startled upright. She'd been sleeping? What time
was it? Did she miss the audition?

The SUV was moving again, having left behind the
busy highways for the more compact city streets. Raven

glanced at the dashboard clock. It was only two P.M. She'd passed out for roughly an hour.

"Sorry," she muttered, clearing the sleep from her throat. "Are we going to the theater now?" She glanced in the backseat at Blake and frowned. "You changed your clothes and . . . where's your hat?"

Raven had noticed he'd been growing his hair out over the summer. She'd seen it sticking out from beneath his baseball hat, but now that he was hatless, she realized just how cute he looked with the tiny curls of hair.

But that wasn't the most shocking.

Instead of his usual jeans and sponsor freebie T-shirt, he wore a pair of dark washed Diesel jeans that fit him nicely and a black button-up shirt with a white tie.

Of course, the tie was loose around his neck and slightly crooked, but it looked good in an I-don't-care kind of way.

"You're staring at me," he said, a grin quirking the corner of his mouth. "Do I have something stuck to my face?" He gave his chin a cursory swipe.

"No." Raven blinked and looked away. "You just . . . you look good."

"It's the ice." He tilted his head so Raven could see the diamond studs in his ears.

She laughed. "Actually, I didn't even notice the diamonds until you mentioned them."

"Sure."

A car horn blared behind the SUV. Mil-D mumbled something about impatient taxi drivers. He turned left at an intersection after the SUV's navigation system prompted him.

"So," Blake began, turning sideways in his seat, "I have a surprise for you."

Raven tensed. She suspected Blake's kind of surprise was not a coffee, or a nice good luck card. Blake's surprise would probably be over the top like his life was and that scared her. This was not the time for surprises.

"Really?" she said cautiously.

"Yeah. I wouldn't have dressed in this monkey suit otherwise."

"You didn't have to."

"I know. But this is pretty special, and I think you'll like it."

"But we're still going to the theater? Right? So I can get in line early?"

He grinned.

"Blake?"

"Well . . . not exactly . . ."

Raven widened her eyes. "Blake! I have to get in line! Otherwise this whole trip has been a waste and Horace will —"

"Chill." He put his hand on her bare forearm. Goose bumps popped on her skin despite his warm touch. "The surprise will be rad. Okay?"

She stared at him again for several longs seconds. Instead of admiration, she was annoyed this time. "If I miss that audition . . ."

"You won't."

"Fine," she grumbled and stuck her iPod earbuds in her ears. She had less than four hours to make sure she knew all of Kay-J's music. And Blake better get her to that audition.

♥   ♥   ♥

Less than twenty-five minutes later, Mil-D pulled up in front of a hotel that said THE CARLYLE in cursive gold lettering on a black awning. A doorman in one of those silly hats stood near a topiary that had been trimmed to look like a poodle's tail.

"What are we doing here?" Raven asked after she'd turned off her iPod. Was Blake trying to get her into his hotel room? Try to score with her or something after he fed her that I'm-a-faithful-boyfriend speech?

"Your surprise is here."

Raven turned on him and gritted her teeth, hoping to get the point across. "I need to get to the concert hall! This is not the concert hall! Blake! I'm going to be last in line."

"Tell her, son," Mil-D said, "before she pops a blood vessel."

Blake sighed. "I wanted it to be a surprise."

"If I miss that audition, it'll be a surprise. A bad one."

Raven could just imagine Horace's disappointment. And then he'd wonder where she'd been if she hadn't gone to the audition and then . . . what would she say? Blake tried taking her into his hotel room because she'd told him that she was attracted to him?

This whole trip was a bad idea!

"All right." Blake pushed the hair off his forehead. "I got you a private audition."

Raven frowned. "You what?"

"An audition. With Kay-J."

"With Kay-J?"

Blake nodded.

"But . . . how . . . I mean . . ."

"I know her," he said, figuring out the question Raven couldn't seem to get past her lips. "We've partied before." He shrugged. "It's no big deal."

Raven raised her brow. "No big deal? Are you serious? I mean, seriously, you're serious?"

He laughed. "Yeah, I'm serious."

The anger slipped away to be replaced by guilt. She shouldn't have jumped to conclusions. Blake had never done anything sleazy — why had she assumed he was trying to hook up with her?

"A private audition?"

"Yeah. Are you ready to go up?"

She gripped her iPod tightly, sweat slicking her fingertips. No, she wasn't ready. She'd run over this moment in her head a thousand times, but that moment had been on stage, with lights blinding her, and Kay-J so far back in the theater that Raven would need a pair of binoculars just to see her face.

Raven hadn't expected a private audition with Kay-J sitting right there!

"I don't know," Raven said.

"Well, it's too late." Blake opened his door. "She's expecting us, and you can't back out now."

He came around to Raven's side and opened her door. "Come on."

"But . . ."

"Come on." He grabbed her hand and dragged her out. "I'll call you when we're done, Mil?"

Mil nodded. "I'm going in search of Krispy Kremes. The navigation system says there's a store ten minutes from here. Ten minutes to heaven." He sighed, then, "Have fun, son."

"Later."

Blake set his hand on the small of Raven's back and guided her over the gold *C* in the pavement in front of The Carlyle. The doorman tipped his hat and said good morning.

"What's up, dude," Blake said before pushing Raven into the revolving door. She went in. Blake took the next open slot and followed.

The lobby of The Carlyle felt like a different world entirely, which made Raven feel extremely out of place. The floors were black, maybe marble, or something else equally expensive. They were polished to the point that Raven could see her reflection when she looked down. It was as if she were walking on water.

There were two orange sofas diagonal from the reception area with big mirrors behind them.

Wherever she looked, Raven could see her reflection. It was unnerving, especially when her eyes looked too puffy from sleep and her lips dry and her eye shadow too dark.

"Good morning, sir," the man behind the desk said. "How can I help you?"

"I'm here to see Kira James."

"One moment." The man picked up a black phone and punched in a number.

"Kira James?" Raven whispered.

"It's her real name."

"You can go up," the man said, setting the phone back

in its cradle. "Go to the tenth floor. Someone will meet you at the elevators."

"Thanks."

"This is all so . . . elegant," Raven muttered as they crossed the lobby to the elevator banks. The floor inside the elevator was black, too, the trim gold.

Blake pushed in the button for floor ten, and the doors dinged shut.

"This place is official," he said. "You don't get much better than this."

"Have you ever stayed here?"

Blake laughed. "Hell, no. I can't afford this place."

The screen above the elevator doors counted the floors. A bell dinged again when they reached the tenth floor and the doors slid open. A man in a black suit and sunny yellow tie greeted Blake and Raven.

"I'm Manuel," he said. "Follow me and I'll take you to Kay-J."

"Awesome. Lead the way, Man." Blake smiled.

Manuel didn't.

The bulky bodyguard headed down the hallway, his hands clasped in front of him. He stopped at a door and slid in the key card. The lock clicked open and he pushed the door in.

Raven's heart thudded a warning in her chest. She was about to make a fool of herself!

Sure, in Birch Falls, people liked her singing, but they had no one to compare her to. Besides, being in a band in a small town had a cool factor attached to it. Maybe part of Raven's appeal was that she sang in a band with guitars and drums that masked her suckiness.

This was such a bad idea.

They entered into a foyer where they were greeted with the sound of a hair dryer and music playing from an iPod docking station.

The bodyguard surged ahead of Raven and Blake and announced their arrival. Kay-J sat in a plush green chair, a magazine open in her hands as a man worked on her hair.

"Hi!" she called, waggling her fingers. "Give me a sec, Don?"

Don, the hairstylist, nodded and disappeared into another room.

Raven tried to focus on Kay-J but there was so much else to admire in the room. The décor was expensive, with an Old World feeling, the furniture plush and lined with throw pillows. Candles flickered on a table behind the sofa.

But it was the view of 76th Street out the picture window that really threw Raven. She went over to it and looked down at the people and the cars. Several taxis drove down the street, their yellow paint the dominant color in traffic. New York was so . . . alive.

"Wow," she breathed.

"It's nice, yeah?"

Raven looked over at Kay-J standing right next to her. Raven had never been a huge fan of Kay-J's. Her music was good and Raven respected her talent, but Raven had always been into rock more than anything.

Even so, she found herself starstruck. It was weird seeing the face that had been plastered all over magazine covers right there in front of her.

"Yeah," Raven muttered. "I've never seen the city so high up."

"It's pretty. Sometimes I forget to look, though." Kay-J flashed that brilliant white smile. "So you're a singer, huh?"

Raven shrugged. "Kinda."

Kay-J was the same age as Raven, but she couldn't help but feel like the younger amateur. It didn't help that Kay-J looked stunning. Her brown hair hung around her shoulders in soft waves. Blond highlights brightened her tanned face.

And she had flawless skin.

Raven was green with envy. Blake was friends with Kay-J? How did he ever stay faithful to Lana when he had a goddess as a friend?

"Come on." Kay-J grabbed Raven's hand and dragged her past Blake where he sat in the corner of the couch. "We'll be back," Kay-J said.

Blake just nodded.

Kay-J took Raven to one of the bedrooms and shut the door. There were suitcases lying on the floor, clothing spilling out of them. Several pairs of jeans had been slung over a chair in the corner along with a skirt and a flowy summer dress.

"Ready?" Kay-J pushed several shirts back on the bed and sat down. "Go whenever you'd like."

Raven just stood there.

Anyone would have killed for this opportunity, and she was freezing up.

"Don't be shy," Kay-J said. "I know how it is singing in front of someone new, but pretend I'm a friend? Your mom? Sister?"

Raven nodded and took in a deep breath. She tried to imagine Horace on her right side, Hobbs on her left, with Dean behind her on the drums. She tried to imagine the drum beats vibrating through the floor of Horace's garage, the bass chords ringing in her chest, and Horace's guitar riffs sending chills up her spine.

She opened her mouth and sang.

♥   ♥   ♥

Raven clasped her hands together and shrieked as the elevator doors closed. "She said I was good!"

"I heard," Blake said. "I heard you singing, too, by the way. That was sick."

"Sick means good?"

He grinned. "Yeah. Beyond good."

She shrieked again, unable to stop herself.

Kay-J had said she liked Raven's unique voice. She said she thought Raven had a good chance in the competition but that there were still two days of auditions to get through. However, Kay-J promised to send Raven notice personally, either by a phone call or a letter.

And to think, a few weeks ago Raven hadn't wanted to come at all. Now that she'd gone through the experience, she couldn't imagine giving the opportunity away.

"I cannot thank you enough," she said to Blake. She bounced over and hugged him, wrapping her arms around his neck. Tiny wisps of his hair tickled her face. He smelled like cinnamon gum and a sweet cologne.

Blake wrapped his arms tentatively around her waist.

"It's no big deal."

"It's a huge deal." She pulled back to kiss his cheek, but he moved his head at the same time and they ended up locking lips.

Raven was surprised at first and she tensed up instantly.

Until Blake's hands slid up her hips and the breath shuddered out of her lungs. He pressed into her more, and she leaned into the corner of the elevator, the kiss having gone from accidental to fierce in two seconds.

Blake ran his tongue along her lips and a chill breezed through her spine.

It was like she'd been waiting for that kiss the entire summer. Every thought disappeared from her mind until Blake pulled away.

"Raven," he said, his voice husky, "we can't."

She knew that, but she didn't want to listen to reason right now. Not with her heart thundering in her chest or the butterflies dancing in her stomach.

The elevator dinged and the doors opened on the first floor. An older couple peered inside at Raven and Blake still pressed into the corner of the elevator.

Blake pushed off the wall and hurried through the lobby, leaving Raven still warring with the pleasure and guilt mixing in her gut.

FORTY-THREE

Rule 7: *Be adventurous and daring! See life as an adventure!*

Rule 26: *Do not feel you have to tell your friends who you are crushing on!*

Drew was taking Kelly on their first official date, but Kelly had insisted they do something privately. What if they went out to a restaurant, just the two of them, and someone saw them?

It would be suicide. Kelly didn't want anyone to know about her and Drew. At least not yet. Eventually it'd come out. And she was so *not* looking forward to that day.

Kelly had left the date plans up to Drew because he was good at plans and final decision-making. Kelly liked to go with the flow. Whatever he wanted was fine with her.

"Who wants to drive?" Kelly asked when he showed up at her house around six.

"We're taking your car," he said. "Todd is borrowing my truck."

Kelly frowned. "For what?"

"Birthday stuff."

"What are you guys getting for my birthday party that needs to be hauled in a truck?"

He grinned. "Tables and stuff, but don't concern yourself with birthday plans. Tonight is you and me and dinner."

"Speaking of which,"— she lowered her voice —"did you tell my brother . . . you know . . ."

"About us? No. He thinks I'm taking you out shopping tonight for streamers." He shrugged. "I already bought a whole bag of pink ones, if that's all right with you."

Kelly couldn't help but smile. Drew knew her so well. "Pink is good."

"Give me two seconds to go talk to Todd and then we'll go." He disappeared down the hallway, and Kelly went into the kitchen, where her mom was doing dishes.

"Going out tonight?" Mrs. Waters asked.

Kelly nodded excitedly. "With Drew."

Her mother turned around. "With Drew?"

"Yeah. But don't tell Todd! Please."

"You have my word." She pushed her long strawberry blond bangs behind her ear. "What happened with Drew and Sydney?"

Kelly's animated expression fell. "Syd broke up with Drew over a week ago."

"But does she know you and Drew . . ."

"No." The guilt came back full force. Kelly bit her lower lip. "At least not yet."

"Well," Mrs. Waters set a hand on her hip, "just be careful. And smart. Okay?"

Kelly nodded just as Drew came into the kitchen. "Ready?" he asked.

"Ready," Kelly said, following him out the door.

♥   ♥   ♥

Drew drove Kelly's car because he knew where they were going and didn't want to tell Kelly until they arrived. About ten minutes after leaving home, Drew pulled into Eagle Park.

"This is perfect," Kelly said, clapping her hands together. "A picnic in the woods?"

"Not quite." He smiled and got out, grabbing the shopping bags from the back seat. He'd picked a few things up earlier, though he hadn't let Kelly look at the goodies.

Drew went to the concession stand near the lake's edge and Kelly went over to the shore while she waited. The lake was placid today. It almost looked like glass, reflecting the surrounding woods in a near perfect upside-down picture.

When Drew came up to Kelly's side, he had a key in his hand.

"What are those for?" she asked.

"We're taking out a canoe."

He went to the row of canoes locked to a railing. He undid the lock on a blue canoe and shoved it into the water. "Get in."

"A canoe? A picnic on the lake?"

"Is that okay?" He took off his glasses and slipped them over the collar of his T-shirt. "We could do something else. . . ."

"No! I love it."

With Drew's help, Kelly climbed into the wobbly canoe and slowly made her way to the front. Drew got in the back end and pushed the canoe into deeper water with the oar.

They glided over the glassy surface. Kelly grabbed her own oar and pushed it through the water.

"Where are we going?" she asked.

"Let's go around the bend." He steered and Kelly kept paddling, switching sides every few minutes. Twenty yards off the shore, her arms felt the burn of rowing. Adam would be proud.

A few swans swam off to the left side of the canoe. A motorized boat trolled the lake in the distance, a few fishing lines extending out from the boat's side into the water.

Drew and Kelly rounded the bend in the lake where the land jutted out like a thumb. Once they were on the other side, Eagle Park disappeared from view and they had total privacy.

"This is so nice," Kelly said, resting her oar on her lap. "I've never been out here on a canoe."

"You haven't?"

She shook her head. "Never even thought about it."

Overhead, smoky clouds blew in, covering the blue sky. A breeze kicked up, disrupting the placid lake and tossing wispy strands of hair around Kelly's face.

Drew paddled until they were about thirty yards away from the lake's edge and still hidden by the mass of land behind them. He set his oar in the back of the canoe and stood up.

Kelly shrieked as the boat rocked. "Drew!" She clutched to the canoe's sides.

He laughed. "It's all right." He sat down on the middle seat right behind Kelly. "See, we're not going overboard."

She set her oar down and turned to face Drew.

"I do not want to go in the water."

"Yeah, but then I could be a hero and rescue you."

Kelly grinned. "Well, when you put it that way . . ."

He set the shopping bags between them. "I brought all your favorites. Something chocolately. Something salty. And something healthy. You know, so you can choose."

"Yeah, because I'm really going to turn down the chocolate for the . . ."— she looked in the bag —"for the grapes."

She pulled out the bag of peanut butter M&M's. "Oh my god, I haven't had these in forever."

Drew twisted open a bottle of water. "Remember when we were little we'd suck all the chocolate off till they were only balls of peanut butter?"

Kelly laughed. "Yes! And then we'd eat several mushy balls of peanut butter at one time."

He nodded, then scooted off the bench of the canoe and sat on the cool fiberglass bottom. "Come here."

She did the same, turning again so that they sat shoulder to shoulder, their backs leaning against the middle bench. Water lapped at the sides of the canoe, pushing it through the lake, farther out from shore.

Drew wove his arm around Kelly, his thumb rubbing circles over her bare shoulder. Goose bumps popped, racing from his fingertips clear down to her forearm.

With his other hand, he touched her cheek, brushed hair from her eyes. "You look so pretty right now."

She grinned. "Thanks."

He kissed her, softly and slowly, using only lips on lips, his fingers on her flesh. And then his tongue grazed hers.

A misty rain fell from the smoky clouds as the breeze shifted again. It wetted Kelly's face, cooling her cheeks where the blood pooled from Drew's touch.

Kelly could have sat there with him on the bottom of the canoe in the middle of the lake for forever, but all good things must come to an end, right?

And their good time ended when Drew's cell rang.

"It's Sydney," he said, after seeing the screen. "Should I answer it?"

Kelly ran her teeth over her lip. "I don't know." She paused, then, "Yes, answer it. But I'm not here."

He flipped the phone open and hit the SEND button. "Hello?"

He eyed Kelly, his arm still around her as he listened to Sydney on the other end.

"No," he said. "I'm at Todd's."

Kelly's heart sunk. It felt so bad going behind her friend's back so she could be with Drew. If she didn't like him so much, she'd call the whole thing off. But she'd go insane if she had him for only a short week and had to give him up.

"That's because we just got back," Drew said. "We were shopping for stuff for the birthday party." He sighed after hearing Sydney's reply. "I don't know why you even care. We're not together, Sydney, in case you've forgotten. I shouldn't have to tell you where I'm at or what I'm doing."

He looked at Kelly and rolled his eyes, then, "I'm hanging up, Syd. Good-bye." He flipped the phone closed and hung his head back.

"What?" Kelly asked.

"She caught me lying about being at your house with your brother."

Butterflies, and not the good ones, slashed through Kelly's stomach. "What did she say?"

"Apparently, she went over to your house and your brother told her me and you left together an hour ago."

Kelly winced. "This is not good."

"It's all right, Kel. We don't have to answer to Sydney."

"But she's my best friend!" Kelly rubbed her forehead. "I can't believe I'm doing this."

"Do you want to stop seeing each other?" Drew grabbed a lock of her hair and twirled it around his finger. She shivered.

"No."

"Then we'll figure it out, okay?" He squeezed her shoulder and kissed her quickly.

The misty rain fell harder.

"We should probably go in." Drew got up and navigated his way to the back of the canoe. Kelly got onto the front bench.

"I love you, Kels," he said softly.

The worse thing about it was, Kelly desperately loved him, too, and if she had to make a choice between Sydney and Drew? Who would she choose?

Deep down, she knew she'd already chosen.

FORTY-FOUR

Rule 12: *Be agreeable and easy to get along with!*

Sydney quietly opened her bedroom door and stuck her head into the hallway. Her mother and father's voices were soft murmurs in the kitchen. They were talking divorce. Sydney knew because she'd overheard the word late last night when she'd gotten out of bed to use the bathroom.

Now her parents were probably talking terms or maybe other options.

At this point, Sydney didn't care and maybe that was worse than being upset.

Back in her room, she grabbed her keys and her bag. She had to be at work in fifteen minutes. She seriously considered sneaking out her bedroom window to avoid her parents, but she didn't want them thinking she'd run away like her mother had.

Groaning to herself, she headed down the hallway, her pace quick, her head down. She hoped to slip past the kitchen without being noticed. Unfortunately, as soon as she entered the kitchen, both her parents stopped talking and looked up.

"Sydney?" her mother said.

Sydney hesitated between the kitchen and the living room. That stupid fish clock on the wall ticked, filling the awkward silence. Sydney hadn't said more than ten words to her mother since she arrived, and she didn't plan to say more than twenty total.

"What?" She quirked a brow.

Sydney looked from her mother to her dad. Her mom was put together like always, as if at any moment she'd get a call for another business meeting and have to leave town. Her black hair was pulled into a chignon. Pearls adorned her ears and wrapped around her neck. She wore a black suit and pointy heels.

Sydney's father, on the other hand, looked like he'd just climbed out of bed. His dark brown hair stuck up around the crown. Stubble covered his chin. There were dark bags beneath his eyes.

"Do you have any free time tonight or tomorrow so we can talk?" her mom asked.

Why had her mother even come back? Guilt? Money?

Sydney tightened her grip on the car keys, the points of the key digging into her flesh. Did she have free time after work? "No," she answered and marched out the door.

The hospital seemed unusually cold today. Sydney zipped up her hoodie and shoved her hands in her pockets as she waited for the elevator to make its slow crawl up to the third floor. You'd think for a hospital, it'd move a little faster, but Sydney would bet that if she raced to take the stairs, she'd get to the third floor before the elevator even cleared the second.

She just didn't feel like stair climbing today.

The doors dinged open on the second floor and Sydney stepped back into the corner to make room for any new passengers. Except there was only one person waiting and it was Quin.

"Hey," he said, stepping inside. "How are you?"

She frowned and shook her head. "Not good. Today isn't a good day."

"Is it your mom?"

"Yes."

They got out on the third floor and hung there by the elevator banks. Quin leaned against the wall, his white Oxford shirt blending in with the equally unappealing white walls. Now that Sydney knew what Quin was like outside of work, she hated seeing him inside the hospital. He had to shield himself here, cover his tattoos, and tie back his hair. She hated that he had to edit himself like that.

"Do you want to talk about it?" he asked.

Sydney shook her head. She felt more comfortable talking about how she felt with Quin, but she just didn't have the energy right now.

"I just kinda want to get my work done today and have some time alone, if that's okay with you."

"Whatever you need, and when you want to talk or hang out or whatever, you know where to find me."

"Thanks. Really. I appreciate it."

They parted, Quin going to West One and Sydney to West Two. She stopped at the nurses' station to get a to-do list from Jannie.

"Just visit each room and see if the kids want anything," Jannie said.

It sounded good to Sydney. She certainly didn't feel like dressing in a dragon costume today. In the first couple of rooms, the kids wanted movies and Sydney fetched those. In the fourth room, with the nurse's permission, Sydney gave the boy some microwave popcorn along with his movie.

In the last room she visited, she said hello to the little girl lying in bed, her tiny frame drowning in the starched white blankets. She'd been there for over a week and her parents had yet to visit. There were no balloons in her room, no flowers.

Sydney didn't know the specifics of the little girl's hospitalization, but Sydney did know the little girl wasn't doing well.

"Hey, Haley," Sydney said as she entered the room. Cartoons played from the TV. The machines behind the girl's bed beeped. The IV dripped steadily at her bedside.

"Hi, Sydney!" Haley grinned wide. "I was wondering when you worked again."

Sydney pulled up one of the guest chairs and sat down. "How are you?"

"I'm good. It's a nice day out."

Sydney glanced over her shoulder out the window. The sky was overcast and rain fell in sheets. "A nice day?"

"I like the rain," Haley said, dialing down the volume on the TV. "The rain is pretty."

Sydney looked out the window, trying to see what Haley saw. It was so dark and dreary, how could it be pretty?

"You don't see it?" Haley asked.

"Not really."

"People see things differently," she mused. "That's okay."

Sydney turned back around.

Haley was about ten years old, with acorn brown hair and hazel eyes. Freckles peppered her nose and chubby cheeks. There was always a smile on her face, no matter how many times the nurses had to poke her or check her blood pressure or hand over foul-tasting medicine.

"How do you stay so upbeat when you're stuck in a hospital?" Sydney heard herself ask. She quickly regretted it. She was talking to a child, a sick child, and she was bringing up the girl's illness. Quin had told her over and over again that it was their job to try to make the kids forget why they were here. And Sydney had just broken that rule.

Of course, she was breaking a lot of rules lately. Certainly there wasn't a rule in the Crush Code that said to break up with the boy you were supposed to love.

Haley glanced at Sydney, unfazed by the blunt question.

"You can't let the bad things get to you," she said. "Bad things must happen to you in life. The bad things teach us how to appreciate the good things. Well. That's what my grandpa used to tell me before he died." She widened her smile, her eyes focusing again on Sydney. "My grandpa always said," she added, "there can be no rainbow without rain."

Sydney laughed and somehow the conversation veered from chocolate to knock-knock jokes to weird dreams.

And when Sydney left Haley's room an hour later, her day didn't seem so bad anymore.

FORTY-FIVE ✬

Rule 32: *Do not act shy, speechless, or tongue-tied around your crush!*

Less than twenty-four hours after that misguided kiss, Blake called Raven and said they had to "talk." Which couldn't be good. Yesterday, on the ride back home, Blake hadn't said a word to Raven. She couldn't tell if he was angry or sad or confused.

She was still having a hard time reading him and now he sat across the table from her at a nearby Starbucks.

With the milk steamer whistling in the background and the smell of ground coffee beans thick in the air, it almost felt like Raven was at Scrappe. She half-expected Horace to walk up and that would be bad. Really bad, considering Raven was having a hard time focusing on anything but Blake right now.

She knew it was wrong, but she wanted to kiss him again. And maybe part of the reason why kissing him was so exciting was because she knew she wasn't supposed to.

Still, she was ninety-four percent certain she'd never do it again. The guilt was a heavy weight in her gut because she loved Horace and she knew, deep down, she was better off with him than with Blake.

It'd been stupid to kiss him. She'd just gotten caught up in the excitement.

"So," Blake began, holding his coffee cup between both hands, "we need to talk about what happened yesterday."

Raven nodded and took a sip from her frappé. They weren't as good as the ones they made at Scrappe.

"Don't get me wrong," Blake went on, "I like you. I really like you and that kiss . . ." He ran his hand over his hair. "The kiss was rad, but I love Lana and I can't hurt her like that."

Raven nodded. She was having a hard time getting anything out.

"So we agree that the kiss was a mistake?" he asked.

Raven liked the kiss and if she were single, she'd want to have more kisses between them, but right now, with their situation, it *was* a mistake. "Yes," she finally said.

Blake let out a relieved breath. "Are you going to tell Horace?"

Knots twisted in Raven's stomach. What if he broke up with her? What if he told her he never wanted to see her again? She couldn't live with it. She couldn't live with knowing she'd hurt Horace like that.

And was it so wrong for her to keep the kiss a secret? It was just one kiss, and like Blake said, it was a mistake.

"No," she answered, "I don't think I'll tell him."

Blake turned toward the windows, the sunlight playing over his face. "Yeah, I don't think I'll tell Lana, either." He glanced at her then, his voice having gone low. "How about we let that secret die here, then?"

Raven nodded. "Agreed."

♥   ♥   ♥

When Raven came home later that evening, she found her mother waiting for her at the kitchen table.

"What were you thinking?" Mrs. Valenti shouted.

Raven froze. She didn't need clarification; she knew exactly what her mother was referring to. Somehow she'd found out about the trip to New York. How, exactly, Raven couldn't begin to guess. Had Jordan said something?

"Um . . ." Heat fluttered in her face. Raven hated feeling caught like this. She wasn't sure where to begin.

"Well," she said, "I guess I was thinking that I wanted to compete in a singing contest. And it was only in New York."

Mrs. Valenti gritted her teeth. Her nostrils flared. "I can't believe you went to the city by yourself, Raven! And for a silly contest! You could have gone there to visit a college, but no, you had to sneak off for music."

Raven clenched her hands into fists at her side. "Horace and I thought it'd be a good opportunity. You know . . . something to get me out of Birch Falls, something to make me successful like you always wanted."

Mrs. Valenti sighed, rubbing at her forehead. "I never should have called Horace. . . ."

Raven frowned. "What? When did you call Horace?"

Her mother stared straight ahead, her lips pursed tightly.

"Mom?"

"I called him when he was in Detroit."

Raven widened her eyes, her lower jaw dropped. "You what?"

"I was doing it for you, honey. I just want you to have a good life. I don't want you to regret anything and sticking around Birch Falls for a boy and a garage band . . . well, that's not exactly the kind of life I want you to have."

Raven was speechless. That's why Horace had been acting so weird since he got home from Detroit, why he'd pushed her into the contest — because her mother had called him and planted ideas in his head, because he'd been afraid of holding Raven back.

"I cannot believe you did that," Raven said.

"It wasn't like I threatened him. I just wanted to discuss with him what he wanted for his future. And yours. We both think you have talent, but I want you to have a backup plan, Raven. When I was your age . . ."

She licked her lips, shifted in the chair at the kitchen table. "When I was your age, I thought I had all the answers, but I didn't and I didn't plan ahead like I should have. And it took me a long time to do what I wanted to do with my life. I don't want you following someone else's ideas or dreams."

Mrs. Valenti was silent for a long time, then, "I loved your father, don't get me wrong, but he wanted different things in life than I did. I was young and optimistic. I figured I had all the time in the world to follow his dreams and mine. But that wasn't the case. We just followed *his* dreams and mine were shoved to the back burner for good.

"That's why I've pushed you girls so hard. I want you to have everything you've ever dreamed of. I don't want you to sacrifice anything for anyone."

Raven grabbed the musical note necklace Horace had given her. She rubbed the cool silver between her fingers as she let her mother's explanation settle in.

Finally she took in a deep breath and said, "I get what you're saying, Mom, but this dream of going off to an Ivy League university, that's your dream, not mine. I love to sing and that's what I want to do."

She stilled, waiting for the wrath of her mother, for a lecture of how irresponsible it would be for Raven to skip college.

But the lecture never came.

Instead, her mother stood up. She crossed her arms over her chest, went to the window looking out over the backyard. "I think I see that now." She turned to Raven, cocked her head to the side. "If that's what you want, if you're one hundred percent sure, then I support you."

Raven raised her brow. "Really?"

Her mother reached over, grabbed her hand, and squeezed. "Really."

Raven dropped the music note pendant. Was this really her mother? Maybe it was an alien, because she wasn't acting like her mother.

"Listen," Raven said, "I have an idea."

"I'm listening."

"How about if I take a year off to do what I want to do. Whether that's music or a road trip, whatever. I'll take a year off and then, if nothing has come of the music, I'll apply to some colleges."

Mrs. Valenti grinned. "I think that's a smart plan that pleases everyone. I just . . . you know . . . I want you to have a backup plan."

"I know."

"Sounds like a good deal," Mrs. Valenti said. "I'm fine with it."

When Raven had walked inside the house and her mother had yelled at her, she was certain this argument would rival a dogfight. It turned out, the conversation was one of the better ones Raven had had with her mother in a long time. And at least she wasn't grounded.

"By the way," her mother said, "you're grounded."

Raven exhaled loudly. "I was wondering when you were going to say that. For how long?"

"A long time."

"Well, I guess I'll have plenty of time to fine-tune my singing voice, then."

Mrs. Valenti gave Raven a hug. "By the way," she said, "I heard you singing at work, and I thought you sounded good."

Raven smiled. Coming from her mother, that meant a lot.

FORTY-SIX

Rule 1: *Be playful, fun, and flirty! Boys like girls who know how to have a good time!*

The number one rule of the Crush Code was to be playful, fun, and flirty. The good thing was, when Kelly was with Drew, she didn't even have to *try* to be fun. Drew automatically brought out the fun side in her.

And what was the point of flirting when she could just kiss him?

She gave her bedroom door a shove, wrapped her arms around him, and planted her mouth on his.

"Mmm," Drew muttered against her lips, then, "Shouldn't I be the one kissing you today? It is your birthday, after all."

"Right," she said, "which means I get to kiss you whenever I want. And *do* whatever I want."

He grinned and took off his glasses, setting those neon blue eyes on Kelly. "I'll be more than happy to let you do whatever you want."

A dog whined from behind Drew.

"Aww," Kelly said, ducking down to Bear's level. The husky sat quietly on his hind legs, his tail swishing over the carpet. Drew had brought him over because, according to Drew, Bear wanted to wish Kelly a happy birthday before the party. Now, unfortunately, the dog had to go home.

It was so cute.

"Are we ready?" Kelly asked, scratching the dog beneath the chin.

Bear barked.

Kelly slipped on her pink flip-flops. "Birthday party, here I come."

Tonight was proving to be the best night of her life.

Drew turned his truck down an unmarked road and the woods instantly swallowed them up. Todd had wanted to have Kelly's party at Matt Turner's barn, but Kelly had quickly vetoed that. The abandoned barn had no bathroom, which meant she'd be using the woods and Kelly really didn't feel like going au naturel.

Somehow, Todd had talked their parents into renting part of the park on the east side of Garver Lake. The slot they had was tucked back in the woods and down a long gravel drive. It was secluded enough that the party's music wouldn't bother anyone else.

Drew pulled onto the grass on the side of the road and parked in a row of five other cars. Todd was already there with Adam, Kenny, and Matt, but judging by the group beneath the pavilion, a few people had carpooled. There were at least twelve guys.

Kelly and Drew got out, loading their arms with supplies. When they reached the pavilion, Kelly pulled off her sunglasses and looked around. Gold Christmas lights hung from the rafters and wove around hot-pink streamers. Pink and gold balloons floated from weights on several of the picnic tables.

"It's so pretty!" she exclaimed and lunged at Drew with a hug. "Thank you." She pulled away quickly when she got the urge to kiss him. She didn't want her brother finding out about her and Drew. At least not yet, and certainly not on her birthday. Kelly wasn't sure how he'd react, but she didn't want any drama at her party.

Kelly went to her brother next to give him a thank-you hug. Todd grimaced, but managed to mutter, "You're welcome," before pulling away from her and patting her back.

As the guys broke away to finish a few last-minute things, Kelly went over to Adam. He looked more than hot today in a pair of cargo shorts and a black T-shirt. The sleeves of his shirt definitely showed off his muscles.

It would have been so much easier if Kelly had fallen for him this summer. Part of her regretted not trying harder. If she were with him, there wouldn't be the risk of losing a best friend. Or alienating all of her other friends.

"Happy Birthday," Adam said, wrapping her in a hug. "You look good today."

She glanced down at her cut-off jean shorts and white baby tee. "Thanks to you. I've lost about fifteen pounds this summer because of kickboxing."

"Well, you did great at the lessons."

"Yeah." She looked over her shoulder for Drew. He and Todd were plugging in more Christmas lights.

"So," Adam said, "you guys are together finally?"

Kelly blushed and looked down at the concrete floor. "Yeah, but please don't say anything. We haven't told anyone yet."

"When are you going to tell people?"

Kelly shrugged. "Just not today."

"Secret is safe with me," Adam said.

She gave him another hug and whispered in his ear, "You and Drew are the best things that happened to me this summer."

♥   ♥   ♥

Raven parked along a row of cars and got out, tugging down the hem of her skirt and then straightening her loose gray tunic. She had to promise years of servitude to get her mother to lift the grounding restrictions for one night. She'd be working at Scrappe without pay until she was eighty.

Dropping her keys in her shoulder bag, Raven headed down the gravel drive to the main part of the park. Kelly had told her the party was starting at seven. Raven was only twenty minutes late, but already the park was crowded with clusters of cliques.

Kelly had always had a knack for befriending just about everyone. She belonged to no clique at school, but she had friends in almost every circle.

Music blasted from a stereo system hidden in the enclosed food area. A song by the rock band A Mighty Saint finished up as Raven neared. A Kay-J song replaced the rock. Raven smiled to herself.

She was still having a hard time believing she'd met Kay-J in person. Raven hadn't heard the contest results yet, but she would be content with either answer. If she were rejected, she still had Horace and the band. She'd be more than happy sticking with them.

Speaking of Horace . . .

He stood by the brick fire pit near the lake's edge. Dean and Hobbs were there poking the fire with sticks as if it were some feral animal.

When Horace saw her, he nodded. Raven hurried over, kissing him eagerly. Being grounded sucked, but it did make the heart grow fonder.

"Dudes!" Hobbs said. "Get a room."

Raven chuckled as she pulled away. "I'm so happy to see you."

"Me, too." Horace smiled. "Your friends here yet?"

Raven scanned the crowd. "I'm sure they are. Mind if I go look for them?"

"No. That's fine. I'll be here with Dean and Hobbs." He kissed her quickly on the cheek before she broke away from the fire pit, heading for the pavilion. Beneath the roof, Raven looked up at the twinkling gold lights and pink streamers. Balloons bobbed over the picnic tables. There was a table near the back, covered in presents.

"Raven!" Alexia called, waving above the crowd.

Alexia looked absolutely adorable in a pair of longer khaki shorts and a chocolate-colored blouse. Her hair was half pulled back in a barrette and the rest hung around her shoulders.

305 ——

"I'm so glad your mom let you come," Alexia said over the music. "How long do you have tonight?"

"Midnight."

"Me, too."

"Are you still grounded?" Raven asked.

Alexia shrugged. "My parents aren't home as much as they were. They finally found a new office, and they're remodeling a lot."

"That's cool."

Alexia nodded. "It's given me a little more time to hang out with Ben before he leaves."

"Have you talked to him about that?"

Alexia frowned and shook her head. "It's been so much easier not thinking about it."

"You'll have to confront it soon. Isn't he leaving in a few days?"

"Six, to be exact, but I really don't want to think about it tonight. I'd rather just enjoy the party."

Raven could understand that.

"Is Sydney here yet?" she asked.

Alexia shook her head. "She's coming soon, though."

"What about Kelly? Where is she? I wanted to wish her a happy birthday."

"I think she's in the enclosed eating area. I'll come over there with you."

They left the pavilion and walked over to the eating area. It was a long building with two large openings on each side. Picnic tables made two neat rows, their tops covered in pink tablecloths. There were bowls of chips and tubs of dip. There were ten different bottles of soda and a cooler full of chilled bottled water.

Kelly was in the corner unwrapping napkins and chatting with Drew.

"Happy birthday, birthday girl!" Raven called, raising her hand in the air as she navigated around the guys setting up more food.

"Hey, Ray!" Kelly said, dropping the napkins on a table.

Raven gave Kelly a hug. She smelled like vanilla and strawberries. She looked thinner, too. Had she been spending more time with that Adam guy? The hot personal trainer? Maybe Raven needed a hot personal trainer.

No, no she didn't. She didn't need any more guys in her life. Horace was enough for her. She hadn't told him about the Blake incident. That was a secret better left unsaid, right?

Raven hadn't seen Blake since their talk at Starbucks. There was a skating tour going on across the United States. She was pretty sure she wouldn't see him for the rest of the summer. He'd texted her a few times to ask how she was and whether or not she'd heard from Kay-J.

Raven was still attracted to him, but she wasn't afraid of that attraction anymore. She could deal with digging another guy while keeping her hands to herself. It wouldn't be that hard. Especially when she had a guy like Horace.

"Is there anything we can help with?" Alexia asked, fidgeting with the hem of her shirt.

"Yeah." Kelly nodded at the napkins and plastic silverware. "Unwrap all those and set them on the tables?"

Alexia nodded and the girls set to work.

FORTY-SEVEN ✒

"Come here," Drew said. "I have something for you." He grabbed Kelly's hand and tugged her out of the enclosed eating area and around the back of the building, away from the chaos of the party.

They had total privacy back here. The woods grew in close to the building. Leaves tickled the back of Kelly's neck. She batted them away, leaning a shoulder against the cool aluminum siding of the building.

"Here is fine," Drew said, keeping his voice low.

Kelly bit her lower lip, trying not to smile too wide. She had to stop being such a goof around Drew.

On second thought, Drew knew better than anyone that she was a total dork. She didn't have to hide anything from him.

"Happy Birthday," he said when he pulled a small white box from his jeans pocket.

Kelly gasped. "Drew. You didn't have to get me anything."

"Of course I did. It's your birthday. Open it."

She took it with nervous fingers. A small white box almost always meant jewelry. More specifically, jewelry from Adorn Jewelry Shop, the most upscale place in town.

Kelly slowly popped open the lid. Sitting on a velvet bed was a sterling-silver infinity knot pendant, a silver chain attached to it.

"Drew!"

"What?" He smiled.

"This is . . . I . . ." She swallowed back the stinging of tears.

"I've known you longer than anyone here," he explained. "And this symbolizes our past and present and hopefully our future. I want to keep you in my life forever."

Kelly's lower lip trembled, and she knew she'd lost the battle with the tears. A few slipped over her lids and slid down her cheeks. She swiped them away and laughed.

"I hope those are happy tears," Drew said.

"Definitely happy tears." She pulled the necklace from the box. "Could you put it on for me?"

She turned, lifting her hair. Drew draped the necklace around her neck and fastened it at the back. The silver was cool against her too hot skin.

"I so love you," she said, kissing him quickly, her heart thumping in her chest.

Something clicked behind them.

Kelly pulled away from Drew and saw Craig Theriot, his cell open in his hands.

"Craig!" Kelly shouted. "Tell me you did not take a picture."

He chuckled. "Just wanted to take a snapshot for the

birthday girl so she can remember this special day." He hurried off as Kelly lunged at him.

"Kelly." Drew grabbed her hand and stopped her.

"He just took a picture of us kissing!" she said, her breath coming quicker. Craig had the biggest mouth at school. He was going to tell everyone.

"So what?" Drew said. "People are going to find out anyway. Let's just try to enjoy tonight, huh?"

"But . . ."

He tilted her chin up with a finger and kissed her, pressing her back against the building wall. His tongue glided over her lips, and she couldn't seem to think straight.

"I'll find Craig," Drew said softly between kisses, "and ask him to keep quiet just for tonight."

"Thanks."

Drew kissed her once more before disappearing around the building.

♥　　♥　　♥

Sydney turned down the long gravel drive toward the park. A sign at the entrance read: HAPPY BIRTHDAY, KELLY! in big block letters with balloons tied behind it.

"Well, I'm at the park," Sydney said to Quin in her cell phone. "Want me to call you later?"

"If you'd like. If you feel like talking."

In the last week, Sydney's mood had been up and down, but Quin had been there for her whenever she needed him. And it helped that when she asked for space, he gave it to her without question.

He was cool like that. And Sydney, for the most part, tried to remain calm and collected, despite her mother's presence in the house. Quin's laid-back attitude really helped keep Sydney above water.

He was a great friend. A lot different from anyone she'd ever known, but maybe that was a good thing. He'd opened her eyes to new things.

"I want to call," Sydney said.

"Then I'll be waiting."

Sydney said good-bye to Quin just as her cell rang with a new picture message. She parked near Kenny's truck and shut the car off.

She checked the sender: Craig Theriot.

"Great," she muttered. It was probably a picture of his butt or something. He was notorious for sending stupid picture texts.

Sydney hit the OK button and the picture popped up.

She froze. The breath stalled in her throat. Her jaw slowly dropped open.

Was she seeing what she thought she was seeing?

Her eyes instantly stung with angry tears.

Was that really Drew and Kelly kissing?

Sydney got out of her car and stomped down the gravel drive. Music thudded through several speakers, reverberating through her chest. People greeted Sydney as she passed, but she couldn't even manage to nod.

She scanned the faces, looking for Kelly or Drew. It didn't really matter which one because she'd find both of them eventually.

At the pavilion, Sydney wove through the picnic tables and spotted Alexia near the back corner with Ben. His arms were wrapped around her and they were whispering to each other.

Sydney tapped Alexia on the shoulder. "Where is Kelly?"

"Um . . ." Alexia pulled away from Ben. "I just saw her and Raven going into the bathrooms."

Sydney whirled around. She went past the bonfire, the fire crackling in the pit, throwing heat out in a twenty-foot radius.

How could Kelly do that? And how long had they been going behind Sydney's back? Had they been hooking up ever since open-mike night?

Nausea rolled in Sydney's gut.

Or maybe they'd been seeing each other long before that. Maybe that was why Drew had broken up with Sydney in January.

Oh god, she thought as she neared the white brick bathroom building. That long? Could they possibly have gone behind Sydney's back for over half a year?

How could she be so stupid? And how could Kelly and Drew be so cruel?

"Sydney, what is going on?" Alexia asked, running after her.

Sydney clenched her hands into fists. She pushed open the green metal door on the girls' bathroom and it slammed against the wall behind it. Kelly and Raven both looked up.

Kelly leaned against the sink counter while Raven stood, arms crossed over her chest.

"How could you?" Sydney screamed. She crossed the

bathroom, grabbed Kelly by the shoulders and shook. "How could you do that!"

Tears streaked down her cheeks, blurred her vision.

"Sydney!" Raven yelled.

"How long, Kelly?" Sydney said, getting right in her face. "How long have you been seeing him? Since open-mike night? Longer? I was right all along, wasn't I? You two were seeing each other the whole time!"

Sydney's fingers were like claws now, twisting the material of Kelly's T-shirt in her grip. She let go, swiped her eyes. Kelly froze, horrified, her eyes glossy.

"I . . . I . . ."

Sydney gave Kelly a shove, and she slammed against the sinks.

Raven stepped in between them, blocking Kelly from view.

"What is going on?" she said.

The music of the party was a distant noise outside the bathrooms. Someone whistled, another guy shouted.

Sydney took in several measured breaths.

"Sydney?" Alexia said.

Kelly was sobbing now, her face buried in her hands.

Good, Sydney thought. I hope she feels terrible. I hope she feels guilty and ashamed.

"Sydney?" Raven said.

Sydney blinked, focused on Raven's face.

"What is going on?" she said again more slowly.

Sydney pulled out her cell and scrolled to the new picture message. She brought up the picture, heat rising in her throat as she looked at it again.

Drew. Her Drew.

It wasn't supposed to be like this.

Why had she ever broken up with him in the first place? What was she thinking? What was *he* thinking hooking up with Kelly?

"Look," Sydney said, thrusting the phone into Raven's hands.

Raven looked at the picture, frowned, and glanced over her shoulder at Kelly. "Kel? Is this really you and Drew?"

Kelly didn't say anything. She only cried harder.

"How could you be such a bitch?" Sydney said, the anger taking over every other emotion. It burned through her veins, made her heart thump harder. Sydney wanted Kelly to hurt the way she hurt.

"And why the hell is he with you anyway?" Sydney went on. "How could he like you? You're a ditz!"

"That's enough," Raven said.

Sydney gritted her teeth. "You're such a slut," she said to Kelly.

Kelly's knees almost gave out. She slumped against the counter, and Alexia went to her, holding her up.

"That's not true, Sydney," Alexia said. "And you know it."

"She's going out with my boyfriend!"

"Ex-boyfriend," Alexia reminded her.

Raven stepped aside, shifting her weight to one foot. "Kelly, can you tell us what happened?"

Kelly wiped the tears from her eyes and tried to catch her breath. "I never meant to . . ." She sucked in a breath. "I don't know what to say."

"How about you start with how long you and Drew have been seeing each other?" Raven asked.

"Not long." She shook her head. "We just . . . just the last few weeks. We never did anything." She looked at Sydney. "I swear it, Sydney. We never even kissed or anything when you guys were together."

"So you waited until I broke up with him and saw your chance?"

"No! I didn't want to hurt you! But . . ."

Sydney narrowed her eyes. "But what?"

Kelly took in a shaky breath. "I . . . I love him," she said.

Alexia and Raven both stilled. Sydney's heart was a rampant drumming in her head. She just wanted to get out of this bathroom, away from this party, away from everything. Everything felt like it was falling apart.

She straightened her back, clenched her hands at her sides. She looked at Kelly and said, "No friend would ever, *ever* go out with another's ex-boyfriend. You can have Drew, Kelly, but we're not friends, and we'll never be friends again."

She whirled around and whipped the door open as Kelly erupted into sobs.

FORTY-EIGHT ~๑

Rule 41: *Do not crush on a boy who has a girlfriend!*

Alexia sat on the edge of her bed. Raven sat next to her. They'd left Kelly's birthday party thirty minutes ago. After that fight with Sydney and Kelly, Alexia didn't feel much like partying.

Raven dialed Sydney's cell again and must have gotten the voice mail. "Sydney," she said, "we're at Alexia's. If you need us, come over here, please."

"If she's not at home," Alexia muttered, "where did she go?"

"Somewhere to cool off, I'm sure." Raven tossed her cell on the bed, where it bounced once and lay at rest.

"Kelly said she saw Sydney with a guy the other day at Bershetti's," Alexia said.

"Really?"

Alexia nodded.

"She hasn't said anything to me about a new guy."

"Yeah, me neither."

The door opened in the front of the house and slammed shut a second later.

"Is that your parents?" Raven said.

Her parents were supposed to be out to dinner with some friends of theirs and usually they were out late, but maybe they'd come home early?

"Hello?" someone called.

Alexia shot upright when she recognized Sydney's voice.

"We're in the bedroom," Raven yelled.

Sydney poked her head in a second later. Her eyes were bloodshot, her hair twisted up into a messy ponytail. Mascara was smudged in the corners of her eyes.

Alexia rarely saw her friend in such a bedraggled state. Raven got off the bed and went over to Sydney, wrapping her arms around her. As soon as Sydney lay her head against Raven's shoulders, she started bawling. Alexia joined the girls in a group hug. They remained there for several long minutes, letting Sydney get it all out.

When she pulled away, wiping her eyes with the back of her hands, she took in a long breath and then laughed.

"I must look like hell."

"You've had a rough day," Alexia said. But so had Kelly. Alexia was trying not to side with anyone, but the things Sydney had said to Kelly's face . . . poor Kelly. She'd left her own birthday party bawling. Everyone was talking about it.

At least she'd left with Drew. As soon as he found out what had happened, he came to her side and never left her.

Alexia had to admit, Drew seemed to love Kelly, but she'd never tell Sydney that.

Of course, maybe Sydney already knew.

"So," Alexia said, "how are you doing?"

Sydney leaned against the wall and closed her eyes, rubbing at the bridge of her nose. "I don't know what I am, to be honest."

"It was wrong what she did," Raven said. "I totally agree with that, but do you really hate her?"

Sydney shrugged. "Maybe."

"Come on, Syd," Alexia said, "that's not true. Kelly and Drew, they've been friends longer than they've known us and . . ."

"So that makes it okay?" Sydney interrupted. "I'm just supposed to forgive them because they've known each other longer than they've known me?"

"Well, no."

"I just can't believe they'd do that to me. I mean, seriously. Hooking up behind my back? How would you feel, Raven, if you and Horace broke up and I hooked up with him?"

Raven licked her lips. "I'd probably be pretty pissed."

"Exactly. And with everything else going on with my parents . . ." She shook her head. "I just don't want to deal. It's so screwed up that thinking about it gives me a headache."

"Just consider forgiving her," Alexia said. "Please? For all of us?"

Sydney bit her lip, but didn't say anything.

Their group was broken right now, and Alexia wasn't sure how to get them back together. The Breakup Code had brought them together at the beginning of this year and The

Crush Code was supposed to give them something else to bind them, but it'd torn them apart.

Alexia suspected Kelly had been using the Crush Code on Drew. Maybe Alexia should have paid more attention to the rule about boyfriends.

Rule 41: *Do not crush on a boy who has a girlfriend!*

FORTY-NINE ⤳

It'd been a week since Kelly's birthday party. A week since Sydney found out her ex-boyfriend was seeing her supposed best friend, and Sydney was still steaming about it.

But could anyone really blame her?

Kelly and Drew had gone behind Sydney's back. That was the worst kind of betrayal. Right up there with having your mother take off across the sea.

Why was Sydney's life so screwed up right now?

Because the people in her life were screwed up. That was why. And she couldn't control their actions. She could only control what she did and how she behaved.

So when Kelly knocked on Sydney's front door, Sydney seriously considered not answering. After all, ignoring Kelly would be a whole lot easier than confronting her, but school was starting next week and Sydney would have to face her eventually.

Maybe it was better to get it over with.

Sydney pulled the front door open and crossed her arms over her chest.

Kelly wrung her hands. "Hi," she said.

Sydney didn't say anything.

"Umm . . . I just wanted to come over to talk to you. You don't have to say anything, but please give me the chance to explain."

Sydney arched a brow. Did Kelly really deserve the chance to explain? And did Sydney even care what she had to say?

Kelly had said she and Drew didn't get together until after Sydney broke up with him, but there had to have been something else going on long before that. Maybe they'd been into each other and just hadn't touched.

That made Sydney feel like an idiot. She was embarrassed that she hadn't noticed something between Drew and Kelly sooner. How could she be so oblivious?

"I just wanted you to know," Kelly began, "that I never meant to hurt you."

Sydney snorted.

Kelly hesitated before taking a deep breath and surging on. "I didn't want to like Drew, and I certainly didn't plan for this to happen. . . ." She swallowed and looked down at the porch floor, wiggling her toes in her flip-flops.

"I just don't want you to hate me," Kelly said. "Can you forgive me? Someday maybe? I don't expect you to forgive me now or next week or next month, but . . . someday?"

Sydney parted her lips to say no, but the word wouldn't come out. She flashed back to Haley in Birch Falls Children's Hospital, to her frail frame in that hospital bed, her room void of balloons and parents.

Haley had even less than Sydney had and she didn't let any of it get to her.

"You can't let the bad things get to you," she'd said. *"Bad things must happen to you in life. There can be no rainbows without rain."*

Was it easier to forgive than it was to hate? Haley didn't seem to hate her parents and they'd barely visited her in the hospital.

But maybe Sydney was asking the wrong question. Maybe it wasn't about forgiving or hating . . . maybe it was about acceptance.

Accepting what you couldn't control.

Sydney couldn't control Drew or Kelly or what they did. She couldn't control her parents and make them okay, nor make the divorce go away.

What Sydney could do was not let the bad things get to her.

She took in a breath and uncrossed her arms. "What you did was wrong," she said to Kelly. "I trusted you, and you went behind my back. I really don't want to talk to you for a while. I don't know how long, but a while. So I just ask that you give me some space. Maybe someday we can be friends again. But not any day soon and maybe never. All I can do is try."

Kelly nodded fervently. "I completely understand." Tears welled beneath her lids. She sniffed, trying to hide them. "Thanks, Syd."

Sydney nodded and shut the door.

FIFTY ✑

Sydney plopped down on the bench near the fountain in the middle of Eagle Park.

A family played in the open field off to Sydney's left. The dad threw a Frisbee and the oldest daughter caught it, tossing it quickly to her little sister. The mother snapped a picture. The sprinklers had shut off a few minutes ago and the grass glistened in the sunlight.

That picture would be perfect when developed.

Sometimes Sydney wished her family had more moments like that, moments to capture on film. They weren't together enough to take pictures.

After Kelly left, Sydney hadn't felt much like sitting at home in her empty house. She'd grabbed her camera and come to the park.

She snapped a few pictures of the sun-dappled grass and then a few more of a squirrel bouncing from tree to tree. The squirrel brought back the memory of her and Drew breaking up the first time so many months ago. Sydney was devastated back then, as she was now, but for an entirely different reason.

Kelly's visit had been a surprise to Sydney. Kelly wasn't very forward. It'd probably taken her the entire day to work up the courage to come over, and maybe a tiny part of Sydney respected her for the effort.

But the fact remained: Kelly had gone behind Sydney's back. And if she'd lied about Drew, what else had she lied about?

It was the deception that hurt worse than the act itself.

Sydney and Drew had been over for a while; they just hadn't realized it yet. So the fact that he'd found someone else wasn't that big a deal to Sydney. It was who he'd hooked up with and how they'd hooked up.

Sydney couldn't stop wondering why he'd picked Kelly out of all the girls in Birch Falls.

Footsteps pounded the paved bike trail off to Sydney's right. She readied her camera, thinking she'd snap a few shots of the jogger as he or she passed, but when she saw who it was, she froze.

It was Drew.

When he saw her, he stopped running, setting his hands on his hips, his shoulders rising and falling with quickened breath. He hesitated on the trail as if trying to decide whether he should approach.

Finally, he walked over the freshly cut grass, his black tennis shoes wet at the toes from the wet grass.

Sydney's heart jumped just once seeing him. They had such a long history together. He was her best friend, no matter what they'd gone through or how they would be in the future. She would always consider him her first love and that was an intense kind of relationship. She wouldn't ever be able to let go of Drew completely.

"Hi." Drew plopped down beside her, wiping sweat from his forehead with the sleeve of his T-shirt.

"Hey."

They sat there in silence for a minute as each collected their thoughts.

Drew was the first to speak, his voice low. "How are you?"

"The truth?"

He nodded.

"I'm . . . okay."

"Okay in general or okay with me and Kelly?"

Me and Kelly.

They were "Drew and Kelly" now?

Sydney suppressed a shudder. Drew had always been hers. It'd always been "me and Sydney." Now he was replacing her. It was enough to make Sydney explode.

But no, she wasn't letting it get to her.

"I don't know if I'll ever be okay with you and Kelly," she said. "But I'm okay in general."

Drew hunched forward, propping his elbows on his knees. He watched the family in the clearing toss their Frisbee around. "You said some hurtful things to her, Syd."

"She did a hurtful thing."

He glanced over his shoulder. "Don't blame Kelly. I went after her, not the other way around."

Sydney swallowed down the heat rising in her throat.

Drew had chased after Kelly?

"How long have you liked her?"

He straightened and draped his arms over the back of the bench. "I don't like her."

Sydney frowned.

"I love her," he finished.

"What?"

"I've loved her for a while, Syd, I just never realized it."

The blood seemed to freeze in Sydney's veins. Her chest felt hollow. "Are you serious?"

"Yeah."

"So . . . you've loved her . . . what, for months? Years?"

He licked his lips, turned those intense blue eyes on her. "Does it really matter now? I loved you when we were together. I was your boyfriend one hundred percent, Syd."

It did matter, but Drew had a point. Knowing now would only ruin what they'd had and they had had a good relationship.

"But why Kelly?" she asked. "Couldn't you have found someone else?"

Drew shrugged. "Maybe eventually, but I wanted her. I wish it wasn't her. I wish it was someone else, because I knew how much it'd hurt you. But . . ." He sighed and ran his hand through his hair. It stuck up in the wake of his fingers. "I don't know. I just . . . I love her. I can't stop thinking about her. I can't stay away from her, even when she pushed me away."

Sydney arched a brow. "She pushed you away?"

"I admitted I was in love with her, like, a month ago and she didn't talk to me for, like, a week. And then when we did talk, she told me we couldn't be friends."

"Really?"

He nodded.

But a month ago . . . Sydney and Drew had still been together. And Kelly had done the right thing by pushing Drew away.

Maybe Sydney had crossed the line by saying all those hurtful things to Kelly. At least Kelly had tried to be a good friend. At least she hadn't hooked up with Drew while Sydney and Drew were still together.

"When were you going to tell me you were in love with someone else?" she asked now that she knew the truth.

"I don't know. I guess I was hoping that things would work themselves out. You know me, I always have a plan, but this time . . . I was kinda lost."

Sydney smirked. "Love is like that, I guess."

"Yeah."

The two girls in the clearing laughed as their dad did a victory dance after catching a high Frisbee toss. The mom snapped another picture. Sydney clung to her own camera, her finger itching to snap some shots.

"So that's it, then," she said, looking over at Drew now. "I mean, I guess we're saying goodbye to 'us.'"

Drew nodded. "We've been done for a while anyway, haven't we? I heard you . . . well, I mean . . . it's water under the bridge now."

"What is?"

He took in a breath and trained his eyes on her. "You and that guy Quin."

Sydney went wide-eyed. With all the drama going on, she'd forgotten about that run-in with Drew and Quin at Bershetti's.

"Oh? What did you hear?"

"That you were hooking up with him."

Sydney laughed and shook her head. "No, it's not like that. We're friends. He's leaving soon for school again anyway."

"Oh. Well, if you were together, that'd be cool, you know. He seemed like a cool guy."

Sydney smiled to herself. "Yeah, he is."

The Frisbee family clustered into a small, tight-knit group and headed for the bike trail. The girls chatted animatedly about the lake and the canoe they were going to rent next weekend.

Sydney and Drew watched the family disappear.

"I guess I should go." Drew stood and Sydney got up with him.

"Friends?" he said.

"Friends." She hugged him, and he squeezed her tightly.

This was the official end to their two-year relationship, and this time, Sydney was okay with saying good-bye.

♥　♥　♥

Sydney shut the front door and heard jazz music playing from the den. That usually meant her mother was home. Her dad hated jazz. He was more into classical.

Sydney had finally settled things with Drew and she was at least content with the situation with Kelly, but the issue with her mother was a loose end and there was a lot Sydney wanted to say.

She went to the den and poked her head around the door. Her mother was there on her laptop, her fingers clicking the keys. She didn't even notice Sydney.

Sydney cleared her throat and her mother looked up. She smiled, but it was strained. "Hi, sweetie. Come on in."

Sweetie?

Sydney's stomach knotted. Her mother used to call her sweetie or honey but hadn't much in the last year or two. Her mother used to do a lot of things before her promotion at work.

"Sit down," her mother said, gesturing at the leather wingback chair in front of the desk. "Let's talk."

Sydney went inside but hovered by the chair, her arms crossed over her chest. "I'd rather stand."

The smile fell from her mother's face. "Okay. Do you still want to talk?"

"Yeah."

There were so many things Sydney wanted to say, but she didn't know where to start.

Maybe there was no perfect lead-in to this conversation. This was her mother and yet she felt so distant from the woman sitting in front of her. Like they weren't even on the same planet anymore, let alone in the same family.

Was it possible to fall out of love with your own mother? She'd hurt Sydney so many times that Sydney wasn't sure if she could trust her mother. And without trust, what kind of a relationship could they have?

Sydney took a deep breath. She just wanted to set the record straight.

"When you left for Italy, I was angry and upset."

"I know," Mrs. Howard said, "and I never meant . . ."

Sydney held up her hand. "Wait." She knew if she let her mother talk that she'd twist everything around, and before

Sydney knew it, she'd be forgiving her mother and they'd hug and make up.

As good as that sounded, Sydney knew the bliss would be fleeting.

"I know you're probably sorry about what happened and maybe you had a lot of things going through your mind, but I'm your daughter. You never should have left the way you did.

"And it was just a few months ago that you promised me you'd be around more, that you'd cut back your hours at work and we'd be a family again. I'm tired of you breaking promises, Mom. I'm tired of being disappointed, and I'm tired of dealing with your drama. I've accepted the fact that you've changed, that you've become a businesswoman more than a mother. I'm okay with that, but I think you should leave. I think you should pack up and leave and stop stringing me and Dad along."

Mrs. Howard sat there staring at Sydney like she wasn't sure if she'd heard her daughter right. Finally, she blinked, inhaled deeply. "Wow. Well . . . I'll take what you said into consideration, but this is an issue your father and I have to discuss, and we'll make the final decision. I know you're angry, Sydney, but please know I never meant to hurt you or your father. It was all on my part. It had nothing to do with you. I'm considering going to therapy. I've got a lot going on in my head."

Sydney wanted to believe her mother. Therapy could work . . . but it only worked if you made an effort, and Sydney didn't see her mother sticking with it.

"That's nice," she said, backtracking for the door. "But

I still think you should leave. The longer you stick around, the worse it'll be the next time you leave. And you'll leave again, because it's what you're good at, Mom.

"If you really love us, you'll go."

With that, Sydney turned and walked away.

FIFTY-ONE

Alexia leaned back in the passenger seat of Ben's Jeep and looked through the open roof to the sunny sky. It was hard to believe summer was over and Ben was leaving. His fingers lightly stroked the inside of her palm and she closed her eyes, liking the warmth of the sun on her face and the feel of Ben so near.

The state park on the other side of Garver Lake was quiet for a Friday afternoon. It was perfect for today.

"Do you really have to go?" Alexia asked Ben.

"Yeah. Besides, having the title 'college freshman' makes me automatically ten times hotter. All the girls will be jealous of you."

"College," she mumbled to herself. Just a few short months ago, Ben had been a high school student — her boyfriend. "College freshman" sounded so . . . official, like he was becoming an adult far too quickly.

Why couldn't they just stay here like this forever?

"It's only like ten weeks before Thanksgiving break."

Alexia bit the inside of her cheek when she felt the sting

of tears behind her eyes. She looked away from the sky and glanced at Ben. "What's going to happen to us?"

Ben stopped rubbing her hand. "I'd like to think nothing would happen. I don't want to break up, if that's what you're thinking."

He was so serious right now, it was almost scary. Ben hardly ever did "serious."

"You think we can make a long-distance relationship work?"

"Are you kidding?" Ben wove his fingers through hers. "If anyone can do long distance, we can."

Alexia nodded, but she knew to expect the unexpected. There were a hundred what-ifs to consider. What if Ben found another girl at Pepperdine. California was the land of skinny blond women, after all. Or what if he spent months away from her and fell out of love? What if *she* fell out of love?

The idea made her ill because she loved Ben *that* much. He was her first of everything. Her first boyfriend. Her first intimate relationship. She might have regretted losing her virginity the way she had, but she didn't regret losing it with Ben. He was the best possible guy to share that memory with.

Could their relationship survive the distance? The tears bit again at her eyes.

"Lexy?" Ben said.

"What if we grow apart?"

"We won't."

"But you don't know that. And you can't promise it." Tears rolled down her cheeks, and she caught them before they rolled off her chin. "It's so much, you know. I just love you so much."

He reached over the console and took her in his arms. He ran his hand over her hair. "I love you, too."

They sat there like that for a long time, or what felt like a long time. Alexia didn't want to let him go, but she knew he had to leave soon.

"I should go," she said. She got out of the Jeep. She'd driven her car to the park and met Ben there. He got out, too.

"So this is it," she said.

"No, this is the beginning."

Alexia frowned. "To what?"

"To the next step of Ben's Four Step Relationship Program. First comes love, then comes separation, then comes marriage and babies. I have it all figured out."

She giggled and wrapped her arms around his neck. "I'm so going to miss you."

He hugged her back. "Me, too. Promise you'll Email me often."

"I will."

He kissed her softly at first, then tightened his arms around her and leaned her back in a dip.

"Ben!"

"I can't help it. You make me want to tango."

"Stop!"

He pulled her up. "I should go."

"Yeah."

He kissed her again. "I love you, Lexy."

"I love you, too."

They waved good-bye and climbed into their vehicles. Ben was the first one to pull out of the parking lot, his Jeep disappearing around a bend in the road. Alexia stared after him, wishing he'd come back, wishing he'd change his mind and stay with her.

Anxious butterflies filled her stomach.

He wasn't coming back — that she knew — but it wouldn't stop her from hoping.

September

FIFTY-TWO

Rule 38: *Carry yourself like you are the stuff! Any guy is lucky to have you!*

The next weekend, the girls all met at Bershetti's to lay The Crush Code to rest.

Sydney hadn't wanted to go. It'd only been two weeks since Kelly's birthday bash and that wasn't nearly enough time to heal the hurt. Also, this was Sydney's last weekend with Quin for a while. He was flying out the next day to go back to school at the Brooks Institute in California.

He looked at her now and smiled. "What would your friends say if I came in with you?"

"They'd probably kick you out. It's girls only."

He took off his fedora and brushed back several locks of hair that had escaped his ponytail. "Fine. But call me as soon as you're done. I want to get in one more photo session before I have to take off."

"I'll call, you can bet on it."

Quin was easily the best thing that had happened to her this summer.

Then again, the things one might consider as bad — her relationship deteriorating, her mother leaving — those had been good things, too. At least in the end they were.

Sydney waved as Quin drove off.

Inside Bershetti's, the air-conditioning blazed, driving off the September heat. Sydney was thankful for the white gauzy long-sleeve shirt she'd slipped on over her cami.

"Hey, Syd," Jordan greeted her at the host podium. "Everyone's already here. Follow me."

Jordan led the way to the round table where Alexia, Raven, and Kelly all sat. There were six chairs total around the table. Sydney made sure to take the chair next to Alexia and far away from Kelly.

Kelly avoided eye contact. She fidgeted with her napkin, folding the corner over and then flattening it. They were all here technically for her. The new Crush Code had been designed for her, after all.

"Can I get you guys anything to drink?" Jordan asked.

They all ordered and Jordan disappeared in the back.

"So," Alexia said, "here we all are."

Sydney looked from Alexia to Raven and then to Kelly, catching quick eye contact. Kelly flushed and glanced down.

"Here we all are," Raven said. "And here"— she reached beneath the table and into her bag, pulling out a familiar shoe box —"is the Code Casket."

She set it on the table among the glasses of ice water and rolled silverware. She flipped open the lid.

Sydney peered inside. A copy of the Breakup Code lay in the bottom along with four four-leaf-clover bracelets and a picture of all four girls. They hadn't opened that box in months. It seemed so long ago that Sydney had used the Breakup Code for Drew. And at the time, when she got Drew back, she figured they'd be together for eternity. It was amazing how one summer could change so much.

Alexia lost It (which Sydney had found out way too late!). Sydney broke up with Drew, had an amazing summer at the hospital where she found Quin. Kelly . . . well, Kelly was in love. Sydney couldn't deny that. And Raven . . .

"Hey, Ray?" Sydney said. "Did you ever hear on that singing contest?"

"Oh yeah. I was going to show you guys the letter I got yesterday." She dug in her bag again and brought out the letter. "Kay-J wrote it. Here's what she said:

'Dear Raven,

'I think you have a tremendous talent for singing. Your voice is awesome and your style is unique. You rocked that song you sang for me. I got chills up and down my arms.

'The only thing I can suggest is to watch your rhythm and pitch.

'Unfortunately'— Raven wrinkled her nose and continued —'you didn't make it to the next round of auditions, but let me explain why. I don't think you're right for the competition. I don't think you should be singing backup. I think you should be singing with a band like Blake said you were. Focus on that because you have all the right elements of a total rocker chick.

'If you ever need anything, let me know. I'd be happy to help.

'XOXO

'Kay-J.' "

"Oh my god," Kelly said. "That's so cool, Raven!" A smile graced her lips for the first time since Sydney had arrived.

"Despite the fact that I didn't make it," Raven said, "I'm not that upset."

"You shouldn't be," Sydney replied. "That letter wasn't a rejection, it was all praise."

They chatted about the band October for a few minutes and how Raven and Horace were planning a Halloween party with a huge show. It was going to be a blast, and Sydney couldn't wait to see Raven sing her heart out.

Alexia cleared her throat. "So, you guys want to get down to business?"

They all went silent.

"We're here today to lay The Crush Code to rest. Do you guys all agree?"

"I agree," Raven said.

Kelly nodded. "Me, too."

Sydney looked across the table at Kelly. Had she used The Crush Code on Drew instead of her friend Adam?

Does it really matter? Sydney thought. No. It didn't. Not now anyway.

"I'm ready to lay it to rest," Sydney said.

Maybe the Code hadn't been designed for her specifically, but Sydney had gotten some use out of it. Now that they were laying the Code to rest, she was going to repeat one rule to herself and use it like a mantra. This was for the new and improved Sydney, the Sydney that was going to focus more on herself and stop trying to control the things that were out of her hands.

Rule 38: *Carry yourself like you are the stuff!*

"Jordan?" Raven said, stopping her little sister as she walked past. "Could you take a picture of us?"

"Sure." Jordan took the digital camera from Raven.

The girls leaned into one another. Raven put her arm around Kelly. Sydney smiled as Alexia leaned closer to her. There was an obvious divide between the girls, especially between Sydney and Kelly, but at least they were together. That's what mattered most to Sydney. Maybe eventually they'd be one big happy group again. She didn't hate Kelly, she just needed time to heal the rift.

"Say cheese!" Jordan snapped the picture and then handed the camera over.

"It's perfect," Alexia said, passing the camera around the table so everyone could see. "Okay, you guys, ready?"

They all nodded.

Alexia set the copy of The Crush Code in the Code Casket.

"As women of the Code," they all said in unison, "we hereby lay The Crush Code to rest."

They all laughed as Alexia set the lid on the casket.

Rule 1: Be playful, fun, and flirty! Boys like girls who know how to have

—— it drives boys wild! Rule 4: Find out what your crush likes —— hobb

eyes! Make eye contact throughout your conversations with him. Never

world! Rule 7: Be adventurous and daring! See life as an adventure!

lies within you! Rule 9: Be yourself! He will like you for the real you!

but interested! Guys love a challenge! Rule 12: Be agreeable and easy to

Rule 14: Make him notice you! Get his attention! Draw him into you!

interested in things that interest him! Rule 17: Always look your best in the

respects you as well! Rule 19: Do not allow your crush to pressure you to

comfortable with! Rule 20: Take chances and appear to live life on the edge

mystery about you! Rule 22: Don't answer questions right away! Take a

Rule 24: Become his friend! Talk to him but do not become one of his boys

have to tell your friends who you are crushing on! Rule 27: Do not keep cr

you are! Rule 28: Do not spend more than two months trying to find out if

or letter, because he might think someone else sent it! Rule 30: Do not tell

to tell your crush! Rule 31: Do not send your friend to tell your crush you l

Rule 33: Do not stalk or stare at your crush! Rule 34: Do not get depress

know your crush slowly! (You may discover that you don't like him!) Ru

37: Learn to listen! Do not just talk about yourself! Rule 38: Carry you

indecisive. Once you make up your mind stick to it. Rule 40: Do not be n